FIRST LIGHT

FIRST LIGHT

*The First Ever
Brady Coyne/J. W. Jackson Mystery*

PHILIP R. CRAIG

AND

WILLIAM G. TAPPLY

KATE'S MYSTERY BOOKS
JUSTIN, CHARLES & CO. PUBLISHERS
Boston, Massachusetts

First Paperback Edition 2005

This book is a work of fiction. All characters and events portrayed in this
work are either fictitious or are used fictitiously.

Library of Congress Cataloging-in-Publication Data
Tapply, William G.
First light: the first ever Brady Coyne/J. W. Jackson novel/
William G. Tapply and Philip R. Craig.
p. cm.
1. Coyne, Brady (Fictitious character)—Fiction. 2. Jackson, Jeff (Fictitious
character)—Fiction. 3. Private investigators—Massachusetts—Martha's
Vineyard—Fiction. 4. Martha's Vineyard (Mass.)—Fiction. 5. Boston
(Mass.)—Fiction. I. Craig, Philip R., 1933– II. Title.

PS3570.A568 F57 2002
813'.54—dc21
2001049053
ISBN 1-932112-39-1

Published in the United States by Kate's Mystery Books,
an imprint of Justin, Charles & Co., Publishers
www.justincharlesbooks.com

Distributed by National Book Network, Lanham, Maryland
www.nbnbooks.com

1   3   5   7   9   10   8   6   4   2

Printed in the United States of America

For
Shirl and Vicki

To anticipate, not the sunrise and the dawn merely, but, if possible, Nature herself! How many mornings, summer and winter, before yet any neighbor was stirring about his business, have I been about mine! No doubt, many of my townsmen have met me returning from this enterprise, farmers starting for Boston in the twilight, or woodchoppers going to their work. It is true, I never assisted the sun materially in his rising, but, doubt not, it was of the last importance only to be present at it.

—HENRY DAVID THOREAU

FIRST LIGHT

Chapter One

J.W.

I had arranged to meet James Bannerman in the Fireside because it was close to the ferry landing, so he could catch the boat and go home to Connecticut after we talked. I was the only customer when he came in. He was a medium-sized guy in his mid-forties. He had flat, dark eyes and hair, and he looked in shape. He wore white-collar clothes. He glanced around, saw only me and the bartender and Bonzo wiping tables in the corner of the room. He came over to the bar.

"Are you Jackson?"

"My friends call me J.W."

The bartender drifted down while Bannerman and I were shaking hands. Bannerman pointed at my glass of Sam Adams. "Bring a couple more of those to us over in that booth, please." The "please" softened it, but it was clear that Bannerman was used to giving orders.

Bannerman and I went to the booth. He shoved a photograph at me. "That's her. That's my wife, my Katherine."

The photo was of an attractive blonde woman

about my age, which made her only a few years younger than Bannerman. I drank from my glass. "Look," I said, "I'm only here because Jason Thornberry asked me to meet you. We've worked together a couple of times before, but like I told him on the phone, I don't think I'm the right man for this job. Your wife is legally separated from you, so where she goes and what she does is her own business."

"Don't say that. I'm desperate. Thornberry's people finally managed to trace her this far last year, but then they lost her. She was here on the Vineyard, but then she dropped out of sight just before Labor Day. I've been here several times this summer, trying to find her, but my work won't let me stay long. You're my last chance."

"You really need a professional. I haven't been a cop for years. I'm retired. If you don't think Thornberry Security can do the job, you should hire some other private investigator, but I think Thornberry is about as good an outfit as you'll find."

"Money's no problem, if that's what's holding you back. I've got plenty. And I don't need some other PI, I need you. Thornberry himself recommended you. He said he's been trying for years to get you to work for him, but you won't. He says you live here, you know the people, and you know this island. He says local knowledge might make the difference. Don't let me down. Please. I love Katherine. I have to find her!"

He dug out a handkerchief and wiped his face. I let myself feel sorry for him and looked at the photo again. He mentioned a sum of money that was large enough to capture my attention. When you live on

Martha's Vineyard and don't have a regular job, you always need money.

"Maybe she's still here on the Vineyard," he said. "We honeymooned here, and she loved the place. I think that's why she came back here. Maybe she's living here, using another name. If she is, I want you to find her. If she's gone, find out where she went. Please."

Bannerman was a tough-looking man, but he wasn't acting tough at all. He looked like he wanted to cry. I wondered if he was an amateur thespian, pulling my strings, or if he was one of those people who fool themselves about their own virtue, or if he was really as concerned as he was acting. I had no real reason to think it wasn't the latter.

I thought of the things I was planning to do. Fishing in the annual Derby was highest on the list. I was tired of being the only surf caster on Martha's Vineyard who had never caught a forty-pound bass.

"Look," said Bannerman, leaning forward, "if Katherine doesn't want to see me, that's fine. All I really want to know is that she's well and happy. I love her. Frankie, that's our daughter, loves her. Kathy's the most important thing in the world to us. Please help me."

His words were consistent with feelings I also had. I was in love with my wife. If Zee ever left me, I'd be miserable, but I'd want her to be happy.

"Please," said Bannerman for the fourth or fifth time.

I didn't want the job, but unlike Sam Spade I was a sap when it came to love or its appearance.

"All right," I said. "I'll see what I can do. But don't get your hopes up. If Thornberry Security can't find her, the chances are that I can't either. And a couple of other things. I can't spend all of my time on this job. I have other commitments. And if I do find her, it'll be up to her whether or not I tell you where she is. I'll tell you if I find her, but I may not tell you where."

"Thank you," said Bannerman. "I appreciate your help more than I can say." He wiped his face again and put the handkerchief away. I poured more beer into my glass and drank it. It was cool and smooth.

"Here," said Bannerman, who had been digging in his briefcase. He put a checkbook on the table and handed me a large envelope. "In there you'll find all of the information I gave Thornberry when they went to work for me and all that they've given me since. Maybe there's something there that will help you. If you need to know more, let me know, and I'll tell you what I can." While I pulled a file from the envelope and glanced at it, he scribbled a check and pushed it at me. It was too much, but if that was fine with him, it was fine with me, so I didn't make an issue of it.

"I'll look at this later," I said, pushing the file back into its envelope, "but you can tell me some things right now. First, why did she leave?"

He'd heard the question before, probably from both his local police and certainly from Thornberry, since detectives in both agencies would understand that husbands usually know why their wives disappear.

"I honestly don't know," he said, looking me right in the eye. "We had our ups and downs like everybody else, but nothing serious. Then one morning after I went to the office, she just drove away from our house there in Hartford and I haven't seen her since. The neighbors saw her go. She was alone. That was a year ago last spring. I've been looking for her ever since, but all I've found out is that she was here on the Vineyard last summer."

"You never heard from her?"

"Our daughter, Frankie, got a postcard from her about a week after she left. It was mailed from New York City. It said she was fine and not to worry. That was all."

"I might want to talk with people you know. That includes your family and friends and the people you work with."

He nodded, then frowned. "Do you have to talk with our daughter? This business has upset her terribly."

"If I do, I'll try to make it painless."

"I'd rather you didn't do it at all. Frankie's a freshman at UConn, and she's got the jitters about that on top of this other thing." He rubbed his forehead. "This is a terrible situation. I'm afraid something has happened to Kathy. Otherwise I'm sure we'd have heard from her."

"I'll see what I can do, but, like I said, you shouldn't get your hopes too high."

We finished our beers and he went away. I ordered another and drank it while I looked over the file he'd left. Thornberry Security had been thorough and their information was useful. About the only thing I could do that they hadn't already done was talk to some people they hadn't interviewed here on the island.

Tomorrow was soon enough for that. Today I had

to get ready for the Derby and meet Brady Coyne when he came down from Boston. Brady used his law practice to support his fishing habit, and his plan was to combine some fly fishing in the Derby with some legal work for Sarah Fairchild, who owned two hundred acres up on the north shore overlooking Vineyard Sound.

My father and Sarah had met before I was born, and Sarah had taken to him enough to give him, and after his death me, lifetime access to Fairchild Cove, which consisted of Fairchild Point and Fairchild Beach, and which was one of the best bass-fishing and bluefishing spots on the island.

But now Sarah was old, and Brady was going to help her decide what to do with her estate. The very idea of trying to deal with that can of worms made me glad I wasn't a lawyer.

I left the Fireside, pushed Katherine Bannerman to the back of my mind, and headed home, thinking Derby thoughts. In September the bluefish are back, heading south after their summer sojourn to cooler northern waters, and to celebrate this return and to extend the tourist season, the Vineyard hosts a month-long fishing derby from the middle of September to the middle of October. Hundreds of fishermen and fisher-women come over from America and join island anglers in pursuit of striped bass, bluefish, bonito, and false albacore. Local plumbers, carpenters, landscapers, doctors, lawyers, merchants, and chiefs close up shop and go fishing. They become haggard and thin as they lose sleep and money to chase fish, and their customers grow surly when they're unable to find anyone to do work for them. In mid-October, when the Derby ends, normalcy returns and you can finally get somebody to rake your lawn or fix that leaky pipe in your basement.

The Derby thrives in spite of the increasing difficulty fishermen have getting to traditional angling spots. The problem is a familiar one in all resort communities, where local land is owned by outside people. On Martha's Vineyard, more and more off-islanders, both individuals and corporations, are buying property and closing off access routes to the woods and shore. NO TRESPASSING signs are tacked on locked gates that previously were open to fishermen and hunters. Local folks, who once felt welcome to cast a line or pop a cap almost anywhere on the Vineyard, now can't get close to hunting stands or fishing spots. Only a lucky few, like me, have permission to open gates and cross private lands. I was happy to be among the chosen, although I wasn't sure how much longer my privileges would last.

I spent the early afternoon with Zee on our screened porch lubricating our reels, replacing rusty hooks with new ones, and checking lines and leaders and rods. Katherine Bannerman refused to stay out of my mind, so while we worked I told Zee about the job I'd taken.

"People don't just leave without a reason," said Zee. "If you find out why she left, maybe you can find out where she went. What did you think of Bannerman?"

"I'm not sure. People wear different faces in different situations. I'm pretty certain he wants to find her, because he's spent a lot of time and money trying to do it. But on the other hand, he's made a lot of money in the last few years, so he can afford to finance an expensive search even if it's just for appearances."

"Is there another woman in his life?"

"None that Thornberry found."

"How about another man in hers?"

"No, but apparently she likes to dance and socialize more than her husband does, and it was a point of contention between them. According to Thornberry, Bannerman is either at the office or at home getting rested up so he can go back to the office. She wanted more than that in her life. Is that enough to send her packing, do you think?"

"Could be. Maybe she was having a midlife crisis."

"I thought only men had those. They divorce their wives and go off with blonde bimbos."

"It happens to both genders. The difference is, nowadays more women have enough money to leave boring hubbies. That wasn't always the case."

When our gear was in good shape, I drove with the kids to Fairchild Cove to make a few practice casts with each of the rods while Zee stayed home to wash her hair and muck out the guest room for Brady. The master plan was for us to take Brady, between lawyering stints, with us as we roamed the beaches in search of that prizewinning fish.

Joshua and Diana and I drove up to Vineyard Haven and managed to make a left turn at the infamous Tee intersection of State Road and the Edgartown Road, the site of one of the three worst permanent traffic jams on the island, the other two occurring at the Five Corners near the Vineyard

Haven ferry docks and between Al's Package Store and the A&P in Edgartown. Smart Vineyard Haven cops do nothing to correct the situations at the Tee or at the Five Corners, because the traffic jams slow cars to a crawl, which is the speed for which island roads are constructed. The jams, of course, are caused by people making left turns. I've been pointing this out for years, but does anybody listen? No. When I'm king of the world, I'm banning left turns.

We drove to West Tisbury, then turned into the narrow, sandy driveway that led to the Fairchild place. A hundred yards along, a smaller lane split off to the right. We took that and came to a locked gate. I had the key.

"How come there's a gate, Pa?" asked Joshua.

"Because the people who own the land don't want other people to come in."

"How come you have a key?"

"Because we're special."

The lane led down to Fairchild Cove. It wound through the trees and past some big rocks left behind by the glacier that, before its eventual retreat back north, had created the Vineyard, Nantucket, Long Island, and other south coastal islands by pushing part of what is now New Hampshire down into what is now the sea. On the far side of the big rocks, we curled over a rise and dropped down toward the shore.

"Look, Pa. A haunted house." Diana pointed.

It did look something like a haunted house. Actually, it was the stone cottage that some nineteenth-century Fairchild male had built as a hunting and fishing lodge for himself and his buddies. As cottages go, it was pretty fair-sized, and in its day it had all of the amenities. But for as long as I had been driving to the cove, the place had been in ruins and, as empty and abandoned houses do, it had taken on an increasingly forsaken air. Maybe it *was* haunted. According to tales I'd heard in my youth, it had never been used again after the drowning death of one of the Fairchild buddies who had been staying there with his fishing pals. The victim had, it was said, been done in by that familiar fisherman's notion that they're biting better over there than over here. He had waded out to the rocks at the tip of Fairchild Point, been trapped by the rising tide, and had drowned trying to get back to shore.

Whether his ghost still hung around the cottage was something I'd never thought of until my daughter's remark. Maybe Diana was psychic.

"I don't think that it's haunted," I said, "but it does look scary."

"No," insisted little Diana. "It's haunted, all right. It's got ghosts."

I glanced at her and she looked up at me. "Don't worry, Pa. They're not bad ghosts. You don't have to be scared of them."

The lane turned and we left the cottage behind us and came to the beach. Fairchild Point was to the west. Reaching out from its tip was the underwater sandbar that the drowned fisherman had followed to the fatal rocks that lay thirty yards out in the sound. The beach curved east to other rocks lying at the foot of the embankment that formed that end of the shallow cove. Out across the sound I could see the Elizabeth

Islands and Tarpaulin Cove, where I had anchored more than once while cruising in the *Shirley J.*

There was a battered pickup truck parked in front of us, and fifty yards to our left a large man was reeling in his line and looking in our direction. His grizzled face wore a scowl. Nate Fairchild, Sarah's son. He didn't like me or anybody else that I knew of. I parked and pointed at Fairchild. "You see that man?"

"Yes, Pa."

"Stay away from him. He doesn't like people to get too close to him when he's fishing. When you get out, go in the other direction to play."

"Is he one of those big people who don't like children?" asked Diana, who was particularly perceptive today.

"Yes, he is."

"I don't like him, either, then."

Smart Diana. We got out and I looked at Fairchild and lifted a hand. He made no reply, but turned back to his line. Diana and Joshua went down the beach away from Fairchild. I got the first rod from the roof rack.

The sun was bright, the air was warm, and the tide was just beginning to run west. It wasn't the best time to wet a line in the cove. That happens at first light just before or after the changing of the tide. But when you fish, any time is better than no time.

I tried all of our rods and several lures and never saw a sign of life in the sea. Off toward the point, Nate Fairchild wasn't catching anything, either. I put the last rod back on the roof rack and called to the kids. They were wet and sandy, so I had them go back in the water to rinse off most of the sand, then wrapped them in beach towels and took them home.

Zee was on the phone, so I put the kids into the outdoor shower, dried them again, and sent them into the house to get dressed. I hung their wet bathing suits on the line, and thought happy thoughts about that shower. An outdoor shower is one of the world's best things. You never have to worry about steaming up the walls or getting sand on the floor, and there's a fine feeling of freedom and airiness that you never get in an indoor shower. We used ours almost all year, forsaking it only when winter arrived in force.

I looked at the watch I'd found in the South Beach surf. You should never pay more than nine dollars for a watch, and mine had cost me only the price of a new band. A bargain. The watch said it was after four o'clock.

I had poured myself a Sam Adams and was up on the balcony drinking it when Zee, martini in hand, came up and sat beside me. She was sleek as a leopard, and her black hair gleamed. Joshua and Diana were down in the yard, looking up. The cats, Velcro and Oliver Underfoot, were in the garden doing cat things.

"Can we come up, Pa?"

"No, Josh. This is big-people time on the balcony."

It was the daily answer to his daily question. He tried another familiar one. "Can we build the tree house, Pa?"

The big beech behind the house was an excellent place for a tree house.

"Not today. Now go play. Your mother and I are having some private time."

Joshua and his sister went to look at the beech tree.

"That was Brady on the phone," said Zee. "Plans have changed. He's getting here at six and having supper with us, but Sarah Fairchild wants him to stay with her. So after we eat, we'll take him up there. I'm sorry he won't be staying with us."

"Well, Brady's been her lawyer for years. If she wants him to stay with her, I guess he should. She's business. We're just for fun."

Zee finished her martini and glanced at her watch. "Time to meet the boat. We're having spag for supper. I've thawed out a batch of your sauce, so you can warm that up and make the garlic bread while I go pick up Brady." She kissed me and went down the stairs.

I looked out over the gardens toward Nantucket Sound and thought about Katherine Bannerman. The dark blue waters touched a pale evening sky, and there was a single sail out on the horizon. Maybe Katherine was on that boat. Maybe she was looking at that sky.

Probably not.

Beauty is truth and truth beauty, the poet said, but I couldn't imagine much of either in the Bannerman case. I finished my beer and went down to the kitchen.

23

Chapter Two

Brady

I walked out of my office in Copley Square in Boston at one in the afternoon on the second Friday in September, and five hours later I had left America behind and was lugging my duffel off the ferry and down the long ramp at the harbor in Oak Bluffs on Martha's Vineyard, which locals like J. W. Jackson seem truly to believe is not America at all, but its own special world.

I'd spent the forty-five-minute ride up on the ferry deck, sniffing the salty sea air and watching the low hazy-green mound of the island grow larger as we chugged across Vineyard Sound from Woods Hole. I scanned the water—I never tire of looking at water—hoping to spot a school of blitzing bluefish, or maybe a shark or a whale or a harbor seal. I did spot some gulls and terns squawking and diving a half mile or so off the port side, but the ferry, inconsiderately, did not alter its course so I could see what was going on.

My mission on the Vineyard was business. Sarah Fairchild, one of my oldest and most beloved clients, had decided to sell off her Vineyard property. The

Fairchild estate encompassed about two hundred prime seaside acres in West Tisbury, where Sarah's old summer place was located. A golf course developer called the Isle of Dreams was vying with a nature preserve group, the Marshall Lea Foundation, for rights to the land, and my job was to check out the two parties, help Sarah decide what to do, and then make it happen.

I had all the paperwork in my briefcase. I also brought my fly rods and waders and foul-weather gear. Sure, I'd do Sarah's business. But my mind was on the fishing.

J. W. Jackson and I had been planning to compete in the Martha's Vineyard Striped Bass and Bluefish Derby since the previous winter, me with my fly rod—J.W. calls it a "toy," hoping to rile me, which he does—and him with his long-distance surf-casting gear.

I had cast off the jetties at State Beach and into the Wasque rips with J.W. and his wife, Zee, a few times in summers past, and we sometimes caught a few stripers and bluefish. We'd never managed any keeper bass, but J.W. smoked the blues and converted some of them into pâté. As he liked to say: Delish!—especially as an accompaniment to afternoon martinis on the Jacksons' second-floor balcony overlooking Zee's vegetable garden and bird feeders, and in the distance, the salt pond where J.W. dug steamers and raked quahogs.

But the Derby, he once explained to me, was to normal fishing what the Daytona 500 was to driving to Harry's for your Sunday *Globe*. "Fishing in the Derby is not relaxing," he said. "It's competitive. The point is to win."

"I don't care about winning," I said.

"Of course you do."

Okay. He was probably right.

J.W. liked to get up before the sun and be on the beach just around the time when the eastern sky was turning from black to purple. I liked it then, too. There's rarely any breeze at first light, and if the tide's right, you can often see the swirls and flashes of feeding fish close enough to reach with a fly rod.

In the summer, we usually had the whole beach to ourselves at first light.

During the Derby in the fall, J.W. said, it's different. These guys fish all night and all day. They don't sleep. Reputations—not to mention prizes like cars and boats and money—are at stake.

Nail a big striper, J.W. said, and you should be prepared for swarms of fishermen to materialize out of the dunes and crowd you from both sides.

So it's competitive. I could handle it.

When I told Billy, my older son, that I was planning to enter the Derby, he laughed. "You'll wimp out, Pop. I know you. You've gotta get up early and stay out late to compete in the Derby. Oh, when you were younger you might've done it. But you've gotten lazy in your old age."

"Don't be ridiculous," I said to him. "I will fish every night."

"Sure," he said. "Unless it's raining, or the tide's wrong, or you've had too many old-fashioneds, or you're tired, or you meet some woman, or—"

"Whaddya wanna bet, smart guy?"

"Dinner at Redbones next time I'm home," he said promptly. "I say you will crap out at least one night."

"And I say I won't," I said. "I'm looking forward to you buying me dinner for a change."

"I am totally confident," Billy said.

Two hungry men could gorge themselves on ribs and pulled pork and wash it down with a few beers at Redbones in Davis Square for under forty bucks. That was hardly the point.

A bet with another man might be a matter of pride in accomplishment. A bet with my number-one son, who never passed up a chance to rag on me, was a matter of honor.

So I would work all day and fish every night.

I could do it. It would be fun.

I wasn't too old. No way.

I spotted Zee, J.W.'s wife, before she saw me. She was scooched down beside her little Jeep Wrangler talking to a chocolate-colored Labrador retriever with a faded red bandanna around its neck. Zee's black hair hung in a long braid down the middle of her back. She was wearing jeans and one of J.W.'s old plaid shirts with the tails flapping.

When I dropped my duffel bag onto the pavement beside her, her head jerked up. "Oh, gee, Brady. I didn't see you. You shouldn't sneak up on a girl like that." She gave the dog's muzzle a final scratch, then stood up and gave me a hard hug and a fat smooch on the mouth.

I stuffed my briefcase and rod cases in beside the duffel bag, then climbed in front, and ten minutes later Zee pulled into the dirt turnaround in front of their house.

Joshua and Diana, the two Jackson kids, came scooting around the corner to greet their mother, then skidded to a stop when they saw me.

"You remember Mr. Coyne," Zee told them. "Say hello."

First Joshua, then Diana stepped forward, held out their hands, and said hello. I squatted down and shook hands with each of them.

Then Zee took my hand and led me up to the balcony, where J.W. was slouched in a chair with his heels up on the railing and a martini glass resting on his belly. We shook hands, and he jerked his head at the pitcher and the glasses and the plate of crackers and pâté on the table beside him.

I spread some pâté on a cracker and poured myself a drink.

"Zee filled you in on the fishing, I imagine," J.W. said.

"Yep." I took the chair beside him and propped my own heels up on the railing. I'd decided not to tell J.W. or Zee about my bet with Billy. If I failed, I didn't want to lose face with anybody else. Billy would make it bad enough for me. "Derby starts tonight, eh?"

"Midnight," he said.

"Who won the toss?"

"Me. We'll alternate nights."

"Different with kids, isn't it?" I said.

He grinned.

J.W. didn't ask about my business, and I didn't ask about his. Such polite conversational gambits are okay for people who don't know each other very well or have nothing more interesting to talk about.

So J.W. and I discussed fishing and tree houses and baseball and Hemingway while we sipped our martinis and gazed over the tops of the trees toward the sea until Zee called us down for supper. Spaghetti with J.W.'s secret sauce, a fresh loaf of Portuguese bread, green salad from Zee's garden, and a nice red wine.

After he got the kids tucked in for the night, J.W. and I climbed into Zee's Jeep and drove up-island to Sarah Fairchild's place, where I'd be staying for the week.

Even in the dark, the old Fairchild house looked vaguely ramshackle and run-down. It was a meandering place, originally a classic New England farmhouse with several fireplaces and a wraparound porch. It had been built shortly after the Civil War, and over the years, ells and wings and sheds had been added on to it until it connected with the sway-backed barn. Tufts of grass and weeds sprouted from the gravel turnaround in front, and a shutter flapped beside an upstairs window in the evening breeze. A few yellow lights glowed from the downstairs windows. Even so, the place looked dark and uninhabited.

I unloaded my stuff from the back of the Jeep and thanked J.W. for the dinner and the ride. He said he'd drop by in the afternoon to get me signed up for the Derby so that the monster fish I was sure to catch would qualify me for the new car or the boat or one of the canned hams.

I lugged my duffel and briefcase and rod cases up to the Fairchild front porch. I took a deep breath before I rang the bell. I hoped anybody but Nate would open the door.

The man who opened the door was not Sarah's ne'er-do-well son, Nate. This guy was somewhere in his twenties. He was younger than Nate, and trimmer than Nate, and less tanned and grizzled than Nate, and unlike Nate, who generally scowled, this man had a pleasant, boyish smile.

But like Nate—and like his mother and his grandmother—he had the aristocratic Fairchild look. He was tall and fair, poised and rather handsome.

He held the door wide for me. "Come on in," he said. "You must be Mr. Coyne."

"I am indeed," I said.

I bent for my duffel bag, but he beat me to it.

He lugged it into the hallway and left it on the floor. Then he turned and held out his hand. "I'm sorry," he said. "We've never actually met. I'm Patrick Fairchild."

Patrick, I knew, was Sarah Fairchild's only grandchild, her daughter Eliza's son from one of her early marriages. The first, I think it was. With Eliza, it was hard to keep track.

That made Patrick the last of the Fairchilds. He had taken back the family name after his father committed suicide. Now Eliza had passed childbearing age, and Nate, her younger brother and Sarah's only other child, had shown no inclination to continue the

Fairchild line, at least not in any legitimate way. So that left Patrick.

I shook Patrick's hand and told him to call me Brady.

"You must be beat," he said. "What about a drink?"

I shrugged. "Well—"

At that moment, in a jangle of bracelets and a cloud of musky perfume, Eliza appeared from around the corner. "Of *course* he'll have a drink." She was holding a highball glass in one hand and a lighted cigarette in the other. She threw the arm with the glass on the end of it around my neck and aimed a kiss at my mouth. I got my face turned in the nick of time, and she nailed me somewhere near my ear.

She chuckled. "Dear old Brady. Aren't you glad to see me?"

I patted Eliza's shoulder and managed to slip out of her embrace. "I'm always glad to see you, Eliza," I said.

It was true. Eliza was easy to look at. She was tall and willowy and well preserved, a typical Fairchild, and she looked at least ten years younger than her age, which I knew was approaching fifty. Despite her golf and tennis and sailing and other outdoorsy activities, her skin was still baby-soft and, except for little crinkles at the corners of her eyes when she smiled, wrinkle-free. She wore her golden sun-streaked hair long, and she had it loosely tied back in a red silk scarf that matched her shorts.

Eliza had long, tanned, athletic legs, a slender body, elegant hands, and a mouthful of even white teeth, and it wasn't hard to understand why men had always found her attractive. Four marriages, one dead husband, and three divorces, I thought it was, though I might have missed one. She spent most of her time at Hilton Head, where she shared a town house with Patrick and competed in amateur golf and tennis tournaments. She and Patrick always spent the summer months on the Vineyard with Sarah, her mother. But usually they'd departed by Labor Day.

I hadn't expected her to be here now.

She took my hand and led me into the living room. "What'll it be?" she said. She held up her empty glass. "I'm drinking scotch, myself."

"Maybe a splash of bourbon, handful of ice cubes," I said.

She turned to the sideboard, then smiled at me over her shoulder. "It's about time I found somebody to drink with me," she said. "Patrick is such a poop."

Patrick had followed us into the living room. He stood there in the doorway, smiling uncertainly. "Grandmother will want to see Brady," he said.

"Of course," said Eliza. "But Brady *certainly* needs a drink first."

I shrugged. "Actually, I would like to say hello to Sarah."

She poured our drinks, then handed a glass to me. "When did you see her last?"

"Back in the winter sometime. I've talked to her on the phone several times since she came to the Vineyard for the summer, though."

"Try not to be shocked," she said.

"Shocked? What do you mean?"

Eliza flopped on the sofa and lit another cigarette.

"Just like her," she said, "not to say anything." She sipped her drink, then looked up at me. "I bet she hasn't even mentioned her health."

"I always ask," I said. "She always changes the subject." I took the chair across from her. "What's the matter?"

Patrick came over and sat beside Eliza. She patted his leg. "Patrick has been such a good boy," she said, "caring for his dear old granny, reading poetry to her, angling hard for his little piece of the Fairchild pie, refusing to have a filial cocktail with his mother." She took a sip of scotch. "She's got cancer, Brady."

"Oh, hell," I said. "How bad?"

She took a drag on her cigarette, then laid her head back on the sofa and blew a long plume of smoke at the ceiling. "Very bad. Couldn't be worse."

"How long has she known?"

"Since December. They gave her about a year. That was nine months ago. That's why she's so fired up to settle the matter of what's left of the Fairchild estate. She doesn't trust Nate and me."

"You can hardly blame her," said Patrick.

"At least I've given her a grandchild," said Eliza. "All Nate does is fish and fight and sponge off his mother. Mother has been talking with several extremely unctuous men representing something called the Marshall Lea Foundation. They want her to deed the property over to them for some silly nature preserve for practically nothing. Mother is rather, um, vulnerable just now, and I'm quite fearful that she'll do something foolish."

"'The lady doth protest too much, methinks,'" murmured Patrick.

Eliza snapped her head around and glared at him. "What's that supposed to mean?"

"If she wants to give away her property," Patrick said, "that's her right."

Eliza smiled wickedly at him. "Yes, of course it is. And that would be the end of what's left of the Fairchild family fortune, and then you and your uncle would have to get actual jobs. I don't suppose you've considered that."

Patrick shrugged. "And thank God for alimony, eh, Mother?"

She shook her head, then turned to me. "You have my mother's power of attorney?"

I nodded.

"Well, I do hope you intend to talk her out of this ridiculous nature preserve idea."

"I'll advise her about her options," I said, "and then she'll do what she wants." I drained my drink, put the glass on the coffee table, and started to push myself to my feet. "I'd like to see her."

"Of course you would," she said. "But you'd like another drink, first, wouldn't you?"

"No, Eliza. One was plenty." I stood up. "Where's Sarah?"

"We've set up a bed on the sunporch for her," she said. "She doesn't get around very well anymore. I suppose with autumn coming we'll have to move her inside." She got up and took my hand. "Come on, then. Patrick, darling, why don't you take Brady's stuff up to his room like a good boy."

"Certainly, Mother," he said. He looked at me and rolled his eyes, then left the room.

Eliza led me through the living room and pulled open the double doors that led onto the glassed-in sunporch.

Sarah was slouched in a wheelchair. A blanket was spread over her legs, her hands were folded in her lap, and her chin rested on her chest. Against the wall, a muted television was showing an old black-and-white movie.

Sarah Fairchild was in her middle eighties. For the twelve years I'd been her lawyer, she'd always looked the same—tall, angular, sharp-eyed, and altogether regal. She had a quick wit and a sharp nose for cant and deceit. As a young woman, Sarah had been a skeet-shooting champion and a mountain climber, and in the years since I'd known her, she'd managed what was left of the family fortune, donating generous amounts of it to homeless shelters and battered women's shelters and other causes that I investigated and vetted for her. She lived in a modest condominium in Marblehead during the cold months and spent her summers on the Vineyard, as Fairchilds had been doing since the Industrial Revolution.

Now, suddenly, Sarah had gotten old. Her white hair looked thin and dull, and her skin was papery, and I had to look hard to detect the faint rise and fall of her chest as she slept in her wheelchair.

Eliza went over to her, touched her arm, and shook her gently. "Mother?" she said. "Mother, wake up now. Brady Coyne's here to see you."

Sarah shuddered, then slowly lifted her head. She looked at me for a moment, blinked, and then smiled.

"Brady?" she whispered. "How nice."

"Brady will be staying with us," said Eliza. "Remember?"

Sarah turned her head slowly and looked up at her daughter. "Of course I remember. I'm not dead yet." She shook Eliza's hand off her arm. "Leave us now. Brady and I need to talk."

"Mother," said Eliza, "it's nearly ten o'clock. Don't you think—"

"Shoo." Sarah flapped the back of her hand at Eliza, then looked at me. "I do nothing but sleep these days."

Eliza bent and kissed Sarah's cheek, then straightened up. "Have a nightcap with me when you're done," she said to me, and then she turned and left the room.

"Shut those doors," Sarah said to me. "I want to talk with you."

I went over, pushed the double doors shut, then pulled a wooden chair next to Sarah's wheelchair. I took one of her hands in both of mine. "You haven't been doing a very good job of keeping your lawyer informed," I said.

She smiled, and I saw the old twinkle flash briefly in her eyes. "It's hardly relevant," she said. "I'll die soon, they say. A fairly predictable occurrence for somebody my age. Rather interesting, actually. It does tend to give one focus, make one more alert. I have enjoyed being down here on our blessed isle, watching the seasons change. The angle of the morning sun is quite lovely when it hits the tops of the dunes this time of year. Back in Marblehead, I never paid much attention to the sun." She gave my hand a little squeeze. "I've got to decide what to do, and I've got to do it quickly."

"It's pretty late," I said. "We can talk about it tomorrow."

"I don't feel like anything should wait for tomorrow anymore," she said. She was staring down at her lap, where her bony fingers lay laced quietly together. "I'd intended to do this my way, in my own time. Have you help me explore our options, make my decision, and then just do it. Alas, the word has somehow leaked out that the Fairchild estate is up for grabs, and there's been a parade of men in suits dropping in and calling on the telephone and writing letters and sending prospectuses and generally trying to ingratiate themselves, as if I'd make a business decision on the basis of their manners."

"Which men in suits?" I said.

She smiled. "Eliza is friendly with some golf people. Pleasant fellows, actually. They have taken the liberty of drawing up designs and plans for my approval. I suspect she's sleeping with at least two of them."

"And what about the nature preserve idea?"

"It's rather appealing," Sarah said. "The Marshall Lea Foundation would buy the property and deed it over to the town of West Tisbury with stipulations that they and I will agree to."

"The golf folks will pay you more, of course," I said.

"Oh, indeed, yes."

37

"You have other options, you know."

She nodded. "Yes. I can do nothing and let Nathan and Elizabeth fight about it until they kill each other while this house crumbles around them, and then poor ineffectual Patrick will be stuck with it, and soon thereafter, the town will take it all for taxes." She looked up at me and smiled. "It's a rather tempting scenario, actually. My children have squandered their lives, unless you count prizewinning bluefish and golf trophies productive living."

"We can also just put the place on the market," I said. "There are plenty of people who'd buy it and care for it and live on it the way the Fairchilds have always done."

"Adam, I'm afraid, would turn over in his grave if I did that." Adam Fairchild, Sarah's husband, had died shortly before she retained me. He'd devoted his life to stupid investments and disastrous business schemes—many, but not all, of which Sarah had rescued him from. "No," she said softly, "I owe it to the Fairchilds to keep our legacy alive. The Fairchilds deserve to be properly remembered and honored."

"The Fairchild Country Club?" I said.

She smiled and shrugged her bony shoulders. "If it comes to that. Or the Fairchild Wildlife Sanctuary."

"How are you leaning?" I said.

"Leaning?" She gave me a sad smile. "I am leaning over my grave, dear Brady, and I'm about to topple in. I would like to make it simple for all of us, you included. I want to liquidate everything—this"—she waved her hand around—"and Marblehead and whatever is left of my investments. When I die, I want you to deliver a check to Elizabeth and a check to Nathan and a check to Patrick and be done with it, neat and clean and tidy."

"The golf course or the nature preserve, then," I said.

"So it seems. Unless you have a brainstorm. I want it settled before you leave."

I nodded. "That's why I'm here."

"Now don't try to fool an old lady, Brady Coyne. I know you. You're here to catch fish."

"That, too," I said.

I could hear the distant roll of the surf and the soughing of the breeze through the scrubby pines from my second-floor bedroom in the back of the Fairchild house. Salty sea air billowed the curtains, and yellow moonlight filtered in through the open screened windows. I expected to fall asleep instantly and stay that way. Sea air generally does that to me.

Maybe it was the nightcap that Eliza had talked me into after she got Sarah tucked into her bed on the sunporch for the night, or maybe it was my visions of hooking a giant striper and winning the Derby, but for some reason I slept fitfully. When my eyes popped open in the darkness for the second or third time, I checked my watch. It was around three-thirty in the morning, the darkest hour.

I figured I was awake for a while, so I got dressed, slipped downstairs, and went outside for a smoke.

The Derby had been open since midnight—for three and a half hours. J.W., along with several hundred other competitors, was out there somewhere winging his Roberts plug impossibly long distances into the dark ocean. I wished I was with him.

I went around to the back of the house, where the Fairchild land sloped away over a broad meadow down to their beach. I thought about the big bass and bluefish that were probably herding baitfish against the rocks there. They'd be swirling and flashing their tails and dorsal fins in the moonlight. I was half tempted to go back upstairs, collect my gear, and spend the rest of the night on the beach.

But I didn't. I had a week's worth of nights to fish with J.W. and Zee, and I had an important bet with my son that I intended to win. What I needed to do this night was get some sleep.

I'd just ground out my cigarette under my heel and turned to head back into the house when I heard an engine start and saw headlights in the turnaround out front. As I watched, a car pulled slowly out of the driveway and turned east on the dirt road. A late-night visitor slipping away after a quick visit to Eliza's bed? Nate, heading off to the beach with his surf-casting rod to be there before the sun?

None of my business. Both of Sarah's children were grown-ups, regardless of how they acted.

Eliza rapped on my door around nine the next morning. "Are you decent?" she called.

"I'm always decent," I answered primly.

"Too bad," she said. She opened the door and came in, bearing a mug of coffee. "There are altogether too many decent men in this world." Eliza was wearing white shorts that set off her tanned legs nicely and a pale blue tank top that matched her eyes. Pink lipstick, just a hint of green eye shadow, dangly silver earrings.

She looked quite fetching first thing in the morning, and I told her so.

"I'm glad someone thinks so," she said. She wished she could linger in my bedroom for more compliments, she said, but she was off to Farm Neck for a round of golf. She'd be back by midafternoon, in time for gin and tonics and flattery. She'd be hurt if I didn't join her.

I said I didn't know what my plans were, but if I was here, a gin and tonic would suit me, and flattering her was not difficult.

Patrick, she said, was still asleep, and she assumed Nate was in his room at the end of the wing near the barn, sleeping off his night of fishing. Sarah was on the sunporch. Patrick would be up soon to attend to her.

I should make myself at home, Eliza said. Then she left.

I drank my coffee sitting up in bed, took a shower, then went downstairs. When I peeked in on Sarah, she had an open book lying facedown on her lap, and her chin was slumped onto her chest the way I'd found her the previous night.

So I gathered up my briefcase, a portable telephone, and another mug of coffee, and I took them out to the patio. I had to absorb all the information on the Marshall Lea Foundation and the Isle of Dreams Development Corporation that my secretary, Julie, had collected for me, and then I'd make a few phone calls and set up some meetings. I intended to be finished by midafternoon. I itched to do some fishing.

It was a crystal-clear September morning on the Vineyard. A stiff breeze was kicking up whitecaps out in the sound, and gulls were wheeling around over the water like white scraps of windblown paper.

The Fairchild property was an awfully pretty part of the island. There were rolling meadows, groves of scrub oak and pine, a couple of small freshwater ponds, and a long, curving stretch of beach. I could visualize the golf course they could build here. St. Andrews came to mind.

I turned my attention to my briefcaseful of papers. Julie had dug up business histories and financial statements and résumés of key personnel and photocopies of newspaper and magazine articles, and from what I was able to gather, both the nature-preserve people and the golf-course people were legitimate, which would make my job a lot easier.

After a couple of hours, Patrick summoned me for lunch, so I stuffed all the papers back into my briefcase and called it a day's work.

Patrick had made egg salad sandwiches and a jug of lemonade, and he and I ate with Sarah on the sunporch. After we took our dishes inside, I filled Sarah in and told her that I expected to have some recommendations for her within a few days.

She stared outside while I talked and didn't say much. Once I caught her squeezing her fists in her lap. "Pain?" I said.

She looked up at me and smiled weakly. "Nothing unbearable, honestly. A twinge now and then, that's all."

"Do you have medication?"

"Oh yes. A lovely nurse comes by every day to bathe me and check my vitals. She gives me shots and makes sure I have my pills handy. And don't worry. I don't have any foolish courage. I take the pills when I need them. For now, the shots and the pills do the job."

I couldn't think of anything comforting to say, so I pushed myself to my feet. "Well," I said, "with your permission, I think I'll take my fly rod down to the beach and do some casting, get limbered up. J. W. Jackson's picking me up a little later. I'm fishing in the Derby tonight, you know."

She smiled. "Good for you. I hope you beat Nate. Do give J.W. a kiss for me, will you?"

"I will certainly not kiss J.W. But I'll tell him you'd like to deliver one in person."

Half an hour later I was standing on the beach with my feet bare and my pants legs rolled up and the water lapping around my ankles, casting a Lefty's Deceiver out beyond the place where the gentle waves lifted and spilled over. In the cove, there wasn't much surf, and I could see where the bottom dropped away, within easy reach of a fly rod. I didn't expect to catch anything under the bright afternoon sun, although it wouldn't have surprised me if a few stripers were cruising along the edge of that drop-off. After the sun went down, it would be a prime spot.

Even more prime was the rocky point that jutted

out into the ocean at the left-hand end of the cove. Now, at low tide, the rocks had risen up out of the water, and all but those on the very tip of the point were surrounded by wet sand. When the tide rolled in, it would cover the rocks, and the waves would crash around them. Then the big stripers and bluefish would come in to gobble sand eels and baitfish and crabs and any other unfortunate prey they might find being dashed around in the swirling currents.

So I cast rhythmically, working my way along the beach. Once or twice I thought I saw the shadow of a swimming fish, and it focused my attention. I was casting to one of those shadows—real or imagined, I wasn't sure—when suddenly my line started moving sideways.

My first reaction was to pull back on my line and lift my rod as I would do if I'd had a strike. I realized this was no fish at about the same instant I heard the man's voice growl, "Who in hell are you?"

I looked over my right shoulder. Nate Fairchild was standing about twenty yards down the beach from me. He was cranking on his twelve-foot surf-casting outfit, and his lure had snagged my line.

"Nate, dammit," I said. "It's me. Brady Coyne."

"Oh, yeah. Mama's lawyer. Well, get your ass off my beach." His lure had run down my line and snagged my fly. He reeled it up, then reached down with a knife and cut my fly off.

Nate wore one of those fore-and-aft fishing caps with one bill over the back of his neck and another over his eyes, along with cutoff jeans and a gray shirt with the sleeves rolled up past his elbows. Pale curly hair grew thick on his legs and arms and poked out from under his cap, and in the shadow of his visor I could see that he wore dark sunglasses and had a bushy sun-bleached beard.

"Gimme my fly," I said.

"Screw you, lawyer. Just get the hell offa my beach."

I reeled up my line, then went over to where he was standing. He stood there glowering at me. He was holding his long surf rod in both hands like a lance. I wondered if he intended to run me through. My slender fly rod was no match for his heavy weapon.

"For Christ's sake, Nate, grow up," I said. "This beach belongs to your mother, not you. I have her permission to fish here, and I intend to do that."

He stepped close to me. "Yeah? Well, she's up there dying in her wheelchair and I'm standing right here. So what're you gonna do about that?"

"I'm going to keep fishing. There's plenty of room for both of us on this beach."

He pushed his face close to mine. "I don't share my beach with nobody, never mind some goddam lawyer who wants to sell it off. So if you don't—"

At that moment I heard a shout. When I turned, I saw J.W. coming down the sandy path toward us.

I was glad to see him.

Chapter Three

J.W.

The Derby started at midnight, and I made my first cast about ten seconds later, laying my Robert's Ranger out through the darkness toward the horizon I could not see. I was shoulder to shoulder with other angling hopefuls, each of us quite willing to catch a champion fish on the first day of the Derby. But, like everyone else on the beach, I caught only some small-ish blues, the biggest of which I dutifully took to the morning weigh-in.

The day's winners all came in from somewhere else, unspecified spots such as "the South Shore," "the North Shore," or "Chappaquiddick," for it is one of the curiosities about fishermen that they are secretive about where they catch fish. Of course, the reason for such closed lips is that the fishermen don't want anybody else to know where the big fish are.

However, on Martha's Vineyard there are only so many places where you can fish, and everybody knows where all of them are, so there are no secret spots. Moreover, yesterday's fish may well not be there today, so even if you had a secret spot, the chances of more giant blues or bass being there the next time you go are fairly dim. Still, most fishermen feel obligated to lie about where they caught yesterday's fish. It's an honored tradition.

I annoy my fishing friends by telling everyone where and when and with what lure I managed to catch my fish.

Tony D'Agostine, sergeant of the Edgartown Police, had planned, I knew, to be out on the beaches at midnight with the rest of us, but after I got to the morning weigh-in at the shed that used to be the Edgartown Junior Yacht Club and learned that my nice little five-pound blue wasn't going to be a contender, I went out into the parking lot and ran into Tony. He was looking as red-eyed as I knew I looked.

"Well, at least you got a fish," he said. "I didn't even wet a line."

"You're probably smart not to play with the big boys," I said. "After all, what chance would a mere small-town cop have competing with world-class anglers such as me?"

"A kid went missing last night," said Tony. "Wandered off with his dog while Mom was hanging out clothes. Dog came home when he got hungry, but the kid didn't. So much for man's best friend. Half the cops and civilians on the island hunted for the boy all night. They found him this morning about a quarter mile from home. People looking for him must have walked right past him a dozen times, but I guess he was sleeping. Anyway, he's fine. Good thing it wasn't cold last night."

"Maybe it's something in the island air," I said. "I met a guy yesterday who's looking for a missing wife.

Does the name Bannerman ring any bells?"

"Seems to me that some PIs were asking about a woman by that name a while back. We get missing persons reports every year. Some college girl goes off with one of the local Lotharios and doesn't make it home by two, her roommates call the cops. She's shacked up someplace, and finally shows a couple of days later, but meanwhile we all get stuck with an extra shift."

"Gee, Tony, I never knew you read Nicholas Rowe."

"You don't know a lot of things, J.W. Anyway, the lost kid is home and I'm headed home myself to get some sleep. Not much happening at Wasque, you say?"

"Five- or six-pounders. No big winners that I know about. I'm taking mine home so I can smoke them."

"Where's Zee? Even if you can't catch any real fish, she usually can."

"She's home taking care of her children, like a normal wife."

"Zee is not your normal wife. I'm surprised that she's home and you're out fishing. I'd have thought it might be the other way around."

"The decision was a democratic one. She lost the coin toss. Tonight she'll be out there on the beach and I'll be home with the tots. You, of course, will be back on the street protecting and serving."

"Wrong. I'll be fishing tonight with your wife."

He walked away, and I went to the Dock Street Coffee Shop for a cup of coffee, then climbed into my old Toyota Land Cruiser and went home. There, behind the shed in back of the house, I scaled and filleted my fish and put the fillets in plastic bags. Then I put the bags in the freezer. Fresh bluefish is best for cooking, but, for reasons that elude me, frozen bluefish smokes better than fresh bluefish. It is another unsolved mystery of the sea.

Inside the house, Zee was getting ready to go to work at the hospital. During Derby time, by dint of strategic deals made with nonfishing nurses, she arranged to keep working, but at odd hours and never when the tides were best. Once the Derby was over, she'd go back to normal shifts. Zee loved being a nurse, but had recently been wearing her I FISH, THERE-FORE I AM T-shirt.

She kissed me. "I'll be back at six, and I plan to be at Wasque not much later. Don't forget to pick up Brady and get him registered and bring him here. You'll be the love of my life if you have supper waiting for us in a little cooler, so we can take it with us."

"It shall be done, madam. I'll include a thermos of coffee and another of vodka in case you want cocktails. When can I expect to actually spend some time with you again?"

"In about a month. Unless I land a sixty-pound bass, that is. If I get her tonight, I'll quit fishing and stay home alone with you." She looked up at me and batted her long lashes. "Of course, that means that if you want to stay home with me you'll have to stop fishing, too. But you won't mind, I'm sure."

"I'll see you in a month."

"What a man. And they say romance is dead."

She went out and climbed into her Jeep and drove away.

Joshua and Diana came in. "Pa, will you build us the tree house today?"

I actually liked the idea of a tree house. Tarzan had a good one, according to the old Johnny Weismuller movies. It would be nice to have one like his, complete with Cheeta and Jane, but that was probably beyond my scope. Something smaller, maybe.

"Let's go look at the tree," I said.

We went out and stood beneath the big beech tree in the backyard. It was huge and old and had many branches, some of which swept the ground.

We circled the tree and commented upon possible places to build our tree house. After a while we zeroed in on what seemed to be the right spot. Then, with me giving the children a hand and trying not to grit my teeth too hard as we got higher, we climbed up to our chosen branches and viewed them at close hand. They still looked good.

We inched down to the ground. Why is it that parents are afraid to have their kids do what they themselves used to do fearlessly when they were kids? As the poet said, down we forget as up we grow.

Like a lot of people who were raised without too much money, I keep a supply of stuff that I don't really need right now but might need some day. I store my collection in a corral out by the shed. Included is my private lumberyard, which is made up of scraps of good wood left over from jobs or salvaged from somewhere or other.

We scouted the lumber pile, then had lunch, and then worked for two hours, sorting boards and timber, until it was nap time for Joshua and Diana.

While they slept, I thought about Katherine Bannerman.

Thornberry Security was good at its work. If Katherine was easy to find, they'd have done it. But that hadn't happened, so it was probable that one of three scenarios existed: Katherine didn't know who she was, she was dead or incapacitated, or she didn't want to be found.

Although there are cases of amnesiacs living long lives without knowing their own identities or having them discovered, such people are rare. Usually they attract attention and someone figures out who they are. On an island as small as Martha's Vineyard, it was unlikely that an attractive woman like Katherine Bannerman could be suffering from amnesia without someone knowing about it and trying to help her. So I scratched amnesia from my slate.

Because of the island's size, it also seemed unlikely that Katherine had died or become too incapacitated to identify herself without anyone noticing. Since she had spent a summer on the Vineyard, someone would have reported her injury or death to the authorities.

Unless, of course, someone didn't want her death known. That was always a possibility. People dropped out of sight every year, and some of them were at the bottom of the sea. But murder, in spite of the headlines it garnered, was a rare crime. I didn't dismiss homicide from my index of possibilities, but I didn't put it at the top of the list, either.

The third possibility was that Katherine hadn't been found because she didn't want to be found. If that was the case, she might be elusive indeed, especially if she was smart and if she had planned things out ahead of time.

On the other hand, even people who want to disappear often fail because of their habits. They keep their old Social Security card. If they played mahjongg before, they still do. If they were in a particular profession before, they enter it again. If they liked small towns before, they live in one now. Most important, they find it almost impossible to stay out of touch with family and friends. Many a criminal on the run has found himself surrounded by cops because he just had to call Mom or an old pal or a girlfriend.

I opened the Bannerman file and read through it. Thornberry operatives had been on the case since the previous fall, and they'd talked with everyone I would have talked with—James and Frankie Bannerman, Katherine's friends and neighbors, Bannerman's employees, the cops, everybody who might know something or might have heard from Katherine.

James and Katherine had been born and bred just outside of Hartford, where James and Frankie still lived. They had married young and honeymooned on the Vineyard. Katherine worked in a bank and James in a small computer software firm. A couple of years later they started a business on the side, working out of their garage. James was the engineer and Katherine was the bookkeeper and accountant. Before long they were both working full-time at home. They made something I didn't understand having to do with computers, and after ten years they began to make some real money. They moved the firm out of the garage and into an industrial park and hired professional employees, including some to do the work Katherine had been doing.

That may have been when Katherine began to feel that life had more to offer than a husband who spent all of his time at work. She got a part-time job teaching accounting at the local junior college, and joined a bridge club, and became involved in charities.

She met men and liked being with some of them, but as far as Thornberry knew she had taken no lovers. She tried to interest James in a social life, but he was all business and was making more money every day. He seemed honestly shocked when she left him.

The single postcard to Frankie was the only contact Thornberry knew about. No further communications had come from Katherine to the Bannerman house.

Frankie Bannerman had put up a brave front during the summer but had fallen apart after Labor Day a year ago, so her father had contacted Thornberry Security. Thornberry's operatives tracked Katherine to the Vineyard, where she had sold her car in August. On the Vineyard they'd learned that she'd lived under her own name in West Tisbury, where she had joined a local women's group. They'd talked with some of the women and learned that Katherine had simply gone away on Labor Day weekend, the weekend of the great migration from the island, when the Summer People head back to America.

And that was about it. Thornberry had researched all of the usual paper trails that lead to persons gone astray, but in vain. Katherine hadn't used her Social Security card or driver's license or credit cards, hadn't been reported dead or injured, hadn't phoned or written to friends or acquaintances. She hadn't, in short, left any signs of where she'd gone or why. She'd sold the car and disappeared.

I went over the report again, then looked at my watch. I only had about an hour before I was scheduled to pick up Brady. Too late to sleuth today, but still time to do some more tree-house building.

I took my long ladder and some tools out to the tree. By the time the tads woke up, I had the supporting timbers in place and had started nailing floor beams across them. By gadfry, the house was already beginning to look like one.

"Can we help, Pa? Will it be done today? Can we come up the ladder? Shall I bring up this board?"

"No, no, no, and no," I said, climbing down. "No more work today."

I put the ladder on the ground to discourage temptation when the paternal back was turned. "I've got to drive up-island now, and you two have to come with me."

They brightened. "Where are we going?"

"To get Brady and sign him up for the Derby. Then we'll come back in time to see your mother before she and Brady go fishing, and then we'll have supper."

So we did that. At the house, Eliza Fairchild, Sarah's daughter, told me that Brady had gone fishing down at the cove, so I got back in my truck, went down the driveway, and turned through the open gate. The stone cottage looked emptier than ever as we passed it and drove on down to the water.

Off to the left about a hundred feet down the beach I could see Nate Fairchild and Brady Coyne. They were standing nose to nose. As I got out of the truck and started toward them, Nate raised a big fist.

I shouted his name.

"I wouldn't make that mistake, Nate," I said, coming up to them. "If you plan to do any fishing in this Derby, you'll be smart to keep your hands to yourself."

"Who's gonna make me?" he sneered. "You?" But he hesitated.

"Not me," I said. "But Brady, here, will take your casting arm off at the shoulder and hand it to you on a platter. He may be a lawyer now, but before that he was an instructor in unarmed combat at Quantico."

"You're a damned liar."

"If you think so, take a swing at him. You can spend the next six months in a body cast, and I can't think of one person who'll shed a tear." I turned to Brady, who was eyeing me from an expressionless lawyer's face. "I'll hold your rod for you. I know you don't want to get sand in your reel."

"Thanks," said Brady, "but maybe it won't come to that." He looked at Nate. "It's up to you. I think this beach is big enough for both of us, but maybe you don't."

Nate glared at him, but said nothing.

"You're a lucky man, Nate," I said. "If I hadn't showed up, you probably would have thrown that punch."

Nate rubbed a rough hand across his mouth. "You'll push me too far one of these days, Jackson."

"We're getting too old for fistfights," I said.

"All right," he said. "There's two of you and only one of me, so you've got the edge this time." He turned and started up the beach, then spun around. "But you won't always have it. Remember that." He whirled and walked on.

"Well, thanks," said Brady. "You rescued me."

"I've got orders to get you registered for the Derby," I said. "Then I'm supposed to take you to our place so you and Zee can get to fishing."

"All right," he said, "but I intend to be back here when the tide is right." He held a fly between his thumb and forefinger. "Old Nate, there, cut my line. It did not make me happy."

"He probably won't try that again, now that he knows more about you. Besides, catching a big fish is the best revenge. When the tide is right, we'll come back here at first light and you can nail a winner from those rocks. Anyway, you aren't the only one with fishing problems. A guy named Bannerman has talked me into looking for his wife while I really should be concentrating on the Derby."

"Unlike me, you've brought your grief on yourself," said Brady, "so I don't want to hear any pissing and moaning about not having time to catch fish as big as the ones I'll be getting."

We walked back to the Land Cruiser.

"I didn't know I was a Marine instructor in unarmed combat," said Brady.

"The important thing is that Nate knows it," I said. "Brady Coyne, the battling Boston barrister. It has a nice ring to it."

We drove first to Coop's Bait and Tackle, where Brady got his Derby button, and then to our house. Brady relaxed on the balcony with a drink, while I packed supper for two in a cooler.

At six, Zee's little Jeep came down the driveway. A half hour later it went back out carrying Zee and Brady away toward the beach.

Later, alone in our double bed, I stopped reading my nighttime book and thought about Katherine Bannerman. There were some things I could do, but none of them seemed promising. I envied Zee and Brady, who were out there on the beach chasing bass and bluefish. Looking for fish was certainly more enjoyable than looking for a missing woman. I was sure they were having happier thoughts than I was.

Chapter Four

Brady

We were bouncing over a narrow strip of sand in Zee's little red Wrangler. She had two long surf-casting rods on her roof rack. My fly-fishing gear was in back, along with the cooler that held the supper J.W. had put together for us.

You've got to be a truly manly man to prepare a picnic for your wife and her male companion and then wave them off for a night of fishing while you stay home with the kids, I was thinking. Good for him. Good for Zee.

And tonight, good for me. Zee knew every inch of the Vineyard. She could find the fish. Chappaquiddick was our destination.

On Chappy we'd crossed the Dyke Bridge, scene of Teddy's terrible and mysterious accident, then driven down East Beach to Wasque, where we found a long row of pickup trucks and SUVs with deflated tires parked along the beach. A few people were down at the water's edge, casting far out into the sea. Their plugs made little water spurts when they landed, and the arcs of their monofilament lines glittered in the low rays of the setting sun. But most of the fishermen were leaning against their front fenders drinking from bottles and talking and smoking and fiddling with their gear and watching the water.

"They're waiting for the rip to build," said Zee. "It'll bring in the blues, for sure. There might be some big bass behind the blues, too, and maybe some bonito and albies will come in. It's good here. But everyone knows about Wasque. It's gonna be a zoo. It always is during the Derby."

So we headed for Cape Pogue, and as we putted along the beach, the number of vehicles and fishermen that we saw thinned out. The soft tires on the Jeep crunched quietly over the packed sand. On our right, the ocean stretched all the way eastward to Spain. On our left was what Zee identified as Pocha Pond.

We passed several long stretches of beach where there were no trucks and nobody was fishing. I asked Zee if these were barren areas, and she said not necessarily. Depending on the tide and wind direction, and at certain times of day or night with certain species of bait in the water, not to mention water temperature and time of year and, oh, there were a lot of other variables she couldn't think of at the moment, not the least of which were the smell in the air and a certain feeling in her bones . . . depending on all those things, she knew some holes and troughs and drop-offs scattered all along this beach that could hold some monster bass.

She didn't say it, but I inferred that few other people knew these things, and I was thinking that I probably had two of the best guides on the island to fish with this week.

With J.W. and Zee to find fish for me, maybe I'd catch a Derby winner. Why not?

J. W. Jackson was a retired cop from the Boston PD. He'd been shot or something. He never talked about it, any more than he talked about his time in Vietnam, where, I gathered, he'd also been wounded.

He lived year-round on Martha's Vineyard. It wasn't clear to me what he did for a living, if anything. He didn't talk about that, either, and I had the good sense not to ask.

I first met him four or five years earlier. He'd come to Boston for reasons he kept to himself, and a mutual friend, a *Globe* reporter named Quinn who knew J.W. from his cop days, had invited me to join the two of them for a night game at Fenway Park. J.W. and I hit it off right away. He liked history and fishing and baseball and classical music, and he disliked cities and high society and neckties and all newfangled technology except spinning reels. By the time the Sox blew a two-run lead in the ninth inning, J.W. had invited me down to the Vineyard to fish with him and his wife, Zee.

I took him up on it the next summer, which was when I met Zee. She was a black-haired, dark-eyed, sleek-bodied stunner, and I might've been jealous of J.W.'s good luck in finding her if I didn't admire what a great pair they made.

On that first visit, J.W. and Zee drove me all over the island in her little Jeep. I'd been on the Vineyard a few times, but I'd never really gotten the lay of the land before then. We drove the roads from Chappaquiddick to Aquinnah, both the paved inland roads and the packed-sand beach roads. It was mid-August, and the bluefish and bass had mostly left the Vineyard to find cooler waters up north, although from time to time we stopped at a place where they'd had luck in the past and tried to catch something.

We drank martinis on the Jacksons' balcony while the sun went down, and we barbecued in their back-yard. We raked quahogs and dug clams while J.W. sang "Oh, my darlin' clammin'-time," and we smoked bluefish in the smoker J.W. had made from an old refrigerator, and we sailed the waters in their little catboat.

Pretty soon, the way those things go, we were friends, and after that, I always spent a summer week-end or two with J.W. and Zee on the Vineyard. We usually fished a little, and sometimes we did pretty well. We ragged on each other about our angling preferences. J.W. teased me about my flimsy fly-fishing equipment and my usual practice of putting back the fish I caught. I told him I didn't need a stiff eleven-foot rod or a dead fish in the back of my truck to prove my manhood.

He accused me of Rod Envy.

I gave Zee some fly-casting lessons. She picked it up instantly. J.W. admitted it looked like fun, but declared himself too old and fumble-fingered to take it up. In fact, J.W. is several years younger than I, and he's one of the least fumble-fingered men I know.

So thanks to J.W. and Zee, I learned my way around the Vineyard. I didn't know the water very well, or the shops or the restaurants or the art galleries. But I like language, and I like knowing where things are, so I made a point of noticing where the landmarks were and learning what they were called—those lovely Wompanoag Indian words like Squibnocket and Tashmoo and Sengekontacket, as well as the solid Anglo-Saxon place names like Aquinnah and East Chop and Oak Bluffs.

Cape Pogue is a long, skinny finger that sticks straight up, pointing due north, at the very northeast corner of Chappaquiddick. A lighthouse perches on the edge of the sea, and when you're there, it seems like it has to be the farthest-from-anything place on the entire Vineyard. Zee kept going past Cape Pogue Light and swung around a long curve of beach until we'd reversed ourselves and were heading south around the other side of Cape Pogue Pond. On our right, the sun was setting over the low greenish mound of the Vineyard, and the pond was off to our left.

"This beach is pretty good on this tide," said Zee. "The fish work their way right along the edge, following the bait into the pond. Sometimes the bass come right into the wash. We can fish our way down into the Gut. That's the narrow opening where the ocean pours into the pond. A pretty good current will be running there."

When we got to the Gut, three or four trucks were parked along the beach, and half a dozen widely spaced fishermen were casting into the water. Some were throwing plugs, and one guy was squatting by his rod, which he'd propped up on a spiked holder he'd stuck into the sand. Bait fishing with an eel, I guessed.

A man and a woman, I noticed, were standing beside each other fly casting. Farther out, a few boats were chugging back and forth.

"Not too bad," said Zee. "A lot of people will probably come down to fish the Gut from the other side when the tide gets running. But we should have this place to ourselves—or at least as much to ourselves as you can get during the Derby."

While I set about rigging up, Zee snagged one of her surf rods from the top of her Jeep and strolled barefoot across the sand down to the water's edge. I paused to watch her cast. She was wearing black shorts and a black T-shirt, and with her dark hair and tawny skin, she was a semi-silhouette against the pink western horizon. She cast her plug amazing distances with the effortless grace of a world-class athlete, and just about the time I got a fly tied onto my leader, I heard her shout.

I looked up. Her rod was bent and something was splashing in the water in front of her. She was hauling back, then dropping her rod as she reeled up, all the while backing up the beach.

I put my rod into the Jeep and jogged down to the water. "What've you got?" I said.

"Oh, just a bass," she said. "Not a keeper. I thought at first it might've been a blue."

Both J.W. and Zee preferred bluefish to stripers, mainly because there are no size restrictions on blues, while most of the bass you're likely to catch run smaller than the thirty-two-inch legal minimum. Small bluefish won't win any Derby prizes, but they can be killed and brought home and eaten. Like most

Vineyard natives I know, the Jacksons think of fish as food, and they like to live off the land and the sea.

I, on the other hand, grew up fishing for trout with a fly rod, and I think of fish as a source of entertainment and sport.

I'm not sure how the fish feel about it.

Zee had herself a fine striped bass. It looked to be just a few inches shy of thirty-two. She dragged it up onto the wet sand, then knelt beside it to back the hook out of its mouth.

She held it upright in the shallow water to revive it. After a minute, it flapped its big tail, drenching Zee, and swam away. Zee laughed, then stood up and wiped the spray off her face. "Well, they're here," she said. "I had a couple other hits. You better get casting. You never know how long it's gonna last."

I jogged to the Jeep for my rod. When I started back for the beach, I noticed that several of the other fishermen had edged closer to Zee so that they were all throwing their lures out into the same general vicinity. She didn't seem to mind. I'd seen this before—the communal attitude of the surf casters. We fly fishermen are more secretive and antisocial and possessive of our hot spots. We resent being crowded. Surf casters seem to welcome it.

I'm not sure what to make of this, but it's tempting to observe that there are two kinds of people in this world: surf casters and fly fishermen.

Of course, there really *are* two kinds of people: those who think there are just two kinds of people, and those who understand that there are many more than that.

Anyway, being a fly fisherman, I walked for about a hundred yards down the beach along the Gut until I'd put plenty of space between me and the last fisherman in line, and then I started casting a big white Lefty's Deceiver out into the water. A little current had started running into the pond, so I cast a bit to my right and let the fly sink and swing past before I began to twitch it in.

I soon got into the rhythm of it—throw it out there, swing it around, strip it back, take two steps to my left, throw it out again. Time becomes fluid and irrelevant out on a quiet beach in the evening twilight, and I may have been casting for an hour, or maybe only for ten minutes, when my fly stopped halfway through a swing. It just stopped, as if it had snagged a piece of sunken wreckage. I instinctively pulled straight back on my line, and I felt the hook bite into something. I raised my rod. It was on something solid, and whatever it was didn't move.

A rock, I thought.

Then it exploded, yanking my rod down and ripping the line out of my fingers.

Then it was gone.

I stripped in my line and saw what I expected to see. My fly had been bitten off.

A bluefish.

A big, razor-toothed bluefish.

Small bluefish slash and crash at bait—and flies—but big bluefish sometimes just chomp down and hold on, the way stripers do. That's what this one had done.

Damn. A really big bluefish. Gone.

Without a foot of wire at the end of your leader, bluefish of all sizes will bite you off.

I sat down on the dry sand, laid my rod across my lap, and lit a cigarette.

My hands, I noticed, were trembling. Hell, that was a *big* damn bluefish. I'd caught enough blues on the fly rod to know the difference, and I'd been attached to this one long enough to feel its weight. That was my Derby winner, right there, in the first hour of trying.

I figured I'd blown my one chance by neglecting to add some wire to my leader, and I could fish my ass off for the rest of the week without hooking another fish that big. The Fishing Gods rarely gave you a second chance.

I was glad that my bet with Billy required me only to go fishing, and not to actually catch anything.

I was aware that the sun had set and darkness had settled over the beach. The breeze had died down, and some fog had begun to gather. The fishermen off to my right were faint, fuzzy shadows, and across the Gut from where I sat, the island was a dark, shadowy mound.

After a while I stood up and trudged back to Zee's Jeep. In my haste to get fishing, I'd forgotten to stick my box of extra flies and my flashlight into my pockets.

When I got there, Zee was sitting on the front fender. Two smallish bluefish lay on the sand next to her.

I sat beside her and pointed my chin at her fish. "Good going," I said.

"They won't win any prizes," she said. "But they're perfect eating size. What'd you do?"

I showed her the frayed end of my leader.

"Blue, huh?"

I nodded. "Guess so. Felt like a good one."

She smiled and shrugged, and I was grateful that she didn't give me a lecture about using wire when there were bluefish in the water. "Hungry?" she said.

I realized I hadn't eaten since early afternoon. "Starved, actually."

Zee got out the cooler J.W. had loaded for us, and we sat there on the front bumper of her Jeep eating sandwiches and watching the ghostly fishermen cast into the misty black water. J.W. had made a salad of smoked bluefish, with mayonnaise and horseradish and chopped onions. Spread on thick slices of homemade bread, it tasted like tuna, except better.

"So how's Alex?" said Zee after a few minutes.

"We split," I said.

She nodded. "I'm sorry. I liked Alex."

"Me, too." I'd brought my then–lady friend Alexandria Shaw down for a weekend with Zee and J.W. the previous summer. Alex and Zee had hit it off.

"So," she said, glancing sideways at me. "You, um, dating anybody?"

"Dating?" I laughed. "At my age, I don't date. Haven't for a long time. There is a woman . . ."

Zee looked at me, shrugged, and said, "Oh."

"Her name is Evie Banyon," I said. "She's the assistant administrator at Emerson Hospital."

"Is it serious?"

"Serious?" I looked out over the dark sea. "I don't

know where it's headed. I'm here and she's there, if that tells you anything. Why?"

Zee was quiet for a few minutes. Then she said, "Well, I have a friend."

I laughed softly.

"I'm sorry," she said.

"No, no," I said. "Tell me about your friend."

"She's been through some tough times. Came down here to get away, start over. She'll be heading back to America in a few weeks."

"Where in America?"

"The South Shore somewhere. She's bright and very pretty. Your age, I'd say. Maybe a few years younger. J.W. disapproves of me playing matchmaker. I think he's worried that it would spoil our friendship. Yours and ours, I mean."

"Why would it spoil our friendship?"

"I don't think it would, or I wouldn't've mentioned it."

"I don't see how it would, either," I said.

Zee and I fished in the darkness for a few more hours, and neither of us caught anything. We quit a little after midnight.

It was a long drive over the nighttime beach, back all the way around Cape Pogue, across the Dyke Bridge to Norton Point Beach and then across the island to the Fairchild place in West Tisbury. It was around one-thirty when Zee dropped me off at the front door.

"One of us will pick you up at cocktail time tomorrow," she said as I climbed out of the Jeep and gathered my gear from the back. "It's J.W.'s turn to fish. Maybe he'll be a better guide than I was."

"You put me on to a big fish," I said. "I had my chance."

"J.W. might keep you out all night," she said. We were talking in whispers, standing in front of the Fairchild house, which was dark except for the glow of an orange bulb over the front door that they'd left on for me. "He loves to fish at first light."

"Suits me," I said. "Fish till you puke, I always say."

"Fits right into the Derby mentality," she said.

She waved and putted up the driveway. I raised my hand, then went into the house.

I suddenly realized I was exhausted. One night of fishing had about done me in, and I had six more to go to win my bet with Billy.

Maybe he was right. Maybe I was getting old.

I slept late on Sunday and spent the morning doing paperwork. When I took my coffee out to the patio early in the afternoon, Eliza and two men I didn't recognize were sitting at the table passing around a pitcher of Bloody Marys. Eliza was wearing a white sleeveless blouse, a short white tennis skirt, and sandals. The two men, who appeared to be in their late twenties or early thirties, wore pastel polo shirts and shorts and wraparound sunglasses and admirable tans. One had black hair and a big mustache, the other had straw-colored hair and a pronounced widow's peak.

Eliza waved me over. "Have a Bloody," she said.

I held up my coffee mug. "I'm fine, thank you."

"Brady," she said, "I want you to meet a couple friends of mine. This," she said, indicating the dark-haired guy with the bushy mustache, "is Luis Martinez."

I shook hands with Luis Martinez. He had great white teeth and a manly handshake.

The other guy's name was Philip Fredrickson. He had nice teeth and a good grip, too.

"Sit with us, Brady," said Fredrickson.

I remained standing. "I've got work to do, Mr. Fredrickson."

"Oh, don't be a poop," said Eliza. "I've been telling Philip and Luis about you."

"What about me?"

"That you're Mother's lawyer," she said, batting her long eyelashes and flashing her seductive smile. "That the future of the Fairchild estate rests squarely on your gorgeous shoulders."

"Why should Philip and Luis care about that?" I said.

The three of them exchanged who-wants-to-tell-him glances, and then Martinez cleared his throat. "Actually, Brady," he began, "Eliza asked us over to meet you. We—"

I held up my hand. "Whoa," I said. "Stop right there. I meet with people when I schedule a meeting. Otherwise, I don't do business. Period." I turned to Eliza. "Don't ever do this again. Do you hear me?"

She shrugged. "You don't have to get all bristly, darling. No one's trying to do anything underhanded. Luis and Philip"—she put her left hand on Philip's leg and her right hand on Luis's shoulder—"are friends of mine, and they're up from Hilton Head to play some golf and tennis, do some sailing, get some sun."

"Then why did you invite them over to meet me?" I wondered if she was screwing them both at the same time, or if they were taking turns. "This doesn't have anything to do with turning the Fairchild estate into the Fairchild Country Club, perchance?"

She smiled wickedly. "Well, of course it does. You know perfectly well that I'd love to see that. Philip and Luis represent the Isle of Dreams Development Corporation. They've put together some lovely courses on Hilton Head and in Florida. They've brought some financial projections and computer models, and we were hoping—"

I waved my hand. "Good-bye. Nice talking with you." And I went back into the house.

A woman carrying what looked like a doctor's black bag was walking through the living room as I was walking into it. She was tall and slender and had short curly blonde hair. She wore a pink-and-white-striped blouse and a blue skirt that stopped at her knees. She looked to be in her late thirties or early forties.

I said hello, and she stopped and nodded and smiled.

I jerked my head at the bag she was carrying. "Are you the doctor?" I said.

"Not quite." She had a very pretty smile. "I'm the visiting nurse."

"Where's your funny-looking cap and your crisp white uniform?"

She laughed softly. "Here on the Vineyard we visiting nurses don't wear uniforms. We dress for glamour." She held out her hand and said, "Molly Wood," just about the time I read the plaque that was pinned over her left breast. It read AMELIA WOOD, RN.

I shook hands with her. "Brady Coyne. I'm the family lawyer. How's Sarah doing today?"

She shrugged.

"That good, huh?"

"I gave her her shots. She's comfortable right now. She's been very up and down lately."

"Okay if I visit with her?"

"I'm sure she'd love it."

We stood there awkwardly for a minute, and then I said, "Well . . ." and she smiled and said, "Well," and she headed for the front door and I headed for the sunporch.

Sarah was in her wheelchair in front of the television, which was showing the Red Sox game with the sound turned off.

I sat in the chair next to her. "Who's winning?"

"We are," she said. "I just love Nomar, don't you? You should've seen the play he just made. Went way to his right, backhanded the ball on the short hop, and winged a bullet over to first." She frowned at me. "What's the matter?"

"Oh, nothing," I said.

"It was Eliza and those two lapdogs of hers, right?"

"She brought them over to lobby me," I said.

"I guessed that's what she was up to. Figured you could handle them. They appear to be a couple of lightweights."

"I didn't really handle them," I said. "I just walked away."

"That's what I meant." She turned to look at me. Her face was pinched, and I saw the glow of pain deep in her eyes. She took a long breath, and the glow dimmed. "Please don't hold it against Eliza," she said. "I want you to make the best decision regardless of her."

I reached over and took her hand. It felt bony and flaccid. "I know that," I said gently. "Personalities have nothing to do with it. This is business."

She laughed quickly. "You sound like the Godfather. Oh, look."

I glanced at the television in time to see a man in a Red Sox uniform jogging around the bases.

"I always hoped they'd win a World Series before I died," said Sarah. "Alas, if it's not this year, it's not going to happen."

"I hate to tell you," I said.

"I know," she said. "It's September and they're nine games out. It's not going to happen."

We watched the game in silence. Sarah held my hand in her lap with both of hers, and when I glanced at her a couple of minutes later, her eyes were closed and her chin had slumped down onto her chest. I gently retrieved my hand from her weak grip. Then I tucked her blanket around her, touched her cheek with the palm of my hand, and slipped out of the room.

When I went into the living room, I saw Patrick standing by the window peering out. Both of his fists were clenched, and he held them pressed tight against his thighs.

I walked over to him. Through the window past

his shoulder I could see Eliza sitting there with Luis and Philip. They were drinking their Bloody Marys and laughing and pawing at each other, and as I watched, Eliza turned to Luis, the one with the black mustache, and kissed him hard on the mouth.

Philip, the blond guy sitting on the other side of her, was stroking her hip.

Patrick apparently didn't notice me standing behind him. He mumbled something that sounded like "Whore." It came out as a low growl.

I cleared my throat, and he whirled around. "Oh," he said. "Brady. Hi."

"If you don't like it," I said, "you shouldn't watch."

"I've been watching it all my life," he said. "It's nothing new. My own mother." He let out a long breath and shook his head.

I took his arm. "Come on, man. Let's go have some coffee."

He took one more glance out at the patio, then allowed me to lead him away. "Sure," he said. "Coffee. Just the thing."

Chapter Five

J.W.

In the small hours when Zee crawled into bed with me after her night's fishing, I woke up and was happy, feeling her skin against mine. She spooned up behind me and her arm came around my chest.

"Catch anything?" I murmured.

"A couple little ones. I've got them on ice, but they're nothing worth weighing in. Brady got a good hit but it bit off his fly. He said it felt big."

"You lose a lot of lures if you fish for blues without a leader," I said. "I've lost my share, leaders and all. But you never know what size fish might win a prize, so you should take your biggest one to the morning weigh-in even if you're sure it's a loser."

"I'm sure, but you're right about going to the weigh-in. Remember when Iowa won a daily with a four-pound blue?" She paused. "I'm going to invite Molly Wood to come to supper tonight, so she can meet Brady."

Does Mother Nature abhor an unattached male? "Who's Molly Wood?"

"Molly's a visiting nurse who's down here for the summer. You'll like her. I think she and Brady both need to meet somebody nice. Brady isn't seeing Alex anymore, and Molly's been a widow for over a year. It's time they got back into the loop."

"The loop is good." I rolled over toward her. "Let me demonstrate one of the benefits of being in it."

She laughed. Her skin was sleek and warm. In the darkness I slid my hands over her, and her arms came around me. I heard her breath deepen as I put my lips to her breasts—golden apples of the sun, silver apples of the moon.

In the morning, Zee slept late. After the weigh-in, she was only going to work half a day, starting at noon, before coming home to play Cupid. Or did women play Aphrodite?

While she slept, I got supper together. Coquilles St. Jacques, an excellent dish that is always worth the time it takes to prepare. Normally I adhere to the principle that you should avoid any recipe over four inches long, but Coquilles St. Jacques is an exception to the rule. Although you have to do a good deal of chopping and stirring, you can make it well ahead of when you'll use it, and thus can take all the time you need. Mine was made of scallops we'd captured and frozen the previous winter, and was sure to be delish.

While I cooked, I thought about fishing, food, my sleeping wife, and the children playing outdoors with the cats. I also thought about Katherine Bannerman. When Zee woke and I could make some noise, I would do a little work on the tree house. Then, when I could be fairly sure that the rest of the world was up and around, I could start earning the money Bannerman had given me.

Joshua and Diana came in. "Pa."

"What?"

"Can we help you cook?"

"Sure. You can go out in the garden and see if we have any green beans left. Pick what you find and bring them in here. Then you can wash them and trim them so we can have them for supper."

I gave them a paper bag for a bean collector and they went out.

By the time Zee had gotten up and gone to the weigh-in with what turned out to be a nonwinner fish, supper was in the fridge, and the kids still had all of their fingers, even though they'd each plied a paring knife to trim the beans. I didn't like having them use knives when they were so young, but sooner or later they'd have to know how, so I sat with them and made sure they cut only the beans.

After Zee got home, Joshua, Diana, and I worked on the tree house for an hour. We finished the floor and got a start on framing the main room.

I liked the work because it brought back the excited feelings I'd had long ago when my sister and I helped my father build our tree house in Somerville. Joshua and Diana didn't mind wearing safety belts attached to upper tree limbs as they handed me nails and tools, and we weren't high enough for my acrophobia to kick in, so we made a good crew.

At ten I called a halt to construction and headed for West Tisbury.

One of the advantages of living in an insular place such as Martha's Vineyard is that you meet and know people you like but might never meet or know if you lived on a bigger hunk of land. As you might guess, there's an opposite side of this coin, since you also meet people you'd just as soon not.

One person I was glad I knew was Gladys White, who lived with her husband, Tom, on Music Street. Tom and I had first met on Wasque Point years before, while both of us were waiting for the fish to arrive. Later I'd met Gladys at the farmers' market, where she sold, and I bought, excellent egg rolls and Oriental soups that she'd learned to make from her missionary parents, who'd been stationed in the Far East.

Gladys and Tom and their neighbors were no doubt happy that an earlier resident of their once rural pathway had purchased a piano and inspired a name change for the road. Music Street was certainly an improvement over Cow Turd Lane.

Gladys had known Katherine Bannerman and had been interviewed by Thornberry Security. When I knocked on her door, she seemed pleased to see me. From behind her came the wonderful smells of cooking foods.

"Come on into the kitchen, J.W. We can talk while I work."

She turned, and I followed her.

"It's about Katherine Bannerman," I said, and told her about the job I'd accepted from Bannerman and what I'd read in Thornberry's file.

"Well, I can't add much to it," said Gladys, stirring a large pot of what smelled like some kind of sweet-and-sour soup. "I told those people everything I know."

"Maybe you know something they didn't ask about."

"Like what?"

"I don't know. According to the report, you told them she was a very nice woman who made friends quickly and worked with you on a support network for battered women."

"That's right. She came here in June a year ago and contacted me not long afterward. I guess she read one of those information sheets we posted at Alley's store. We talked and she volunteered to work. Seemed to enjoy it. A very sympathetic woman. People took to her right away."

"Do you think she may have been a battered wife herself?"

Gladys gave me a sharp look. "She certainly never said anything about it."

"How did Thornberry's people happen to contact you?"

Gladys added something to the soup pot. "They found out that Kathy had sold her car. That happened in August. I guess that brought them to the island. They talked with Pete Blankenship, who'd bought the car. Kathy had told Pete that she was living up there in Chilmark and my name came up. But by that time, Kathy was gone, so I wasn't much use to them."

"Where do you think she went?"

She turned from the stove, spoon in hand. "I haven't the slightest idea. It's perplexing. But Kathy wasn't much inclined to talk about herself. She'd answer questions, but she didn't volunteer much. Except about her daughter, that is. She never said much about her husband, but she loved to talk about Frankie."

"Didn't she have any confidante, anybody special she might have talked to about other things?"

"Well," said Gladys, "if she did, it wasn't me. I was her friend, but I wasn't that kind of friend. Most of our talk had to do with the support network we were working with. Kathy's a lot younger than me, so maybe she did girl-talk with somebody else."

"She was an attractive woman. Did she have a man in her life?"

"You mean like somebody here on the island? Not that I know of, but, like I say, I wasn't the sort of friend she'd confide in about such things."

"Who might have been that kind of friend?"

Gladys thought that question over, then said, "If I was to guess, I'd guess Myrtle Eldridge. Myrtle is about her age, and she's divorced. She and Kathy worked together on several projects and seemed to hit it off pretty well."

"Where can I find Myrtle Eldridge?"

"Up on Menemsha Cross Road just past the place they used to have those Wednesday flea markets. She got the house when her husband ran off with that schoolteacher from Barnstable." She glanced at her watch. "You might catch her at home right about now, in fact. She gives pottery lessons in her barn. Eldridge Pottery. The name's on a sign. You can't miss it."

"I've seen it. Did Kathy ever talk about leaving the island and going someplace else? Back to her family, maybe?"

"No, she didn't. She didn't say she was going anywhere, and she didn't say she wasn't. I had the impression she was keeping her options open, thinking things over. Maybe getting a life, as the young folks say."

"She didn't bad-mouth her husband?"

"She didn't say much about him one way or another. Even if she wasn't wild about him, she might have gone back to him just so she could be with her daughter."

"He says that didn't happen. That soup smells wonderful."

"Come by the market sometime and I'll sell you some."

"No free samples?"

"Get out of here, J.W. And say hi to Zee for me."

I got.

Myrtle Eldridge's pottery class consisted of two women covered with clay from the wheels in front of them and a slightly cleaner girl who looked like she should be in school. The future of ceramics seemed in danger if they were the next generation of potters. The only person in the room wearing a clean apron came over to meet me. She was a woman about my age, one of those who wear their hair and their skirts a little longer than most women do, and shun makeup. She had dark, busy eyes. "Hi. Can I help you? Are you interested in making pottery?"

"Yes, you may be able to help me, but no, I'm not interested in making pottery. My name is Jackson. Can you spare a few minutes?"

"I'm Myrtle Eldridge, and I know who you are. I've seen you at the West Tisbury Library book fair." She brushed at a strand of hair. "Somebody pointed you out to me. You're married to Zee Madieras." She glanced at her students. "What do you want to talk about, Mr. Jackson?"

"Katherine Bannerman."

Her sharp eyes grew careful as they looked up into mine. "Some private detectives talked with me about her some time ago. I told them everything I could."

"I have their report." I told her about the job I'd taken and that I'd gotten her name from Gladys White. "Gladys said that you were close to Kathy, and that she may have confided in you."

She studied me, then nodded coolly. "We talked."

"Did she mention going away? Back to her husband, maybe, or maybe someplace else?"

"I don't think she'd have gone back to him."

"Why do you say that?"

She shrugged. "Men aren't dependable. I should know. My husband left me, and my boyfriend has wandering eyes. They wandered on Kathy Bannerman, among others. If you want to know the truth, I think she probably looked back."

I decided to leave that one alone. "What did Kathy say about her husband?"

Myrtle's voice was icy. "Look, I don't really want to help him find her, Mr. Jackson. If she wants him to find her, she'll let him know."

I nodded. "The deal I have with her husband is that if I find her I won't tell him where she is unless she okays it. He says that all he wants to know is that she's all right."

"Sure he does."

I shifted to safer ground. "How did you two meet?"

She seemed glad to talk about that. "In the stamp

82

line at the Post Office. She had one of the support-group flyers that Gladys White puts up on the bulletin boards all over the island. We got to chatting, and she started working with us. We got on pretty well. Common interests, common problems, you know?"

"What kind of problems?"

"What do you think? Men."

I should have guessed. "Did she ever talk with you about going off-island?"

Myrtle shook her head. "No, and I think she would have, if she had plans. But on Labor Day weekend last year, she just left without a word to anybody. Something must have come up suddenly."

"You haven't heard from her since?"

"No, and I'm a little surprised by that." There was a touch of hurt in her voice.

"Did she have a man in her life while she was here on the island?"

She ran a hand through her long brown hair. "She wanted to make up for lost time, she said, and I knew what she meant. We'd both married slugs, if you know what I mean."

"Maybe I do."

She looked at me, and the corner of her mouth turned up. "And maybe you don't, because you're not the slug type. Zee Madieras wouldn't marry a slug."

While I was deciding how to respond to that, she went on: "Anyway, since we were each alone and she didn't know the island scene, I took her to the Hot Tin Roof and to the Atlantic Connection, where she could meet people and dance."

"And did that happen?"

"Yes. Men liked her and she liked them. She liked being out and around. She was sort of innocent, you know?"

"How do you mean?"

She smiled. "There's only one guy I ever heard of who didn't inhale, but Kathy hadn't even tried it, so we did some dope. She liked it, and we hung around with some people who liked it, too."

"Anybody special?"

"No. She met a lot of men, and dated some, but she didn't go home with any of them. Or if she did, she didn't tell me."

"Would she have told you?"

Myrtle shrugged. "I think so. I'd have told her. I think she just liked having a social life for a change. She didn't have one back with hubby, I guess. He was a drone, just like my ex."

A picture of Bannerman's gravestone leaped into my head. On it was written:

JAMES BANNERMAN
BENEATH THIS STONE
LIES A SLUG AND A DRONE

"So there were men," I said, "but nobody special."

Another shrug. "At first we always went out together, so I could sort of show her around. I also wanted to keep an eye on Jasper—that's my beau, though he may not be for long. Anyway, toward the end of the summer she began to go on her own. Maybe she wanted to be alone with some guy. She was always sort of closemouthed about her private life, even with me. I was her friend, I guess, but not her keeper. Speaking of going out, you don't have a brother, do you?"

"Only a sister, and she lives north of Santa Fe."

"Rats. The man supply gets thinner around here after Labor Day." She rubbed her shoulders as though she was cold.

"Do you know the names of any of the men she dated?"

"I think they were mostly summer guys. I haven't seen the same bunch around this year. Except for Shrink Williams, of course. You know Shrink?"

I nodded. Cotton Williams, known as Shrink, and I had met a couple of times. He was a psychiatrist who'd come to the island and set up a practice following his own divorce. He had stayed single but was well known for his active social life. Shrink liked women, and they apparently liked him, although Zee had noted more than once that none of his relationships lasted very long. She gave the women credit for this, since she didn't think Shrink had much to offer in terms of long-range relationships.

"Shrink met Kathy when I took her to the Connection," said Myrtle. "He can be charming, and he's a good dancer, so they hit it off. A couple of weeks later it was all over, though."

"Sounds like a typical Shrink relationship."

"You know about Shrink and his ladies, eh?"

"Mostly via the grapevine." I changed gears. "Did Kathy strike you as somebody who could take care of herself?"

Myrtle cocked her head to one side. "I never

thought about it. Women can be strong and smart and naive at the same time. Kathy was like that, I think." She paused. "Maybe I am, too."

"Maybe we all are."

From behind her came a sudden yelp. As she turned, I looked over her shoulder and saw a pot disintegrating from the center of a wheel, sending wet clay flying.

"Help!" cried the potter, trying to hold the remaining clay together.

"Sorry I couldn't be of more help, but I guess our conversation's over," said Myrtle. She smiled and walked away toward her mud-covered student.

I went home.

After Zee left for the hospital, the children and I worked some more on the tree house. During their nap time, I was aware of something niggling at the back of my mind. It had to do with my conversation with Myrtle Eldridge, but when I tried to see it clearly, a picture of a clay-spattered woman kept getting in the way.

Irksome.

I reread Thornberry's report. His people had checked all of the possible paper trails and talked to most of the people who had known Kathy, including Pete Blankenship, the guy who'd bought her car, and Kathy's landlady. She had let them look at her room, where they'd found nothing of help. As far as I could tell, Thornberry had done good work. But no investigation is ever perfect, so tomorrow I'd try talking to some people they hadn't mentioned.

When Zee came home, I had her martini waiting for her.

"You're a good man, Charlie Brown."

"Is your temptress coming?"

"Six-thirty is her ETA, but she's not a temptress. She's just a very nice woman who could stand meeting a very nice man. Speaking of which, you'd better go pick up Brady."

"I'm on my way."

As I pulled out of our long, sandy driveway I remembered what had been bothering me: Myrtle had said she and Kathy had met at the Post Office.

Aha, as the detectives say.

Chapter Six

Brady

J.W. picked me up around six o'clock, and when we pulled into his driveway, there was a little red Honda Civic parked behind Zee's Jeep. "Looks like you got company," I said.

He grinned and said nothing.

I followed J.W. onto the screened porch. Zee was sitting there on the sofa. Beside her was a blonde woman, who looked at me, blinked a couple of times, then rolled her eyes and laughed.

I smiled back at her. "Hi, again," I said.

It was Molly Wood, Sarah Fairchild's visiting nurse.

"I don't want to jump to conclusions," I said to Molly, "but I've got the feeling that somebody's been playing matchmaker."

"So *you're* the mysterious Boston lawyer," she said.

I turned to Zee. "Did you call me mysterious?"

"Handsome," said Zee. "That, I think, was the word I used." She frowned at me, then at Molly, then at me again. "Am I missing something here? Do you two know each other?"

"We were high school sweethearts," said Molly.

"Really?"

"No," I said. "But we have met. Molly is Sarah Fairchild's visiting nurse. We bumped into each other in the living room this afternoon."

"Oh, jeez," said Zee. "This is embarrassing."

"Not for me it's not," I said. I held out my hand to Molly. "It's nice to see you."

She took my hand in hers and smiled at me. "Likewise, for sure."

"Well," said J.W., "drinks, then." He disappeared into the house.

Zee leaped up. "I'll help," she said, and followed him inside.

I sat beside Molly. "Sorry about this," I said. "Zee mentioned something about a friend of hers, but I didn't expect it to be you, or here, or tonight. She didn't tell you my name, huh?"

"Nope. But you know what?"

I shrugged. "What?"

"If she had," she said, "I still would've come."

"Aw, shucks," I said.

"What about you?"

"I would've come, too," I said.

Molly was wearing sandals and white slacks and a flowered silk blouse. She'd left a couple of buttons undone at her throat, and a thin gold chain glittered there against her honey-colored skin. She had pretty blue eyes with little crinkles in the corners. I hadn't noticed how pretty her eyes were the first time I'd seen her.

She managed to get me talking about my two boys—now young men—and my divorce, and how I managed living alone, and she said that she, too, was living alone, and hadn't been doing it for very long, and the fact that she didn't have kids made living alone feel terribly lonely, and I was about to ask her if she'd been recently divorced when J.W. and Zee came back out onto the porch bearing drinks and a platter of crackers and bluefish pâté.

Diana and Joshua were right behind them. "We made bread," said Diana. "It's gonna be delish."

"We picked beans, too," added Joshua. "We cut them up ourselves and didn't cut our fingers off."

"Good thing," I said. "I like steamed beans better than steamed fingers."

Both kids giggled.

"Balcony time," announced J.W. "You guys set the table."

So we four grown-ups trooped up onto the balcony, while Diana and Joshua headed back toward the kitchen.

We sipped our drinks, gazed off toward the ocean, watched the evening birds dart around Zee's feeders, and talked about fishing. Actually, Zee and I did most of the talking, trying to include Molly, who apparently didn't fish, in our conversation. Although Zee was a bit embarrassed that she'd arranged a blind date for two people who'd already met each other and could've made a date on their own if they'd wanted to, the fact was that Molly Wood was pretty and funny and smart, and I, for one, was glad Zee had done it. I probably wouldn't have tried to befriend Sarah Fairchild's nurse on my own initiative.

J.W. sat there sipping his vodka martini and saying very little. He had a bemused little smile playing over his face, and every once in a while Zee would glance at him and frown.

When he finished his drink, J.W. stood up and announced that he was going down to be sure the kids hadn't destroyed supper.

A few minutes later Zee said she'd better go down and help.

After she left, Molly said, "They're leaving us alone again."

"Yes," I said. "So that we can get to know each other better."

"She's cute, isn't she?"

"Zee?" I said. "I think she's feeling rather awkward about this. Knowing J.W., he didn't approve of her matchmaking. Wouldn't it be terrible if you and I didn't like each other?"

"Zee would be devastated."

"J.W. would never let her forget it," I said. "It could destroy their marriage."

"And leave those two innocent little children victims of a broken home," she added.

"So I think we have an obligation to like each other," I said. "Out of consideration for Zee."

"Well," said Molly, "I'll give it my best shot. Out of consideration for Zee, and her marriage, and the future happiness of her children."

Molly had a great, earthy laugh, and both of us were laughing when Zee and J.W. called us down for dinner.

Afterward, Zee and J.W. refused to allow Molly or me to help clean up, leaving us alone on the screened porch where we'd eaten.

"They're doing this on purpose," said Molly. "Leaving us by ourselves again so we can get to know each other some more."

"In my experience," I said, "it takes a long time for two grown-ups to get to know each other."

"Longer than just one dinner party with another couple."

I nodded. "Two people can't be expected to figure out if they like each other on the basis of a single, um, whatchamacallit . . ."

"Date?" she said.

"I guess that's the word for it," I said. "It seems like a funny word for two divorced adults to use, that's all."

Molly looked away. "I'm not divorced," she said softly. "I'm widowed."

"I'm sorry," I said. "You mentioned your husband, and I thought . . ."

She turned to me and put her hand on my arm. "It's okay. Really it is. I just think it's very different from being divorced."

"How long ago?"

"A year ago last June," she said. "He had an aneurysm. It exploded in his head while he was sleeping. He was forty-one years old. I woke up in the morning, and he . . ."

I saw tears glisten in her eyes, and since I couldn't think of anything appropriate to say, I had the good sense not to say anything.

After a minute she smiled. "I'm sorry, Brady. I'm okay with it now. It's just, sometimes I remember those first few months after it happened, and it all comes rushing back." She shook her head. "I tried to keep working. I was a surgical nurse. But I realized I had to find something less . . . familiar. So I came down here for a while. I've been renting a room in Edgartown and temping with the Visiting Nurses for the summer. I'll be going back to America in a few weeks. They're holding my job for me. I think I'll be okay with it."

"Where in America?"

"Scituate. On the South Shore."

"I know Scituate," I said. "It's less than an hour from Lewis Wharf on the Boston Harbor, except during rush hour."

"Is that where you live?"

I nodded. "I've got a view of the Harbor Islands in one direction and Logan Airport in another, and the seagulls perch on the railing of my balcony. I like to grill hamburgers and steaks out there and listen to the bell buoy and watch the fog roll in."

Molly smiled at me. "If I didn't know better, I'd say that sounded almost like an invitation."

"Maybe it was," I said. "But right now, I've got a better idea. How about letting somebody else grill something for us tomorrow evening?"

"Why, sir," she said, batting her eyes, "are you asking me for a date?"

"Date," I said. "That word again. But what the hell. Sure. It doesn't preclude grilling on my balcony sometime. But how about a date? You and me. Tomorrow. The restaurant of your choice. Say six-thirty?"

"The Navigator Room is nice," she said. "We can get a table by the window up on the second floor, watch the boats come into the harbor. I'll make the reservations and meet you there. How's that?"

"That's excellent," I said. "Zee will be pleased."

"How about you?"

"I am pleased, too," I said.

A minute or two later, J.W. cleared his throat by way of warning us that he was coming, then appeared in the doorway. He sauntered over to the screen door, stood there staring out at the gathering dusk, and without turning around, he said, "I'm going fishing."

Molly grinned at me, then stood up. "That sounds like my cue."

She went into the house to say good-bye to Zee and the kids, and was back a minute later. She tiptoed up to kiss J.W.'s cheek, thanked him, and wished him good fishing. Then she turned to me.

"I'll walk you to your car," I said.

"Chivalry," she said, "is not dead."

About halfway up the driveway to her car, Molly touched my arm and let her hand slide down to mine. It felt soft and electric, and I held on tight. The walk to her car was altogether too short.

She turned to me and smiled. "I almost turned Zee down," she said softly. "Blind dates at my age."

"I'm glad you didn't."

She reached up, touched my cheek, and sighed. "Well, J.W. is getting impatient." Then she tilted her face, leaned against me, and kissed my jaw. I put my hand lightly on the back of her neck and pulled my head back to look at her. Her eyes were smiling into mine. I arched my eyebrows—may I kiss you?—and she nodded.

It was a tentative kiss, no more than a light brushing of lips, and it lasted only an instant before she laughed softly, gave me a quick hug, and pulled away.

She climbed into her little red Honda. I closed the door for her. She started the engine, then rolled down the window and looked out at me with her eyebrows arched.

I bent to the window, and she reached out with her hand, steered my face to hers, and kissed me hard on the mouth.

I hadn't been kissed like that in a while, and as I stood there in J.W.'s driveway watching Molly Wood's red taillights jouncing away into the gathering dusk, I rubbed my mouth with the back of my hand and let out a deep breath.

By the time J.W. and I parked his truck on the roadside by Squibnocket, it was dark. The clouds obscured whatever moon might've been up there, so we made our way down a long beach and over some dunes by flashlight. The water gathered the night light well enough for me to see that there was a long curving beach and a rocky point off to our right. The tide was coming in, and gentle breakers were rolling rhythmically against the sand.

Squibnocket Point is on the southwestern tip of the Vineyard, as far from Cape Pogue, which is on the northeastern tip, as you can get. J.W. had heard rumors that while Zee and I had failed to catch a Derby qualifier at Cape Pogue the previous night, other contestants had taken several at Squibnocket.

It was worth a try.

I could hear muffled voices on the beach around us and surmised that there were some other fishermen there, though they sounded distant and I couldn't see them. We seemed to have plenty of space to cast right there on the beach. J.W. stood on the wet sand in his bare feet with his pants rolled up to his knees and heaved his heavy lure way the hell out there. I, with my little fly rod and in my neoprene waders, sloshed out past the breakers, stood thigh-deep in the water, and began flailing away.

I had mixed feelings about the fact that there were no other fishermen crowding around us. On the one hand, I liked having some space to share only with my partner. On the other hand, I'm always convinced that other fishermen know what they're doing better than I know what I'm doing, so if I find a place where no one is fishing, I tend to assume that's because the fishing's no good there.

And when I cast in such a place for half an hour without a strike, I become convinced that it's barren.

J.W. seemed content to wait for the fish to come his way. But I got itchy and decided to go try and find some. I began to fish my way along the beach to the right, where the surf was beating against a jumble of rocks. On the incoming tide, I figured the fish might work their way into those rocks, where they could ambush some hapless baitfish.

There was no one fishing the rocks, either. I'd never fished Squibnocket before, so for all I knew, this was a lousy spot. But for lack of anything more promising, I decided to work it over.

I had to wade up to my hips to get my fly out

among the rocks. The currents were surging and swirling around them, and I imagined the baitfish and crabs and eels and squid being tossed around, easy pickin's for big, predatory striped bass.

I'd made a dozen or so casts when my fly stopped. I pulled straight back on my line, felt the hook bite. "Fish on!" I shouted to J.W. as I raised my rod. The fish bulled its way toward the rocks. If he got there, he'd wrap me or fray my leader, and either way I'd lose him, so I dropped my rod to horizontal and tried to turn his head. I had no idea how big he was. Not tiny, I knew that. I'd caught plenty of small stripers, and I knew what they felt like.

The fly held and the leader didn't break. I backed up toward the beach as I fought the fish, and a few minutes later it was sloshing around in the shallow water in front of me.

"Keeper?" It was J.W., who'd materialized beside me.

"I haven't seen him yet," I said. "Shine your light out there."

A moment later, J.W.'s light snapped on. The fish had lost its will and was holding quietly in front of me with its head just out of water against the bend of my rod.

"Might be a keeper," I said.

"Nope," he said. "Nice one. Thirty inches, I bet. But it's gotta be thirty-two. Steer him over here."

I did, and J.W. measured the fish against some markings on his rod. "Twenty-nine inches," he said. "In the old days, he'd make a good dinner for four."

"These days, aside from the fact that he's not legal,

he's too precious to kill," I said. I steered the fish to my side, tucked my rod under my arm, knelt in the shallow water, grabbed the fish's bottom lip between my thumb and forefinger, and used my other hand to back the hook out of its mouth. Then I waded out to my knees, held the fish with one hand gripping its tail and the other under its belly, and moved it slowly back and forth to force water through its gills until I felt its strength return. When I let go, it gave a powerful thrust of its big tail and disappeared into the dark water.

J.W. stuck out his hand and I shook it. "Nice fish, even so," he said. "Go catch his grandmother, why don't you?"

"I'm gonna try," I said.

He shut off his light and sloshed away, leaving me alone again on the beach. I checked the point of my hook, then waded back out to where I'd been standing when that fish had hit. The tide was still coming in, and in the few minutes I'd been fighting that fish, the water had risen from my hips to my waist. I made a couple of casts, but the rock I was aiming at was just a little beyond my range. As I edged closer, I was aware of the current pushing against my hips and the undertow surging in the opposite direction around my ankles.

I needed just a couple of more steps to reach that rock, and as I slid my foot forward, it came up against something hard. I stumbled, then lost my balance. I flailed around with my arms, but the undertow caught my legs and pulled them out from under me, and the surging tide pushed my upper body backward. I managed to gulp a breath of air before I went under, and for an instant I felt myself churning around underwater at the mercy of the tidal rip with no idea of which way was up.

Okay, I thought. Relax. This has happened before. Remember. You float. Let yourself rise to the top. . . .

And that's what happened. I bobbed to the surface and floated there on my back, and the incoming tide carried me toward the beach until I was able to lower my legs and find sand under my feet.

I had not let go of my rod. My line was tangled around my waist and legs and my fly had somehow gotten hooked in the seat of my waders.

I staggered onto the beach. The tight-fitting neoprene waders had kept the bottom half of me fairly dry, but my top half was drenched, and I found myself shivering in the salty onshore breeze.

I shucked off my waders, got my line and fly untangled by flashlight, and stood there hugging myself. I thought of telling J.W. that I'd nearly drowned, that I was wet and cold, and that I wanted to go home and swallow a warm shot or two of bourbon.

Then I thought of that big striper I'd caught, and how the rush of adrenaline had heated me up instantly.

Go catch another fish, I thought. That's the ticket.

So I pulled my waders back on and waded out. But this time I didn't venture in over my hips. There were some rocks I couldn't reach, but the hell with them. I knew I'd never win my bet with Billy if I drowned.

*   *   *

We'd agreed to quit at midnight. I had meetings set up for the next morning, and the lawyer needed to be sharp. Plus I had a date—I was getting used to that word—with Molly, and I wanted to be reasonably bright-eyed, if not thoroughly bushy-tailed, for her.

J.W. and I had each landed a small bluefish, and I pretended to argue about keeping mine for his smoker. Actually, I had no philosophy against killing a fish now and then. But J.W. thought I did, and I didn't want to disappoint him. In the end I gave it to him.

When I told him about wading out too far and losing my footing and getting all tangled in my line and nearly drowning, he said, "Hell, they're only fish."

As we drove back to the Fairchild house, I told him to tell Zee that I intended to borrow Sarah's car for my, um, date with Molly, and that I'd drive over all ready to go fishing. Zee should expect me around nine.

J.W. told me not to cut short my date. The later I was, the more fun Zee would assume we were probably having, and she would like that.

"Look for me at nine o'clock," I told him. But I was remembering Molly Wood's last kiss, and I decided that I'd play it by ear.

I wondered if Molly would tempt me to forfeit my bet with Billy. It was an intriguing thought.

J.W. dropped me off at the Fairchild place a little after 1 A.M. Two cars were parked there—Eliza's Saab and Sarah's Range Rover, but Nate's truck and Patrick's BMW were both gone and, except for the porch light, the house was dark.

A couple of golf bags rested against the rail on the

front porch. One was a big masculine bag that would make any caddy sweat, and the other had pink knitted head covers. Eliza and her partner, I figured. A pair of empty highball glasses sat on the steps.

Sarah was sleeping on the sunporch when I peeked in. Unless Eliza was asleep already, which would've been uncharacteristic, it looked like they'd all left the old woman alone for the night.

I went upstairs to get ready for bed, and I was just coming out of the bathroom when I heard car doors slam out front, then loud laughter. A minute later, the front door opened and shut. I heard Eliza's throaty voice from downstairs, then the rumble of a male voice.

That voice, if I wasn't mistaken, belonged to Phil Fredrickson.

After a minute or two, I didn't hear anything.

I went to bed.

Maybe it was the memory of how I'd nearly drowned. Maybe it was the fishing adrenaline still zinging through my veins. Maybe it was the anticipation of tomorrow's meeting with the golf-course developer's lawyer.

Molly Wood certainly had something to do with it. There was an intensity in the kiss through her car window that had surprised me.

Whatever it was, and in spite of feeling thoroughly exhausted, I couldn't get to sleep.

At 2 A.M. I turned the light back on and read for a while. I'd brought my battered old copy of *Moby-Dick* with me. Usually, Melville put me right to sleep.

At two-thirty I turned the light off.

At three I turned it on again, read a few more pages, and realized I was wide-awake. So I slipped into some clothes and went outside. Maybe a cigarette and a few whiffs of sea air would do the job.

A car I didn't recognize was parked in the front turnaround. The two golf bags still rested against the porch railing.

I wandered out onto the back lawn. Clouds were skidding across the moon, and the ocean was a sort of platinum color. So far, J.W. and I had not pulled an all-nighter. Nor had we fished at first light. We weren't taking our competitive Derby responsibilities seriously enough.

On the other hand, I figured if I could manage a few hours of sleep every night, I might not be tempted to wimp out. Billy would never let me forget it if I did.

Chapter Seven

J.W.

The morning after the Squibnocket trip, I phoned Kathy Bannerman's landlady. Her name was Elsie Cohen. I told her what I was doing and that I'd like to examine Kathy's possessions.

"I'm afraid you're about a year too late, unless you want a bottle of men's cologne," said Elsie Cohen.

"Come again?"

"After those detectives came around looking for her last August, I waited a few weeks in case Kathy came back, then when she didn't I got in touch with Mr. Bannerman and packed everything of hers up and shipped it to him. I'd gotten his address from the detectives. A little later I found the cologne in the closet. I guess I should have sent it, too, but it didn't seem worth it, so I gave it to my husband. But Bill isn't a big cologne user, so we still have most of the bottle. Do you favor Enchanté?"

My ignorance of men's cologne was quite profound. I had never even heard of Enchanté. I wondered if James Bannerman used it and, if not, who did.

"Do you remember anything about her other possessions? Anything that might give me some idea where she was going or who she might be seeing?"

"I didn't read her letters or her other papers," said Elsie Cohen in a voice that was suddenly a bit prim, "and there was nothing special about anything else she had. No snowshoes or scuba gear or ice axes, if that's what you mean. Nothing exotic. Just ordinary things."

"Did she ever talk with you about her life here on the island? People she knew or things she did? That sort of thing."

"You mean like who wears Enchanté cologne? I'm sure I couldn't say. I told those detectives everything I knew, but it didn't seem to help them much. She worked with the local women's service group and did some socializing with people I really didn't know. Mostly down-island, I think."

Down-island meant Oak Bluffs, Vineyard Haven, and Edgartown. Chilmark, West Tisbury, and Aquinnah were up-island, where there are no dance halls, clubs, liquor stores, or bars. Up-island people have to dissipate in private rather than in public places. Some of them only go down-island to buy liquor at the Edgartown and Oak Bluffs package stores, after which they flee home again, to peace and quiet.

Elsie Cohen didn't know the names of any men Kathy Bannerman might have dated. I wondered if Bill Cohen and Kathy might have sneaked out a night or two, and, if so, if Elsie knew about it. You never know what goes on inside a marriage.

"Pa, can we work on the tree house?"

They'd been waiting patiently. "Sure."

So we did that until noon, because life does not stop

for major events, let alone small ones such as my search for Katherine Bannerman. We're gonna stay and we're gonna go, as Sweeney observed, and somebody's gotta pay the rent, but that's nothing to me and nothing to you.

After lunch, I got the kids into the Land Cruiser and headed for Edgartown, running various possibilities through my head as I drove.

When children or infirm adults go missing, it's cause for concern because they're often not mature or healthy enough to fend for themselves. Usually when healthy adults like Katherine Bannerman drop out of sight, they show up again and act surprised that anybody was worried. When that doesn't happen, it's often because they don't want to be found. They're fleeing debts or unwanted lovers or enemies or the cops, or they just want to leave their old lives behind and start again, and they're willing to abandon their houses and families and friends to do it. Sam Spade once dealt with that sort of missing person. The irony was that the guy abandoned one family and lifestyle, then moved up the coast and created a new one exactly like his old one. Sam was both amused and bemused by the case.

Katherine Bannerman's only motive, as near as I could tell, was boredom with her husband and her life.

Of course not all missing people disappear intentionally. In some cases some hunter's dog, years later, brings his master a bone that the hunter recognizes as human and which, after the authorities finish their investigations, finally answers the question of what happened to so-and-so.

Martha's Vineyard, with its wealthy and famous Summer People, has the same percentage of criminals as any other place, as the local cops, nurses, social workers, and lawyers can tell you. If you doubt it, just show up at the courthouse in Edgartown on a Thursday. Yeah, slimy things do crawl with legs on the Blessed Isle as well as upon the slimy sea.

The existence of snakes in Eden notwithstanding, murder is rare on the island, so it seemed unlikely to me that Katherine Bannerman had met with foul play. An accident, possibly, or some unexpected call back to the mainland that left her no time to inform friends or fellow workers, or some combination of both. Kathy hadn't been brought to the hospital, and if she'd been killed in an accident, her body would probably have been discovered long since. There are a hundred thousand people on the island during the summer, and it was hard to imagine all of them failing to see a body if there was one to be seen. Still, you never know. I once talked to a guy who'd been to Africa, and he'd said you could be ten feet from a pride of lions and never see them.

I drove to the police station, once the finest on the island but recently challenged for that honor by the new station in Vineyard Haven. The Chief was in his office.

He looked relaxed for a change, another sign that most of the tourists had gone home for the winter. As soon as he saw Joshua and Diana, he opened a drawer in his desk and brought out a package of Farley's gummy worms, the world's finest. He had grandchildren about the same age as my children, and he knew how to be a kid's best friend.

Joshua and Diana both accepted his offer and said thank you.

"How about me?" I asked.

"Oh, all right." He held out the package and I took a half dozen lovely, bright-colored gummies.

"Easy there!" The Chief yanked his gummies back, took a handful, and put the rest back in the drawer.

"Thank you, Chief."

"You're welcome. What do you want? I know you want something, because you always do when you come in here. Say, would you kids like to have a tour of the building? Kit! Come in here a second."

Kit Goulart, all six feet and 275 pounds of her, came in from the front desk. Kit and her husband were about the same size and looked like matched Percherons when they walked down the street together.

"What is it, Chief?"

"How'd you like to take these two tykes for a tour of the premises while I fend off their father, here."

"Sounds like a deal." She looked down at them and smiled a smile that would melt a tax collector's heart. "I'm Kit. I work here. Do you want to see the police station?"

They did, and the three of them went off. The Chief looked at me. "Well?"

"A woman named Katherine Bannerman disappeared from the island last year about this time. Her husband has hired me to try to find her. I wonder if you remember the case."

He nodded. "Yeah. Some agents from some big PI outfit in Boston were down here looking for her. As far as I know they never found her. You should be talking with the Chilmark PD, because she lived up there."

"I've read the report that Thornberry Security gave to the husband. There wasn't much in it that helps, but they seem to have done a pretty thorough job."

"I'm not big on private eyes nosing around, but you're right. They seemed pretty good. The Chilmark PD put out a GBC, but nothing came of it."

I nodded. A General Broadcast Call would have alerted all of the island police forces to be on the lookout for the missing woman.

"Later," said the Chief, "they put out Kathy Bannerman's physical description on NCIC, in case she was on the mainland. Another zero. It's a big country, and if she wanted to disappear, she could be anywhere." He tapped a finger on the papers he'd been working on when I'd come in. "You were a cop, so you know people go missing more often than most folks would think."

I did know that. In the United States, thousands of people disappear every year, for one reason or another.

The Chief went on: "Usually the missing people turn up safe and sound, but we don't always learn that. During the last few years we've had a half dozen or so disappear off the island into thin air about Labor Day. I imagine most of them just went home and didn't tell whoever it was that got worried about them, and then we didn't get told, either. Unless they've committed a crime or are suspected of being victims of a crime, the authorities don't really have a lot of reason to look for missing people."

"And you don't have any ideas about where I might look for this one?"

He shrugged. "Try back home with her husband."

"He says she's not there."

Kit and the kids reappeared.

I got up. "Well, Chief, if you hear anything, let me know."

"I will. You do the same. And don't do anything that might hamper an investigation."

"You can trust me, Chief."

"Sure I can."

After we left the station, the kids and I had ice cream cones, and as we walked back to the truck, we passed a shop that had expensive-looking soaps and lotions in its windows. Feeling serendipitous, I took the kids inside and asked the woman behind the counter if she had Enchanté.

She not only had it, but she let me have a sniff. "Would you like to buy some?"

"I don't think it's my fragrance. Do you sell much of this?"

"Usually to women who are buying it for men."

"Do the men use it?"

She smiled. "You'll have to ask the women."

At home, filled to the brim, the tots were ready for naps. So was I, but I had a phone call to make first. So while they fell into those sweet swoons that the innocent enter so quickly, I got directory assistance for Storrs, Connecticut, and asked for the number of

Frances Bannerman. No problem, since it's a rare college freshman who doesn't have her own phone these days.

A feminine voice answered on the second ring, and I asked for Frankie.

"Who's calling, please?"

I told her my name and that I was calling from Martha's Vineyard. That got me a "just a minute" and, in less than that, another feminine voice. "This is Frankie Bannerman. Have you found my mother?"

"No, but we're looking. Maybe you can help."

"Me? How? I haven't seen Mom for over a year."

"Your father told me that he hasn't heard from her since she sent you a postcard from New York."

There was a hint of a pause before she said, "That's right."

"No mail ever came from her to the house again?"

"No."

It was not too great a "no." In fact it was too small.

"Here's what I know," I said. "Your mom was writing to somebody, because she bought stamps here on the island. And she was getting mail from somebody because she had letters among the possessions that her landlady sent back to your father last fall. I also know that she loved you even if she had stopped loving your father, because she talked about you all the time."

I paused and I heard her inhale sharply. But she didn't say anything, so I went on. "And here's what I think. I think she was writing to you last summer and that she probably sent the letters to you in care of your best friend. I don't know who the friend is, but I can find out if I need to, so don't deny anything if

I'm right. I think you wrote back to her, and that those were the letters that were among her possessions when they were sent back to your father. I think that you were home when the package arrived and that you opened it and took out the letters before your father got home."

Her voice was faint. "How did you know that?"

"Because he would have mentioned the letters if he'd seen them, and he didn't. So you were writing to each other."

"Yes. Mom didn't want Dad to know anything about where she was or what she was doing. She was deciding whether to leave him. My dad is a nerd. All he does is work."

There are worse faults in a man, I thought, and soon enough she'd surely find out about them.

"But the letters stopped coming last August," I said.

"Yes. She wrote the last one just before Labor Day. She used to write every week. When her letters stopped, I wrote to her, but I didn't hear from her anymore. I didn't know what to think. I didn't know what happened to her. Do you know? Tell me, if you do."

"I don't know, but I'm trying to find out. I need information from you. Was she seeing anyone here on the island? A man, maybe? Someone she might have gone off with."

"She said she was dating, but I can't remember any names. She wanted me to burn her letters so Dad wouldn't find them. I'm sorry now that I did."

"Was there anybody in particular? Especially toward the end of the summer."

"She never said anything that made me think she was going away with anybody, if that's what you mean."

"Maybe just some guy she was dating and liked."

"Well, in one of her last letters she said she was playing tennis with a guy. She must have liked him if she'd do that, because she'd never played tennis in her life and always said it was boring. I guess she really was playing, because there was a tennis racket in the box we got from that lady."

"Elsie Cohen?"

"Maybe that was her name. I don't remember."

"What did your mother say about this guy?"

"Just that she liked him and he was good-looking and he made her feel young. She got married right out of high school and never got a chance to be a single woman for a while first. She always told me not to make that mistake, and her letters made me think she was trying to make up for things that she missed because she married my clunky dad."

"Think hard. Can you remember the man's name?"

"No. I don't think she ever told it to me."

"Can you remember anything more she said about him? Looks or habits? Where they went, where they played tennis? Did they go dancing? Did they have a favorite place to eat? Anything."

"I don't remember anything like that. They played tennis and had dinner and went to his beach, but I don't think she ever said where. I wish I'd never burned those letters."

Amen to that, but it was spilled milk. "Did this man live on the island year-round?"

She paused for a minute. "I don't know. I don't think she ever said."

"Does your father know about the letters?"

"No! She didn't want him to know. I've never told anyone. Oh, my gosh! Are you going to tell him?"

"I don't know yet, but I think you probably should. You may think he's a nerd, and he may be just that, but he loves you and he loves your mother as best he can."

"He doesn't love anything but his work."

"Does your father use a cologne called Enchanté?"

"Good grief, no. He only uses Old Spice. I should know. It's the only thing he ever wants for Christmas."

She had given me a little, but I didn't think she had much more to offer. "I think you're wrong about your father only loving his work," I said. "Let me give you my telephone number. I want you to call me if you think of anything that might help me."

"Let me find a pen. . . . Okay."

I gave her the number, promised to let her know if I learned anything, and rang off.

I was glad I wasn't eighteen anymore. Once was enough.

Chapter Eight

Brady

On Monday morning I drove Sarah's Range Rover to my meeting with the Isle of Dreams Development Corporation's lawyer in Oak Bluffs to hear their pitch for building a golf course on the Fairchild property. We were scheduled for ten o'clock, which was the precise time that I got there. His name was Lawrence McKenney, and he had a suite of offices on the second floor over a souvenir store.

I presented myself to McKenney's secretary, a roundish woman with white hair and a dark scowl. "They've been waiting for you, Mr. Coyne," she said in the same tone of voice she might've used if she'd caught me stealing magazines from her reception area.

"They?" I said.

"Mr. McKenney and the Isle of Dreams people, of course."

"Of course," I said, although my understanding had been that this first, preliminary discussion would be just between us lawyers.

The secretary ushered me into a conference room. There was a big rectangular oak table with a dozen chairs around it, and five of the chairs were occupied. Four men, one woman.

One of the occupants was Luis Martinez, the guy with the black mustache whom Eliza had been rubbing herself against the previous day.

I pointed at Martinez. "Get him out of here," I said to no one in particular. If Phil Fredrickson, the other guy who Eliza had brought around to lobby me, had been there, I'd have kicked him out, too.

One of the other men stood up. "Mr. Martinez is—"

"Out of here," I repeated. "Him or me."

The man who had spoken had thinning reddish hair, pale skin, and large round glasses. I assumed he was Lawrence McKenney. He blinked at me for a moment, then nodded and turned to Martinez. "You better go," he said.

Martinez looked at the others sitting around the table. All of them shrugged.

So he stood up, shoved his chair back so hard that it cracked against the wall, and came toward the door. When he got to me, he stopped, pushed his face close to mine, and whispered, "Bastard."

Then he went through the door and slammed it behind him.

I looked around the room. "Gentlemen," I said. "And lady," I added, nodding at the woman, who was having trouble concealing her smile. "Let's talk."

I let them do the talking. They'd drawn up aerial maps and sketches of the golf course and clubhouse and practice range and swimming pool and tennis courts they proposed for the Fairchild land, and indicated how they intended to abide by the various zoning and environmental regulations. They were flexible, they said, since they'd need only about half of the two hundred acres for the golf course itself. They wanted to build a few fairways near the ocean, but they were sensitive to environmental concerns.

It wasn't until we returned from lunch to resume the session that money was mentioned. Based on my research, their figure was more than fair. I didn't tell them that. Money wasn't Sarah's main concern, but I didn't tell them that, either. I asked some questions about how they intended to preserve the integrity of the parcel, reminded them that it had been in the Fairchild family for more than two hundred years, and told them that Sarah would never approve any plan that didn't protect the nesting plovers and preserve the areas of wetland where waterfowl bred and endangered amphibians lived. Abiding by the letter of the environmental laws wouldn't be enough, I told them. Sarah had her own concerns, and I pointed out some places on their proposed layout that looked like they'd need redesigning.

McKenney, who did most of the talking for the group, said they'd need to discuss it, which was the response I would've given under the circumstances.

We agreed we'd be in touch and get together again, and we adjourned around four in the afternoon. Just enough time for me to hustle back to the Fairchild house, catch a catnap, and get cleaned up for my date with Molly.

I was just sliding the key into the door of Sarah's Range Rover where I'd left it parked in front of the lawyer's office when I felt a hand on my arm. I whirled around. It was Luis Martinez, and it's a good thing I didn't have a cigarette in my mouth, because his breath would've burst into flame.

I figured he'd been drinking since I kicked him out of our meeting about six hours earlier.

I looked down at my arm where his hand gripped it until he let go. Then I opened the car door.

"You trying to ruin me?" he said. He slurred it into one word: "Youtrynaroonme?"

"I'm trying to go home," I said as I slid into the front seat.

He clenched his fist and cocked his arm, but I slammed the door. The window was rolled up, so I couldn't hear what he said next. But I saw the snarl of his lips and the anger glittering in his eyes, and as I started up the engine, he smashed his fist down on the top of the car, then turned and lurched away.

I got to the Navigator Room on the dot of six-thirty, the time Molly and I had agreed to. The hostess said that Molly had indeed made a reservation for two, that she'd phoned it in the previous evening, in fact, and that I could wait for her at the bar or at our table upstairs. I chose the table. It was near the corner with a good view of the harbor. I told the hostess I'd wait until Molly arrived before ordering a drink.

I watched the boats mill around in the harbor, and fifteen or twenty minutes later a waitress came by and asked if I'd changed my mind about a drink. I told her maybe I'd have one after all.

When I finished it, it was seven-fifteen, and Molly

still hadn't shown up. It was just about dark outside, and the boats were all showing their running lights. There was a party on a big yacht just outside the window. Laughter and shouts and music filtered up to me.

I declined a second drink. Hmm. How long did you give somebody you'd just met before you acknowledged the obvious—that she'd stood you up?

An hour, at least, I thought. That Honda Civic of hers hadn't looked that new. A flat tire, a dead battery, anything could happen. If she'd gotten stranded on the road outside of town without a cell phone, it could take a while to get help.

I decided to give her an hour and a half. That would make it eight o'clock. I wanted to be chivalrous. But I didn't want to be some sad sack who'd wait forever for a lost cause.

At a quarter of eight I went downstairs, found a pay phone, and called the Jacksons. Zee answered. I told her Molly had apparently stood me up, that I hadn't eaten, and that if she didn't appear soon I'd be over to go fishing. I hoped J.W. had some more of that bluefish salad for a sandwich, because I was starved.

"I'm surprised," said Zee.

"How well do you know her?" I said.

"I haven't known her long," said Zee, "and I haven't spent much time with her. But I *like* her. I know I like her. I wouldn't like somebody who'd break a date without at least calling."

"She's a widow," I said. "She's spooked. She changed her mind. I can understand that."

"I would've thought she'd call, at least," said Zee.

"Well, she didn't. I'll wait another half an hour. If she shows up, I'll call you. Otherwise, I'll be along."

I finally gave up on Molly a little after eight-thirty. I debated whether to be pissed or worried, and settled for being pissed. We'd lost a couple of good fishing hours while I was sitting in a restaurant declining food and looking at my watch.

When I showed up at the Jacksons' house it was close to nine o'clock. J.W. came out into the yard as I was getting out of Sarah's Range Rover. "I'm not sure Zee's up for fishing tonight," he said. "She's convinced something happened to Molly."

"Flat tire," I said. "Or, more likely, cold feet."

"She tried calling. No answer."

"Well," I said, "something better probably came along. What do you think?"

I'd given him a good opportunity to nail me with an insult, but he declined. "I think my wife should retire from matchmaking," he said. "And I think I should make you a sandwich."

I gobbled two of J.W.'s bluefish-salad sandwiches on thick slices of Portuguese bread at their kitchen table while Zee dithered about going fishing. I tried to assure her that I'd been stood up before, that it was a normal and predictable thing for a recent widow to do when facing a date with an irresistible hunk of man such as myself, and that an evening on the beach was just the thing to clear our heads.

In the end, we trekked off to State Beach, which was on Nantucket Sound, just a ten-minute drive from the Jackson residence. We cast off the jetties and around the openings to the pond and along the beach itself, where Zee found a school of bluefish blitzing out beyond the range of my longest cast with a fly rod. She beached three of them before they moved along. I didn't get a strike.

Around midnight I noticed that Zee was sitting cross-legged on the sand staring out at the dark sea. "You're not casting," I said.

"It's Molly," she said.

"I'm sure Molly's fine." I sat down beside her. "And so am I. Honest. Don't feel bad. It was a good try, and I appreciate it. She seems like a nice person. You can't expect these things to work out every time."

She turned to me. "I wasn't feeling bad about being a failed matchmaker," she said. "In fact, I feel good about that. She liked you. I know she did. And I could tell you liked her."

"I did," I said. "I do."

"So why didn't she show up?"

"A million possible reasons. She'll probably call tomorrow full of apologies."

"I'm kinda worried," said Zee.

I figured it was her obligation as a woman and as a matchmaker to be worried, so I didn't try to talk her out of it.

In fact, once my annoyance at being stood up finally wore off, I began to worry a little myself.

We sat there watching the water for a while, and then Zee said she really wanted to quit. The tide had filled the ponds, and she figured the fish would be hard to find, and anyway, she had to work the next day.

I understood. Her heart wasn't in it. For Zee to want to quit early, she really had to be upset.

Chapter Nine

J.W.

The morning after her fishing trip with Brady, Zee was still unhappy and perplexed by Molly's failure to show up for her date with him. I was more inclined to pass it off as nothing earthshaking.

"I'm always hearing about how girls suffer while they wait for boys to phone or ask them out on dates," I said, "but guys have to put up with girls rolling their eyes and saying no thanks, or saying yes, then standing them up. It happens all the time."

"But Molly isn't the type to do that."

"Every woman is the type. I asked you to marry me for years before you finally said yes."

She lifted her chin. "Maybe I should have put it off longer."

"Too late."

"It's never too late for a girl to go home to her mother."

"Ha! I can just see you living with your mother."

I had her there. "I feel sorry for Brady," she said with a sigh.

"Brady's a grown man," I said. "Grown men don't need to have people feeling sorry for them,

121

they can feel sorry for themselves. Look at me. Don't make too much of this. There's probably a simple explanation."

"I wish I knew what it was." She fussed with her food.

"All will be revealed in time." I stacked my dishes in the sink. "Since you're going to be home this morning, I'm going to use the time to talk with some more people about Kathy Bannerman."

I started with Shrink Williams. Dr. Cotton Williams lived on West Chop not far from the spiffy new Vineyard Haven Library. His office was attached to his house and had two doors—one for going in and one for going out. I didn't know if many psychiatrists made a practice of having separate exit doors for their patients, but Shrink did. The theory, apparently, was that a patient would just as soon not have the next patient know that the first patient was one, too.

Shrink's office hours started at ten, and I was the first one through the door, edging out a nervous woman who came mincing along the sidewalk right behind me. Inside, Shrink's receptionist, an efficient-looking woman pushing sixty, frowned at her daybook and told me that I didn't have an appointment.

"My name's Jackson," I said. "I have a badge in my pocket if you'd care to look at it, but I'd just as soon keep this informal. I only need to talk with the doctor for a moment. I'd like his advice on a case." I showed her my best Joe Friday face.

I actually did have my old Boston PD shield with me, if it came to that, which I hoped it wouldn't, since there are laws against pretending to be a police officer. Luck, in her willy-nilly way, chose to smile upon me.

"Just a moment, please." The woman went out of sight and came back. "This way, please." I followed her into an office, where she left me with Shrink.

He was about my age and didn't look like the ladies' man he was reputed to be. But who knows what women like, besides shoes?

"How can I help you, Officer Jackson?" Then he frowned. "Haven't we met before?"

"Briefly, some time ago. I'm looking into the disappearance of a woman named Katherine Bannerman. She was here on the island last August, but hasn't been seen since then. I've been told that you dated her, and I'm hoping that you can give me information that might be useful in locating her." I showed him my photograph of Kathy Bannerman.

Shrink assumed a professional air. "If Mrs. Bannerman had been a client, of course our conversations would be confidential. Even so, I'm afraid I can't be of much help to you because I only saw her socially for a short time."

"When was that?"

His brow furrowed. "It would have been in late July of last year. We only went out a half dozen times."

"Did she ever talk about leaving the island, or suggest someplace she might be planning to go?"

"No, not that I recall."

"Did she mention going back to her family?"

"No. She told me she was living apart from her husband and her daughter, but never said anything about going back to them. Although she did speak fondly of her daughter."

"Did she seem happy or unhappy?"

"You mean, was she depressed? Are you thinking that she might have committed suicide?"

I shrugged.

He shook his head. "I doubt it. She was very cheerful. Full of life. She was enjoying herself as a single woman."

"You're frowning."

"Am I?" He shook his head. "I'm supposed to be able to disguise my feelings."

"What feelings are we talking about?"

He smiled. "Wounded vanity? She stopped dating other men so she could go out with me, and that was fine. Then she stopped dating me so she could date someone else, and that wasn't so fine." He looked at me. "Just because I'm a psychiatrist doesn't mean I'm immune to the kinds of emotions any man would have."

Having been divorced by my first wife, I could understand how he might have felt. "And you never dated her again?"

"No."

"Or talked with her?"

"We might have bumped into each other in the grocery store or somewhere and said hello. We weren't enemies, but we didn't talk."

"Who did she date after she dated you?"

He shrugged. "I didn't know him."

"You saw them together?"

"Sure. There are only so many places on this island

where you can dance or listen to music. I saw her with some guy."

"You never heard his name?"

"No."

"What did he look like?"

Again the shrug. "I really couldn't say. Young, not bad-looking."

"Blond or dark?"

"I didn't really pay much attention. I had a date of my own, and I would have been paying attention to her."

"Beard? Mustache?"

"I don't remember. They were across the room."

"Where did you see them?"

"At a club, as I remember. The Connection, maybe, or the Tin Roof, or maybe the Fireside. I'm really not sure." He looked at his watch. "Look, I have a patient waiting."

"Thanks for your time. You've been helpful."

"I don't see how."

My smile was at least as real as his. "I know more than I did before," I said.

I had time for one more stop before heading home so Zee could go to work. I drove to Oak Bluffs and parked off Kennebeck Street behind the Fireside Bar. I knocked on the back door, and Bonzo opened it. He was holding a push broom, and he smiled his wide vacant smile when he saw me. "J.W.! What a nice surprise!"

Long before I knew him, Bonzo had been a very promising young man. Unfortunately, he had gotten hold of some bad acid and thereafter had become a

125

PHILIP R. CRAIG AND WILLIAM G. TAPPLY

kind, mindless, cheerful fellow whose greatest plea-
sures were fishing and watching birds, and whose
dim thoughts prevented him from doing work more
complicated than sweeping floors and wiping tables.
He lived with his adoring mother, who had taught forever in the island schools and who cared for him like
the large child that he was. Still, though Bonzo was
missing some of his original parts, you could never be
sure what he'd remember and what he wouldn't. For
instance, he remembered every bird he'd ever pho-
tographed and every fish he ever caught.

"I'd like to talk to you, Bonzo."

Bonzo leaned on his broom, smiled, and considered this proposition. Then he frowned and said,
"I'm working right now, J.W. Won't be long before
we open for lunch, and the place has to be clean, and
I have to do it." He blinked at me.

"It'll only take a minute, Bonzo."

"Oh, okay. Let's talk. It's been a while since you
been in for a beer, J.W."

"I'm a married man, Bonzo. I stay at home these
days, instead of going out on the town."

He nodded. "I know. You're married to Zee. It's
good that you got married, J.W. Especially to Zee.
Zee is a nice lady."

I showed him the photograph of Kathy Bannerman. "Last year this woman was on the island. You
ever see her in the Fireside?"

He studied the picture, then nodded. "Gee," he
said. "Last year. That was a long time ago, J.W, but
yeah, I seen her here a few times."

"Did you ever see her with Shrink Williams?"

He smiled his biggest smile. "Sure I did. They was here, and then afterward she was here with the man that the doctor didn't like her to be with. She's pretty, J.W., and nice, too. She gave me a dollar every time she was here."

"Who was the other man?"

He gave an elaborate shrug. "Gosh, I don't know everybody, you know. Especially in the summer when this place is full of those tourists and college kids. He's a man I don't know is all I can tell you."

"Has he been back since you saw him with her?"

Bonzo stared through a fog toward his memories, then nodded. "Yeah, he comes in sometimes. I seen him this summer sometimes. In the evening, after dinner."

"But you don't know his name?"

"His name?" Bonzo shook his head. "I don't know his name. We get a lot of people that come in here, and I don't know the names of most of them. Only the people who are here year-round. I know some of their names. The regulars, you know what I mean?"

"I know what you mean, Bonzo. What does this man look like? Can you describe him?"

But that was too much for him. "He's just ordinary, like everybody else."

I tried for some details but didn't get any. The man wasn't tall, short, dark, blond, clean-shaven, or bearded. His hair wasn't long or short, his eyes could have been blue or brown, and there was nothing unusual about his clothes, his behavior, or his spending habits.

He was ordinary.

But he was still around. Not a regular, but still around. "When does he come in, Bonzo? Any particular time?"

"In the evening sometimes, like I told you, J.W. Don't you remember me telling you that?"

"I remember now, Bonzo. If he comes in again, will you telephone me? I'd like to meet him."

"Telephone you? Sure. Your number's in the book. I can do that. You want me to tell him to wait for you?"

"No, just phone me. What did you mean when you said that Dr. Williams didn't like Kathy to be with the man?"

"Well, he didn't like it. I'm not dumb. I can tell things."

"How do you know? Did they have an argument?"

He drew himself up. "No, they didn't do anything like that. Dr. Williams never does that. What he does is, he comes in after the women and the other men and watches them from across the room. That's what I mean. He watches and he watches and he looks funny and almost never drinks his beer, and when they leave he waits and leaves too. He always does that. He did that with this lady in the picture, and he always does it."

Stop. Rewind. "What do you mean, Bonzo? You mean Shrink Williams has done that other times? Not just with this woman?"

He looked pleased. "You got it, J.W. You're smart, just like me. He does it all the time. He brings them ladies here himself, then later when they come in with other men, he follows them in and he follows them out, but he never says nothing to them at all. He just watches them. You want to know something else?"

"Sure."

"He never leaves a tip. He's a doctor, and doctors make lots of money, but he never leaves a tip. Never at all. That's why I always remember him. Otherwise, he's just ordinary. You know what I mean?" Then he brightened. "Say, J.W., I bet you're looking for the woman in that picture!"

"That's right, Bonzo."

He clapped his hands. "I knew it when I saw you with that man."

"What man?"

"That man you was talking with here the other morning. I remember him from before. He's been looking for her, too."

"Yes. She's his wife. He said he'd been on the island several times this summer, trying to find her."

Bonzo nodded. "That's right. And last year, too, just before Labor Day. I remember, because it was right when the bluefish came back. He was looking for her then, too."

That was news I hadn't gotten from either Bannerman or Thornberry's report.

I drove home thinking about the implications.

Chapter Ten

Brady

I was awakened by a hand on my shoulder. I blinked my eyes open. It was Eliza. She was wearing sunglasses and a slinky belted lavender wrap that stopped around mid-thigh. She held a mug of coffee in her hand.

"What's with the shades?" I said.

"Part of the ensemble," she said. "What do you think?" She posed for me with a hand on her hip.

"Yeah," I said. "It works for me. But you didn't knock and inquire if I was decent."

"I already know that you're altogether too decent," she said. "And I did knock. You didn't answer."

"A bit sleep-deprived," I said. "Fishing and whatnot."

"If you ask me," she said, "too much fishing and nowhere near enough whatnot." She put the coffee mug on the table beside the bed.

I hitched myself into a sitting position and picked up the mug. I took a sip and felt the life force begin to surge through my arteries. "Thank you," I said.

She sat at the foot of my bed. "So how's it going?"

"No keepers," I said. "I hooked something big a couple nights ago out to Cape Pogue Gut, but he bit me off. Got a nice striper at Squibnocket, but it was a few inches short. Couple small bluefish."

She smiled. "I didn't mean the fishing."

"If you meant the disposal of your mother's property, I've told you. Don't ask."

"Today's Tuesday. You're meeting with the nature freaks today, right?"

I smiled. "Yes. The Marshall Lea Foundation."

"They don't have any money."

"Eliza—"

She squeezed my foot through the blanket. "I'm sorry. I'll stay out of it."

I took another sip of coffee. "So how's Sarah doing?"

Eliza shook her head. "She's sleeping more and more. When she's awake, she's in pain. It's getting worse. And to top it off, her beloved nurse didn't show up yesterday."

I stopped my coffee mug halfway to my mouth. "Molly Wood? She didn't?"

Eliza smirked. "So you noticed Mrs. Wood, huh?"

I shrugged. "I met her on her way out a couple days ago. What do you mean, she didn't show up?"

"Another nurse came. An older woman. Mother didn't like her, refused to let her give her a sponge bath, insisted I get the Wood woman back. I called the Visiting Nurse office. They wouldn't tell me much, but I inferred that she just didn't check in that morning. I asked them what was wrong, and they hemmed and hawed, which led me to believe that they didn't know.

I suppose she's sick. They assured me they'd have her back today."

I tried to make a chronology out of it. On Sunday afternoon, I'd met Molly Wood on her way out from tending Sarah. That evening, Molly had eaten supper with me at the Jacksons' house. We'd parted around eight. Sometime later that evening she'd called the Navigator Room and reserved a table for two for the following evening. The next morning, Monday, she didn't check in for work at the Visiting Nurse office, and she'd failed to keep her appointment with Sarah that day. Monday evening she did not show up at the Navigator Room. Now it was Tuesday.

Maybe Zee was right. Maybe she should be worried.

If something had happened to Molly, as Zee suspected, it had happened Sunday night or early Monday morning, sometime between the time she and I parted at the Jacksons' house and the time she was supposed to check in for work.

"I'm going to get up now," I said to Eliza.

She smiled. "Go right ahead."

"I'm not, um, decent."

She shrugged, got off the bed, and started for the door.

"Eliza, wait," I said.

She stopped. "What?"

"Come here." I held out my hand. "Please."

She smiled, came over beside me, and took my hand.

"Bend down here," I said.

She leaned over until her mouth was nearly touching mine.

I reached up and plucked off her sunglasses.

"Hey!" she said.

The flesh surrounding her left eye was several shades of purple, green, and yellow.

"What happened?" I said.

She shook her head. "Nothing. I bumped into something."

"What's his name?"

"It's personal, Brady. Okay?"

"Not if his name is Martinez or Fredrickson, it's not."

"Please," she said. "It's my problem. It's got nothing to do with you."

"Somebody hits a woman," I said, "it's got everything to do with me. I'm a lawyer, an officer of the court, and battering women is against the law."

She laid the palm of her hand on my cheek, peered into my eyes for a moment, then bent and kissed me softly on the lips. "I'm okay," she said. "Everything's under control. Okay?"

"You shouldn't let him get away with this."

She stood up and tugged on the belt of her robe. "I can handle it," she said. Then she turned and left the room.

When I got downstairs, I took my coffee out to the sunporch. Sarah was wrapped from chin to toe in a crocheted afghan. She was watching some talk show on the television.

I bent down, kissed her cheek, then pulled up a chair beside her. "Thought I'd fill you in," I said.

She nodded and muted the TV with the remote in her lap.

I told her about my meeting with the golf-course developers, my impressions of their operation, how I'd conveyed her conditions to them, and what they'd offered for the property. I added that I had a meeting with the Marshall Lea Foundation later in the morning, where I expected to get a better handle on their intentions.

"That's just fine, Brady," Sarah said. "You handle it."

"I am," I said, "but it's your decision."

"Insofar as I am capable of a rational decision," she said.

I slid my chair around in front of her so that I was looking into her face. Her mouth was tight and her forehead and eyes were pinched. "A lot of pain?" I said.

"It's tolerable," she said. "I woke up with a headache, that's all."

I stood up. "I'll leave you, then. You should sleep."

She tried to smile. It was a poor effort. "Thank you, dear. I'll feel better when you get back. I promise."

Patrick was coming into the sunporch as I was going out. I touched his arm. "I want to talk to you for a minute."

He nodded. "Sure. What's up?"

I steered him back into the living room. "Your mother tells me that Sarah's regular nurse didn't show up yesterday. I was wondering how well you knew her."

"Who? The nurse?"

"Yes. Molly Wood."

Patrick shrugged. "She comes in, takes care of Grandmother, and leaves. I've said hello and thank-you-good-bye to her a few times. Grandmother loves her. She was depressed all day yesterday when that other nurse showed up."

"Has Mrs. Wood been reliable?"

"Sure. Reliable and punctual and, as far as I can tell, very competent. Like I said, Grandmother's very fond of her."

"Never missed an appointment?"

"Yesterday was the first time." Patrick cocked his head and frowned at me. "Why are you asking about her, Brady?"

I saw no reason to tell Patrick that Sarah's nurse had stood me up the previous evening and that I suspected something had happened to her. "I'm concerned about your grandmother, that's all," I said. "She seems a little down today."

"She had a bad night," he said. "I was on my way in to sit with her, see if I could cheer her up."

"Good for you," I said. I patted his shoulder. "Go for it."

I gathered up my lawyer gear, climbed into Sarah's Range Rover, and headed for the bank in Edgartown where I was to meet with the representatives of the Marshall Lea Foundation.

The MLF, according to the research Julie had done for me, was a well-heeled local organization of preservationists that bought up choice island properties and deeded them over as nature sanctuaries to the towns where they were located, with the stipulation that they, the MLF, would retain control over their uses and that the properties were never to be developed or commercialized. The organization depended entirely on private funds and engaged in no lobbying, thus giving it—and all who donated to it—tax-exempt status.

When I'd mentioned the Marshall Lea Foundation to J.W., he'd snorted. "Plover lovers," he said. "They find one blade of rare grass or some endangered beetle, they surround it with No Trespassing signs. If they had their way, they'd kick all the people off the island and turn it over to the birds."

I like piping plovers and rare grass and exotic beetles just fine. But I like people, too. Except extremists. I don't like extremists regardless of what they're extreme about. True believers scare me.

As far as the Fairchild property was concerned, however, what I liked didn't matter. My job was to help Sarah get what she liked.

It would be interesting to see what the MLF had in mind for the Fairchild property. I knew they couldn't come close to matching what the golf people had offered to pay for it. Sarah claimed she didn't care about money. That left it up to me to care.

At the bank, I was ushered into a conference room behind the tellers and loan officers out front. A florid man with a bald head and an eagle-beak nose sat at the head of the rectangular conference table. His name was Gregory Pinto. He was an MLF trustee and chairman of the committee to investigate the acquisition of the Fairchild property. Two women, both sprightly dames in their sixties, and another man, a gangly towheaded guy who looked like a teenager, all introduced themselves. The woman with the shoe-leather face was Millie, and the round one with the white hair was Roberta. The pale-haired young guy was Kimball G. Warren III. He wanted me to call him Trip.

Pinto was the president of the bank. Millie and Roberta were married to wealthy men who owned summer places on the Vineyard and made heavy annual donations to the foundation. Trip Warren, as it turned out, was another damn lawyer.

Pinto did the talking. Their proposal was simple: They would give Sarah Fairchild a check for her two hundred acres, then deed it over to the township of West Tisbury with a variety of codicils, stipulations, conditions, and requirements, all of which amounted to the foundation's retaining veto rights over any use of the property the township might consider. The beach and dunes, they felt, should be strictly off-limits to human use. Piping plovers nested there, not to mention several other less-threatened avian and aquatic species. The freshwater ponds, likewise, should be out-of-bounds. The MLF would bring in an army of biologists to take a census of the entire property. Any area where a single species of plant or animal they considered fragile, threatened, or endangered, or that might simply be unhappy if people were nearby, would be given sanctuary.

The Fairchild parcel was, said Pinto, "an ecological treasure," and should be preserved and protected from human abuse.

I inferred that "abuse" and "use" were synonymous terms in the MLF lexicon.

They would, of course, raze both the Fairchild house and the stone lodge at the beach. Pinto called them "eyesores." Their aim was to restore the property to its "original unspoiled condition."

Their proposal was, they understood, subject to negotiation with both Sarah Fairchild and the township of West Tisbury.

When Pinto was done, he looked at me. "Well, Mr. Coyne, there you have it. Do you have any questions?"

I shook my head. "I'll bring all this paperwork home with me and look at it with my lawyer's eye. And, of course, I'll have to explain it all to Mrs. Fairchild. Then we'll see what she thinks."

"Of course, of course," he harrumphed. He hesitated, then said, "We haven't, um, discussed . . ."

"Money," I said.

"We cannot match the Isle of Dreams offer, you understand."

"You know what they offered?"

He cleared his throat. "Let's say we have a pretty good idea."

"You don't want to match it?" I said.

Trip Warren, the baby-faced lawyer, reached across the table and put his hand on my arm. "Sir," he said, "the Isle of Dreams is a private corporation. They envision a profit-making operation. It's entirely different."

I shrugged. "We'll see who wants it the most. The final decision, of course, is Sarah Fairchild's."

"The price is negotiable, I hope," said Pinto.

The two ladies nodded vigorously.

"At this point," I said, "everything's negotiable."

We had lunch at the Harborview, and then we all piled into Pinto's van and drove out to the Fairchild property. We parked at the locked gate by the dirt roadway that wound through the meadow and scrubby oak and pine forest, over the dunes, and down to the beach. A big NO TRESPASSING sign was nailed to the gate.

We got out, walked around the gate, and started strolling down the road. I was in front with Trip Warren. Millie and Roberta were right behind us, chattering animatedly, and Gregory Pinto was huffing along, bringing up the rear.

We had just turned a corner by a grove of pines when Nate Fairchild stepped out of the woods into the roadway in front of us. "You again," he snarled, glaring directly at me. "Get the hell outta here." His eyes took in the others. "Goddam nature freaks. I mean all of you. Scram."

Nate was wearing his fore-and-aft fishing cap and a pair of overalls with no shirt underneath. With his bushy sun-bleached beard and scruffy work boots and menacing scowl, he looked like something out of *Deliverance*—particularly since he was holding a pump-action shotgun under his arm.

Millie, the leather-faced old gal, walked right up to him. "Put that silly weapon away, young man," she said. "We have every right to be here. We're the Marshall Lea Foundation, and we're here with the Fairchild family lawyer, and you don't frighten us."

Trip Warren mumbled, "He frightens *me*."

Nate glowered at Millie. "I don't give a shit who you are, lady," he said. "You're trespassing, and I'll pepper your scrawny little ass if you don't get the fuck off my property."

Millie turned to me. "Who is this terrible person?"

"Meet Nathan Fairchild," I said. "Sarah's son."

"I'm out of here," said Trip Warren.

Gregory Pinto was already heading back to his van. Trip turned and started trotting after him. Roberta and Millie continued to stand there in the middle of the road glaring at Nate.

"Come on, ladies," I said. "I'll get this straightened out and we'll come back another time."

"I ain't going away," said Nate. "You come back, I'll be here."

Millie stepped up to Nate. "You're not going to shoot us."

He grinned. "Don't count on it, you shriveled-up old witch."

I put my arm around Millie's shoulders and gently pulled her away. "Come on," I said. "Let's go."

When she and Roberta reluctantly started back to the van, I turned to Nate. "What the hell do you think you're going to accomplish? Do this again and you'll be arrested, I promise."

"Fuck you, lawyer," he said. "It's my property, and it's posted, and that gate is locked."

"It's Sarah's property, not yours. I'll straighten it out with her."

"I doubt that," he said.

I started to ask him what the hell he meant by that, but he just shrugged, turned, and disappeared into the woods.

In the van on the way back to Edgartown, Gre-

gory Pinto and the two ladies told young Trip Warren Nate Fairchild stories, how he was a local ne'er-
do-well, a notoriously bad-tempered drunk and
brawler well known to the local police, a fisherman
and hunter who ignored closed seasons and bag limits and was known to sneak onto beaches that the
EPA had declared off-limits. He was, they agreed,
the Fairchild family's bad seed. One of the benefits
of buying up the property would be to rid the island
of him.

Warren wondered if the MLF ought to reconsider
its offer to purchase the place. He envisioned Nate
Fairchild haunting it, shooting buckshot at people
who came to check on the plovers.

I apologized for Nate and promised to speak to
Sarah about him. We agreed to get together again at
the end of the week.

It was nearly five in the afternoon when I pulled into
the turnaround in front of the Fairchild house. I'd
been thinking about Molly Wood, wondering if she'd
turned up. I'd call J.W. as soon as I got inside. He'd
know.

Patrick came onto the front porch as I was getting
out of the car. I waved at him and started up the
steps. Then I stopped. Patrick was biting his bottom
lip and shaking his head.

"What's the matter?" I said.

"It's my grandmother," he said.

Chapter Eleven

J.W.

At the house I found Zee looking even more upset than when I'd left. "I called the Visiting Nurse Service. Molly missed work yesterday and didn't come in this morning, either."

I had a sense of déjà vu. I'd been looking for one missing woman, and now Zee was fussing about another one.

"It's not like Molly to miss work," she was saying. "She's much too responsible. She would have called in if she was sick. I'm worried."

"Maybe she had to go off-island unexpectedly. An emergency of some kind. Do you have her mainland phone number or address?"

"No. She's staying with Edna Paul here in town, but all I know about where she lives in America is that it's in Scituate." She glanced at her watch. "I have to get to work."

I had a sudden sense of some cosmic decision-maker involving me in a drama not of my own choosing. "I tell you what I'll do," I said, feeling as if I were reading a script, "I'm already looking for Kathy Bannerman. While I'm at it, I'll see if I can catch up with Molly Wood."

"Oh, good. Call me if you find out anything." She picked up her purse and gave kisses to her lunch-chewing children.

I walked her out to her Jeep, where I got my own kiss. "Do you know anything that might help me get started? People Molly knows, places she goes? That sort of thing?"

"Well, she knows the people at the Visiting Nurse Service, and she knows Sarah Fairchild and her family, and of course she knows Brady. There have been other people in and out of the Fairchild house when she's been there. Those golf people and the Marshall Lea people. Maybe she knows some of them."

"Did she ever talk about the people she's been dating? Do you remember any of their names?"

She climbed into the Jeep. "I know she's had a couple of dates, and maybe she mentioned some names, but the only one I remember is Shrink Williams."

Shrink Williams again. "Shrink Williams must date every single woman on Martha's Vineyard. He dated Kathy Bannerman last year. What do women see in that guy, anyway?"

"Well, he's got some money, and he's a good dancer."

"Except for the part about money and dancing, that's a perfect description of me."

She patted my cheek. "Women don't stick to Shrink for long. You've got me for life, though I sometimes wonder why."

I had a thought. "Was Molly one of Shrink's patients?"

"I don't know. It's possible, I guess."

"Isn't it unethical for a psychiatrist to date his patients?"

"Who said psychiatrists are any more ethical than other people? But as far as I know, nobody's brought charges against Shrink. I've never heard of any woman who thought he was exploiting her. I think most women just get bored with him."

She drove off, and I went in to clean up the lunch dishes. After that, the children and I worked on the tree house for a while. It was coming along nicely, in spite of the usual delays caused by dropped tools, continuous modifications in design, and pauses to admire our work.

In midafternoon, I called a halt to construction and we drove into Edgartown. I wanted to talk with Edna Paul, who was Molly Wood's landlady. Edna's house was toward the southwest end of Summer Street. It was a modest place compared with some of its neighbors. Edna was a retired schoolteacher who stretched her pension by renting her spare bedroom to mature single ladies. No college students. Too noisy. Edna belonged to the Marshall Lea Foundation. I hoped she'd talk to me anyway. She liked children, so I was glad I had mine along when I knocked on her door.

"Oh, it's you," said Edna when she opened the door. The smile on her face was replaced by a frown. Edna and I had clashed more than once over how preserved land should be used. She was a No-People person who favored limited human access to let land revert back to its natural state. I held out for traditional uses such as hunting, fishing, hiking, and picnicking.

I got right to the point. "Molly Wood hasn't been seen in two days. I hope you can tell me she's here."

"Well, she isn't. But, she's paid up to the end of the month, so I assume she'll be back."

"When did you last see her?"

"Why should I tell you?"

"Because my wife is her friend and she's worried, and because if Molly stays missing, the cops are going to be looking for her. Did you see her yesterday?"

She looked down at the children and almost smiled, but the smile went away when she looked back at me. "No, I can't say I did, but I don't stick my nose in other people's business like some people I know."

"When did you last see her?"

"Night before last. I was watching television. I heard her, but I didn't see her. She's got her own entrance."

"That would have been after she left our place. She had dinner with us. Where did she park her car?"

"Right there in the driveway. First I heard her drive in, and then I heard her come in and go up the stairs."

"And you never heard her or saw her again."

"I didn't say that. A while later I heard her telephone ring. She has a private line. Said she needed to be in touch with people in Scituate, where she comes from. Anyway, these walls aren't too thick, so I heard the phone ring. Then a little later she went out and drove off. Probably to meet up with one of those men she's been seeing."

One of those men. "Do you know which one?"

"No."

"Do you know any of them or any of their names?"

"Can't say as I do. The girl goes out pretty often for a widow woman who just lost her husband, though. One of them brought her home a few days ago, and the two of them were outside for a long time, sitting in his car. I didn't get a good look at him, but I don't want any hanky-panky at my house, so I flicked the porch light a couple of times and they got the idea. He drove off and she came in and went up to her room."

"What kind of a car was it?"

She shrugged. "They all look alike to me."

I have the same problem. "New or old?"

"It looked pretty new."

"What color?"

"It was night. I couldn't tell."

"What did the man look like?"

"Could have been young or old. I don't stare at people, like some others I know."

"Would you recognize him if you saw him?"

"Doubt it."

"Did you mention him to Molly afterward?"

"I don't pry."

"Did you ever see him again?"

"Maybe he was here one other time. It was night again. I only saw the back of his car when he drove off."

"No long talks in the car that time?"

"I couldn't say. I was coming home from a meeting and I pulled in just as he drove off."

"Do you mind if I take a look at her room?"

"I most certainly do."

"I won't take anything. You can come with me to make sure."

"You can't go in there. My guests have complete privacy."

"The police may want to look in there."

"They have a warrant, they can go in. They don't, they can't."

"Molly Wood is missing, Edna. We're trying to find her."

"Well, you won't find her here."

"If she comes home or calls, please tell the police."

She thought, then nodded. "Yes. I will."

I thanked her, and she shut the door in my face.

I rewarded the kids with ice cream, and by the time it had been eaten and hands and faces had been wiped free of the overflow, I knew what I needed to do. So we drove to the police station, and I told the Chief about Molly Wood's disappearance and what I'd learned from Edna Paul, which wasn't much.

"That's because she doesn't like you," said the Chief, who had been scribbling notes while he listened.

"I know," I said. "I think she knows a lot more than she told me. She said the walls are thin, but that she doesn't listen through them. I'll bet she does. She said she doesn't keep tabs on what her tenants do, but I doubt that. She claims she can't describe the men Molly dated, but I'll bet she can. I came by to ask you to wave your badge and a search warrant at her, so she'll talk with you and give you a look at Molly's room."

"Once again, your simpleminded police department is indebted to a citizen of the town, telling us how to do our work. I'll send Tony D'Agostine down to have a chat with Edna. He won't have a warrant, but I'll bet he gets into Mrs. Wood's room without one."

"If you learn anything, will you let me know?"

"Maybe. How many more missing women do you expect to be looking for in the next day or two? If you tell me now, I can start looking for them right away."

"Two is two more than enough, as far as I'm concerned."

"Amen. Now, if you don't have any other earth-shaking ideas, why don't you run along and let me do my work, which right now is making some calls around the island and to the mainland to see if your new missing lady is still here or went back to Scituate."

As we left, he was frowning and reaching for the phone.

Joshua and Diana wanted to go home and work on the tree house.

"No," I said. "We're going for a drive. We're looking for the red car that Molly was driving when she came to our house for supper. You two can help. If you see a red car, tell me."

"There's one!"

"That's not the right one, but keep pointing them out."

"There's another one!"

It was going to be a long day. I hadn't even gotten out of town before my bright-eyed children had proven that there were a lot of red cars around. Unfortunately, none of them was a Honda Civic belonging to Molly Wood.

I figured that the island's ten different police forces were probably cruising where they normally cruised, and that people living at the ends of private driveways would have reported any strange cars on their property, so I decided to cruise where the police didn't usually go and to ignore private drives.

I didn't have much hope of finding Molly's car, but you never know, so I spent the last of the afternoon driving the back roads that wander through Edgartown's forests and scouting every housing development I could find. There are a lot of these, and more in the making, thanks to the ever-increasing popularity of Vineyard living. I followed roads I'd never been on before and saw houses I'd never seen. I was both impressed and depressed, and I found myself waxing nostalgic for the good old days, before things had gotten so crowded. Of course, when my children were grown they would be nostalgic for days like this one, when life was simpler and there weren't so many crowds.

I didn't find Molly's car, and both children went to sleep in the backseat while I was searching. Nap time waits for no one.

When I'd driven every back road I could find in Edgartown, I moved my search up to Oak Bluffs and repeated the process there. As in Edgartown, there were lots of roads, both paved and unpaved, to be explored, and a lot of new houses. I drove many miles but saw no sign of Molly's car.

Then I thought of the purloined letter. People could say a lot of things about me, but they couldn't deny that I was slow. If you're naked and you don't want people to notice, you go to a nudist colony. If you want to hide a book, try a library.

If you want to put a car in some inconspicuous place, you put it in a long-term parking lot.

After Labor Day, there are more parking spots available than there are in the summer, and the cops are much more lax about enforcing parking limits. Still, there aren't too many places where cars can be parked for several days without being noticed and ticketed. Most towns have a few such places, and the local police probably didn't pay too much attention to them.

I took a look at Oak Bluffs twenty-four-hour parking areas and found nothing. I drove back to Edgartown and tried there. Nothing again. I started for Vineyard Haven but then realized I didn't have time for that, since Zee would be coming home at any minute. I felt impatient and frustrated, as though an unjust fate was keeping me from almost certain success, although I knew that was nonsense. I drove home, where I woke up the kids and had just enough time to put the martini glasses in the freezer and get supper going when the phone rang.

It was Zee. Her voice was filled with anger and fear. "Jeff, something's happened! Come up here right away. I'll meet you in the parking lot."

"Are you all right?"

"I'm fine. Please come."

I piled the kids into the car and was at the hospital parking lot in ten minutes.

Zee was standing beside her Jeep, holding a piece of paper in her hand. I went right to her.

"What is it?" I said. "Are you okay?"

"I'm fine, but look at that." She pointed. A tire had been slashed. "And this was under the windshield wiper." She thrust the paper at me.

It was crudely lettered, but plain enough. "Tell your husband to keep his nose out of places it doesn't belong."

I felt a red fury rise inside me. "Somebody must have seen this happen."

She shook her head. "I've asked. Nobody saw anything. What does that note mean? Who did this?"

The red anger flamed. "I don't know," I said, though I thought I might. "You take the kids home in the truck. I'll change the tire and be right behind you."

"All right. But we should tell the police."

"Good idea. Stop at the OBPD on your way and give them the note and a report." That way I'd probably be home about the same time she and the kids were. I didn't want them there alone.

I hurried with the tire and was home waiting for them when they drove in. By then my anger was the cold kind.

Zee looked tired. "The police are going to talk with people and try to find a witness. They wanted to know what you were doing that might make somebody mad. I couldn't tell them. They want to talk with you."

"All right, I'll get in touch with them." I put my hands on her shoulders. "The note wasn't addressed to anyone, so there's a chance the guy mixed your car up with somebody else's. Maybe it's just another example of OB politics. It's not the first slashed tire in that town."

"Maybe." She looked doubtful, although everyone on Martha's Vineyard knows that everything in Oak Bluffs is political and passions run high.

While she changed out of her uniform I took the chilled glasses from the freezer, sloshed a bit of dry vermouth in each of them, tossed it out, then got the Luksusowa out of the freezer and filled each glass. Two black olives went into Zee's and two green ones stuffed with hot peppers in mine.

Perfect martinis. Different but equally delish.

When Zee came out of the bedroom, I handed hers to her and we went up to the balcony. "Leftover St. Jacques for supper," I said.

"Fine. I don't know how to think about my tire, so I'm not going to talk about it anymore. I'm more interested in Molly. I know they haven't found her, because you'd have told me that right away. What are they doing?"

I was also glad not to talk about the tire, although I'd been thinking about it pretty hard. So I told her about my conversations with the Chief and Edna Paul and about my fruitless hunt for Molly's car. "I've got a very slim chance of finding it, but the police are looking for it, too, so between us we may locate it. And if we do, maybe we can learn something."

"It's totally unlike her to go off and not tell anyone. I know something's happened to her."

"The cops are hunting for her both here and on the mainland. If they can find the car, that could help."

She brushed back a strand of black hair that had strayed over her forehead. "I did want her to meet Brady. He needs a good woman as much as she needs a good man. I'm very worried."

"Come down and have some supper. Afterward I'll call the station and see if they've learned anything. If there isn't any news, we can drive up to Vineyard Haven and look around. We probably won't find the car, but at least we'll be doing something. Maybe we'll get lucky."

Reheated Coquilles St. Jacques is, like most casseroles, even better-tasting the second time around, but worry kept Zee and me from enjoying the flavor of the meal. The children, not sharing their parents' anxieties, gobbled theirs right up.

We washed and stacked the dishes in the drainer, and then the four of us piled into the Land Cruiser and drove to Vineyard Haven, where there are several places you can park a car if, say, you need to go over to America for a couple of days. I started on Causeway Road. We found no red Honda Civic parked there under the trees.

"This is hopeless," said Zee.

"Do you want to go home?"

"No. Let's keep looking."

"Mr. and Mrs. Sisyphus," I said.

Diana laughed. "That's funny, Pa. Say that again!"

I said it again.

More laughter. "That's hard to say, Pa." Joshua and Diana had a fine time saying it over and over.

At the fourth place we looked for the car, we found it. It was right there in plain sight at the rear of a church parking lot off Franklin Avenue.

Zee was out of the Land Cruiser in a flash. I barely had time to say, "Don't touch anything," before she was beside the red Honda peering in through the windows.

"Stay here," I said to the kids. I went over and made my own visual examination of the car. I saw nothing amiss. No signs of violence, nothing unusual. I was turning away when something on the floor in front caught my eye. It was a glove, and there was something slightly unusual about it. I pointed it out to Zee, who put her nose near the glass and studied it.

"It's a golfer's glove," she said. She looked up at me. "I don't think Molly even plays golf."

"I'll stay here and make sure nobody disturbs anything. You go tell the police that we've found the car."

She ran to the Land Cruiser and drove away.

I peeked again at the glove on the floor. It looked like a very nice, expensive glove. Too big for a woman. A clue, maybe, though many of the people who visited the Vineyard played golf. If this was a clue, it didn't narrow down the field very much. The Isle of Dreams crowd came to mind. I didn't know any of those people, but Brady did. Brady and I were scheduled to fish tonight. Maybe he'd have a name or two for me.

I felt like a hound on the scent.

Chapter Twelve

Brady

Patrick looked like he was about to burst into tears.

"What about your grandmother," I said. "What's happened?"

"She's in the hospital," he said.

"Oh, shit." I turned, got back into the Range Rover, and started up the engine.

Patrick ran down the steps and climbed in beside me. "I'll go with you."

On the way to the Martha's Vineyard Hospital in Oak Bluffs, Patrick told me that when he'd gone in to check on Sarah sometime in the middle of the morning, he'd found her lying on the floor. He'd taken a quick check of her vital signs, and—

"You know how to check vital signs?"

"I'm an EMT down in Hilton Head," he said.

"I didn't know that," I said. "I thought all you did was play tennis and golf."

"Very funny," he said. "You're thinking of my mother. Sometimes I play tennis and golf, and sometimes I save people's lives."

"Sorry. Go ahead."

When Patrick knelt beside her, he said, he saw that Sarah was conscious but unable to speak. She appeared not to recognize him or to understand him when he spoke to her. She tried to sit up, but couldn't.

"She fell and hit her head," I said.

"Maybe," he said. "But she fell because she had a stroke."

"How bad is it?"

"At her age," he said, "it's always bad. She's in the ICU. I don't know if they'll let you see her."

I talked my way into Sarah's stark little cubicle in the Intensive Care Unit. The nurses gave me five minutes.

She appeared to be asleep. An oxygen tube was pinched onto her nostrils, and a machine was tracking her blood pressure, pulse rate, and blood oxygen. Another tube snaked down to her wrist from three or four clear plastic bags hanging on what looked like an aluminum hat rack.

I pulled a folding chair beside her bed, held her hand, and talked to her about the Red Sox. When I squeezed her hand, she gave me a weak squeeze in return. I wanted to think that she recognized me, had heard and understood what I'd said to her, and wanted to reassure me that she was okay. But I realized that her hand squeeze was probably just a reflex.

Afterward, I found a doctor who told me that they didn't yet know how seriously Sarah had been impaired, but that she undoubtedly had been impaired, and that, given her age and health, it most certainly was irreversible. The blood flow to part of her brain had been cut off. She might've lost her speech or the use of some limbs. Her personality could be changed, and she would very likely experience memory loss. "Multi-infarct dementia" was the term the doctor used.

Patrick's quick action, he said, had probably saved her life.

They were giving her anticoagulants. Surgery wasn't out of the question, although in her frail condition, and considering the advanced progression of her cancer, the doctor seemed to think it a poor risk.

He didn't say it, but what he meant was that surgery would be a waste of time. Sarah was a terminal case either way.

She would not die, the doctor said. Not tonight, at least. Not from her stroke. That was the good news.

She would, of course, soon die from her cancer.

When we got back to the house, I told Patrick to go find Eliza and Nate and bring them to me, and I went out onto the patio to have a smoke. The sun had just set over America, and from where I sat behind the Fairchild house looking westerly, I had a good view of the sunset's pink reflection on Vineyard Sound. The afternoon wind had died, and the water's surface looked as flat and glossy as a pane of glass. It wasn't hard to imagine schools of stripers and bluefish and bonito swirling and splashing out there, chasing baitfish, just waiting to eat the fly that I might cast in their path. Some dark cigar-shaped clouds hung low and motionless over the horizon. They looked like blimps hovering there. Their backs glowed gold, and their bellies were the same pink as the sea.

I'd just stubbed out my cigarette when Eliza came out. She was wearing a yellow bikini top and a wide-brimmed straw hat and sunglasses and a flowered silk sarong. It rode low on her hips, showing off her flat stomach and girlish belly button. She was, naturally, carrying a glass.

She flopped onto the chaise beside me, crossed her legs, and took a sip. "You heard, huh?"

"About Sarah? Yes. Patrick and I just got back from the hospital."

"She was very upset about the nurse," said Eliza. "She really hated that old battle-ax who came yesterday."

"You think that's why she had a stroke?"

She shrugged. "Who knows?"

"Patrick might've saved her life," I said.

Eliza shrugged. "He's very devoted to her." She held up her glass. "G 'n' T," she said. "Want one?"

I shook my head.

She took another sip. "So now what?"

"We're waiting for Nate and Patrick. I want to talk to the three of you at the same time."

"Oh," she said. "Sounds heavy. Give me a hint."

"Nope."

"So how'd the meeting with the nature freaks go?"

"Eliza—"

"Yeah, yeah." She held up both hands and smiled. "Sorry."

A few minutes later Patrick came out onto the patio. "Uncle Nate's on his way," he said. "Pissing and moaning, but he's coming."

Eliza put a hand on Patrick's arm. "You saved your

grandmother's life," she said. "I'm proud of you, dear."

"It's about time," he said. He looked up. "Here he is."

Nate had come from around the side of the house. He was still wearing his overalls and work boots, but he'd abandoned the cap with two bills and his shotgun. He was holding a beer bottle. His big hand went all the way around it.

I nodded to him. "Sit down, Nate. I need to talk to the three of you."

Surprisingly, he simply nodded and sat.

I leaned forward and looked at each of them. "I wanted to say what I've got to say to you all at the same time, so we could all be sure you don't have different stories or different understandings. Okay?"

They nodded.

"As you know, Sarah has had a stroke," I continued. "The doctors believe she'll be impaired, though they can't yet say how badly or in what way. She may lose some of her memory. She may not regain her speech. She could lose the use of her limbs. She might not be able to process what one of us might say to her."

Eliza started to speak. I held up my hand. "I realize you understand these things. I'm only telling you so that what I have to say next will make some sense." I paused. "It's possible that Sarah will be incapable of making an informed decision about the disposition of her property. As you know, I'm down here specifically to arrange for its sale, which is what she wants. I have her durable power of attorney. Therefore—"

"Wait," said Nate. "You saying you can sell our place without my mother's okay?"

"I can do that, yes," I said. "That's what a durable power of attorney means."

"But," said Eliza, "you really wouldn't—"

"Yes," I said. "I can and I would. Sarah has made her desires very clear to me, and it's my job to carry them out. At this point, both the Isle of Dreams Development Corporation and the Marshall Lea Foundation have made serious offers. If Sarah is . . . impaired . . . it's my job to consider their offers, complete the negotiations, and finalize the sale. I called you here to tell you that that's what I intend to do."

"Just a goddamed minute," said Nate. "You tryin' to tell us that you're gonna sell our property and we got nothing to say about it?"

"It's not your property. It's your mother's."

"But we're her family," he said. "You're just a fucking lawyer."

"I'm not just any fucking lawyer," I said. "I'm Sarah's fucking lawyer. That makes all the difference." I glanced at Eliza, who was peering intently at me through her sunglasses, and at Patrick, who had his arms folded and was studying his lap.

"Look," I said. "I'm very sad this has happened to Sarah, and believe me, I didn't ask for this responsibility. But I've got it, and it's my job to exercise it, and I just wanted to explain it to you."

"So you can sell all this"—Eliza waved her hand around—"without Mother's approval, then?"

"I can do whatever I believe she would approve of,"

I said. "If I didn't, I wouldn't be doing my job. I intend to get it done as quickly as possible, because . . ."

"Because she might die, you're saying," said Nate.

"Yes."

Patrick cleared his throat. I nodded at him.

"What happens if she—she does die?" he said.

"Before we settle the property matter, you mean?"

He nodded.

I shrugged. "Sarah has a will."

"And we're her heirs, right?"

"Yes," I said. "The three of you, equally."

"How would you fit in, then?" he said.

"If Sarah dies," I said, "I'm the executor of her estate."

"Meaning . . . ?"

"Meaning, I will see that her will is executed."

"And you can't sell the property."

"No," I said. "Not after she dies. Her will specifies that her estate be divided equally among you. Then whatever you agree to is what'll happen."

"We've never agreed on anything yet," said Patrick.

I shrugged. "Well, maybe you should think about giving it another shot."

After Eliza and Patrick and Nate went their separate ways, I went into the house, called J.W., and told him what had happened.

"I suppose you don't want to go fishing tonight, then," he said.

"I don't see why not," I said. "There's nothing I can do for Sarah."

"I've been thinking of begging off myself," said J.W.

"Why?"

He told me how he'd spent the day talking with people about Molly Wood and looking for her car, and how he'd finally found it in a long-term parking lot in Vineyard Haven.

"*You* found it?" I said.

"Yup."

"Were the police looking for it?"

"Yup."

"But they didn't find it."

"Nope."

"You did."

"Yup."

"So what makes you so smart?"

"Clean living, I guess."

"But no sign of Molly, huh?"

"Nope. She might've hopped on the ferry. The cops're checking on that. Zee's pretty upset. She doesn't think Molly would just go away without telling anybody. She's convinced something's happened to her."

"What about you?" I said. "What do you think?"

"I don't know Molly any better than you do, but I guess I'm inclined to agree with Zee. She's got good instincts." He hesitated. "Something else, too."

"What's that?"

"Somebody slashed Zee's tire and left a note warning me to lay off."

"Jesus," I said. "So is Zee too upset to let you go fishing?"

"Zee would never not let me go fishing. If I don't go, it'll be my choice."

"Of course it will," I said. "So what is your choice?"

He was quiet for a minute. Then he said, "If we don't go, Zee will be more upset. We could hit Wasque at first light. I'll wake her when I leave, and we can get back before she has to go to work."

"You're okay, leaving her and the kids alone?"

"We're not going to let some cowardly tire-slasher run our lives." His voice was soft, but I heard menace in it. "Let's go fishing."

"Fine by me," I said. "What time is first light these days?"

"Well, the sun actually rises around six-thirty. The sky starts to turn pink about an hour before that. That's first light. The magic time. We should be on the beach about an hour before the sky turns pink."

"Four-thirty, then."

"Yeah. We should be on the beach with our rods rigged at four-thirty. Figure a half hour from here to Wasque."

"And twenty minutes from here to your place," I said. "So I'll set my alarm for three-thirty."

"I'll have coffee," said J.W.

"Lots of coffee," I said.

For years and years, except on weekends, I've been going to bed a little before midnight. I usually read a few pages of *Moby-Dick* until my eyelids droop, which takes fifteen or twenty minutes, turn off the light, roll onto my stomach, and fall asleep instantly. My alarm goes off at seven.

Even when I have things on my mind, I sleep easily and well. Comes of having a clear conscience and a pure heart.

On this night, with my alarm set for three-thirty, I forced myself to turn out the light at eleven. Naturally, I couldn't get to sleep. I kept seeing Sarah Fairchild lying in her Intensive Care bed, her chest barely rising and falling, surrounded by the blinking lights and the ticks and hums of her machines.

And Molly Wood's face kept popping into my head. She had a great smile and a hearty, uninhibited laugh, and I remembered how she'd kissed my mouth when we were saying good-bye at the Jacksons'. I was absolutely convinced that she'd been as eager for our rendezvous at the Navigator Room as I'd been.

And mixed with these visions were mind-pictures of the beach at first light. Peaceful and quiet and utterly, hauntingly lonely.

The magic time, J.W. had called it.

The first time I turned on the light to check the time it was ten after one. Quick calculation: If I went to sleep instantly, I'd get two hours and twenty minutes of sleep.

Hardly enough. I'd be a wreck.

I tried like hell to fall asleep. I concentrated on it. And the harder I tried, the less sleepy I felt.

Tomorrow I had a lot to do. Fishing, of course. Then, maybe, home for a quick nap. But I wanted to visit Sarah in the hospital, and I should check in with Julie back in my office in Boston, and I had to discuss some things with the Isle of Dreams people, and I had a couple of questions for Gregory Pinto, and there was

Molly again, squeezing my hand and smiling up at me, her eyes crinkling at the corners, and her mouth soft on mine . . . what the hell had happened to her? . . . and I remembered how Sarah had squeezed my hand, too, and I figured it was about two o'clock, so I gave up worrying about sleep, because I simply wasn't going to get any . . . and then the alarm went off.

I came close to shutting it off, rolling over, and going back to sleep. But then Billy's taunting voice echoed in my head, calling me a wimp and an old man.

It took enormous strength and courage to stagger out of bed.

But I did it.

Chapter Thirteen

J.W.

The two Vineyard Haven cops who showed up at the parking lot looked like they should still be in high school.

"My guess is that she caught a ferry to the mainland," said one of them. "A lot of people park up here when they do that. The church isn't too happy about it, but they put up with it." He peeked in the window and tried the locked door.

"Either of you play golf?" I asked.

The cop gave me a quizzical look. "Yeah, I do. Why?"

"You'd hardly call the game he plays golf," scoffed his partner. "You'd call it slice and burn."

I pointed at the glove on the floor of the car. "I see that as a man's glove, what do you think?"

They took turns shining their flashlights on the glove and squinting at it. "Either that or a woman with big hands," said the golfing cop.

"Left hand or right?"

He squinted harder. "Can't tell."

"Neither can I, but Molly Wood, who owns this car and has been missing for two days, has average-sized hands. Anyway, I don't think she plays golf."

"Maybe the guy she went to the mainland with does."

"Maybe. But if she went to the mainland with or without some guy, she never told anybody about it. She was supposed to be at work the last two days, but wasn't, and she missed a dinner date last night."

The cop shrugged. "You never know what a woman will do."

"Jeff might, but you sure don't," snapped sharp-eared Zee. "Molly Wood is an honest, hardworking, responsible nurse. She would never abandon her patients and go off without telling anyone. You'll be smart to get your detectives over here to check this car out. That glove could belong to a kidnapper."

The cop's ears got red.

"She's right, George," said his partner. "I'll get on the wire." He turned away and pulled a radio from his belt.

George pulled himself up straight. "Sorry, ma'am. I misspoke."

Zee was edgy with worry. "Forget about it. No, don't forget about it. Remember what you said. It wasn't the brightest observation you ever made."

A detective arrived, and we told him what we knew. He took notes, then walked around the car and shone his light inside.

"No blood that I can see, but we'd better get the state police here. Their lab might tell us something."

"If you don't need us anymore," I said, "we'll head for home. You have our address and phone number."

"You think of anything that might help, call us."

167

We drove home through the darkness. A car passed us.

"Pa."

"What?"

"That was a red car."

"We don't need to find any more red cars, Josh."

"Ma."

"What, Diana?"

"I'm hungry."

Everything changes. Nothing changes.

We arrived home just in time to get a phone call from Brady. I told him about the car, and he wondered if we were still going fishing. We agreed to try Wasque at first light. Then Zee and I got the kids into bed.

"I keep thinking we should be doing more," said Zee. "I feel guilty sitting here while Molly's out there someplace."

I thought of Auden's executioner's horse. "Life doesn't stop for disasters or miracles," I said. "All the normal things keep on happening, too."

"Oh, I know that. I know that babies are born while other people are dying. But knowing that doesn't help." She ran a hand through her hair. "I'm going to make some corn muffins."

Corn muffins. "Corn muffins?"

"Breakfast for you and Brady. If you're going to fish at sunup at Wasque, you won't feel like making them before you go. Besides, it'll give me something to do, so I won't have to think about Molly or that note."

"The person who wrote that note is unlikely to show up here," I said, repressing my anger.

So she made muffins, and then we went to bed, where it took both of us a long time to go to sleep. I set the alarm for three-thirty, and a half hour after it went off Brady's borrowed Range Rover was in our yard. We transferred his fishing gear to the Land Cruiser and went out into the black night, under the stars and a thin moon. Our headlights cast spectral shadows in the trees beside the driveway.

At the highway, we turned left and drove into Edgartown. We were the only car on the road as we passed through the sleeping village and on south to Katama. There, I shifted into four-wheel drive, and we turned east along the beach. To our right, the Atlantic rolled south beyond the curvature of the earth. To our left, through the narrows dividing the harbor from Katama Pond, the lights of Edgartown twinkled. Ahead of us, the eastern sky was just beginning to brighten.

I told Brady of my hunt for information about Kathy Bannerman, and we talked about finding Molly's car and about the golf glove, and we brooded over their significance. We danced around death but finally faced the possibility.

I asked him for the names of any golfers who might have known Molly, and he gave me a couple.

Eliza and Patrick played golf, he said, and maybe Molly had run into a guy named Luis Martinez or another one named Philip Fredrickson, both part of the Isle of Dreams crowd. "But," he said, "you can't question everybody on the island who plays golf."

"I'm trying to narrow it down to the most likely million," I said, and told him again about the slashed tire and the note.

"Someone's pretty mad or pretty scared," he said.

"Or did a number on the wrong car."

"Yeah, maybe that's it. You made anybody mad lately?"

"Sure, but none of them acted scared."

He was quiet for a while, then said, "Nate Fairchild has a knife and a temper."

"Yes."

At Leland's Point, just east of Wasque, we pulled to a stop. One of the good things about fishing is that you don't even have to fish. You can just sit there with your coffee and corn muffins and look. So we did that. Off to the right we could see a flicker of lights from the towers on Nantucket, and to our left were the lights of Cape Cod. Between was the darkness of Nantucket Sound topped by the gradually lightening sky.

I told Brady about my visits with Edna Paul and the Chief. "Maybe you're more Edna's type," I said. "I'd like to know what's in Molly's room, but Edna wouldn't let me get my foot in the door. Maybe she'll fall for your boyish lawyer charm."

We drank coffee and watched the water and the brightening sky. After a few minutes, Brady said, "Do you happen to have a photograph of Katherine Bannerman?"

"Right there in the glove compartment."

He found the photo and flicked on his flashlight. Kathy Bannerman smiled up at us.

"Well?" I said. "What do you see?"

170

"They don't really look alike, but you know who she reminds me of?"

"Who?"

"Molly Wood." He put the photo back in the glove compartment and turned off his flashlight. "Molly is probably fine. There's probably a perfectly logical explanation that we just don't know about."

That was two *probably*s in a row. "You're probably right," I said, making it three.

I turned on the radio and found the classical station over on the Cape. I let it come into my psyche, and it gradually drove questions about Kathy and Molly and the slashed tire from the front of my thoughts.

Then, suddenly, there was a stirring on the surface of the water about a half cast out. Blues!

"There!" I said. Both of us tumbled out of the truck. I snagged my rod from the roof rack and ran down to the water. Before Brady had even rigged up I'd made a cast and felt a fish hit. I set the hook and heard the singing of the line as the rod bent, and I started reeling the fish in. By the time I beached it and got the hook out of its mouth, Brady had shucked off his shoes and socks and was trotting down to the water.

The school moved closer to the beach and Brady made his cast.

Bingo!

They moved up the beach, and we followed, grinning and feeling good.

When the blitz ended, we had a half dozen nice seven- or eight-pounders up on the sand.

"Awesome," said Brady.

I felt a smile on my face. "I don't know if there are any winners here," I said, "but we should weigh in our biggest. We might get on the board. Stranger things have happened. And even if we don't score we might win a mystery prize."

Suddenly the sun rose up out of the sea and light burst over us. It was Eden, and this was the first day.

At home, Zee admired our catch. "You might have a couple of dailies there, guys. Let's have breakfast, then I'll see you later. I'm only working until noon."

"I'll take you," I said, aware that far back in my mind, beneath the layers of civilized emotions I'd placed over it, was a fury that had been there since I'd seen that note.

"No, you won't," said Zee. "We're not going to let some nut change our lives. I'll put my car where I can keep an eye on it."

"I'm not worried about the car."

She patted my cheek. "You don't need to worry about me, either. I'll be careful."

I watched, narrow-eyed, as she drove away.

After we weighed in our biggest fish, Brady and I went back to the house. "Five-thirty," I said to him. "Cocktails and supper with us before you and Zee head out."

After Brady left, I took our fish out to the bench behind the shed and filleted them.

Then I phoned James Bannerman.

"Have you found her?" he said. "Do you know where she is?"

"I found something," I said. "I found out you

were here on the island about the time your wife disappeared. We're not going to get anywhere if you lie to me."

I could almost hear his teeth grind together. "I don't know what you're talking about."

"You get one more chance."

"I didn't lie."

"That's it. Find yourself another sap. I'll send your check back tomorrow."

"Wait. I didn't mean to—"

"We can't work like this. You didn't tell me, and you didn't tell Thornberry."

"I . . . I thought it would look bad for me. You know how the husband is always the prime suspect. Okay, I was there, but I never saw her, so I didn't see any reason to mention it."

"I'll have to tell the cops. They need to know."

"Do you have to? Listen, it was just an impulse. I didn't even know until later that she really was there, but I remembered how much she'd loved the place and I thought maybe she'd gone back to where she'd been happy. I went to the rooming house where we'd stayed. But Mrs. Grady was dead, and the new people didn't know anything. And I went to a couple of clubs and places like that where we'd gone all those years ago. I learned nothing. So I just came home. That's all there was to it, I swear."

"You'll have to tell that story to the cops, because they'll be talking to you. What else haven't you told me?"

"Nothing. Don't waste your time on me. Find my wife."

I hung up, wondering whether to believe him or not. His story was so frail that it sounded true, but maybe he knew that when he told it. I didn't take him off my list.

Joshua wanted to work on the tree house.

I decided that there was a good chance that Luis Martinez and Philip Fredrickson might not be in the Isle of Dreams offices until later in the day.

We worked until noon, and we got the roof shingled and the rail installed on the porch. The tree house was almost done, and not a bad job, either. It was pretty crowded when I was in it, but big enough when the kids were there by themselves.

"That's it for today," I said. "Next time we'll build the ladder so we won't have to scramble up through these branches."

"Pa?"

"What, Diana?"

"We're hungry."

It's nice to have certainties in an uncertain world. We climbed down to the ground and went into the house for lunch.

When Zee got home an hour later, I left the kids with her and headed for Edgartown. The Chief was in his office. He didn't look surprised to see me.

"I was going to call you," he said, "but I knew you were so nosy that you'd come by on your own. I hear you found Mrs. Wood's car. Good work. They dusted it for prints, but don't hold your breath for the results, because everybody who's ever been in that car likely left prints. They also searched the car, but they didn't find anything except that glove."

"Was there something unusual about the glove?"

"The state cops have it at their lab. Dom tells me that it's custom-made and only sells at snazzy shops like they have down South and in Arizona, where they play all year. You know, those places that cost you a quarter million to join and have a five-year waiting list."

"Who made it?"

"An outfit down in Georgia. The Mallet Corporation. You watch golf on TV, you've seen their ad: 'Hit with a mallet.'"

The Mallet Corporation. Did the name sound familiar just because of TV ads? "Can they trace it to a buyer?"

"Doubtful. They make a million gloves a year. But I expect they'll look into it." He peered at me. "You have that lean and hungry look that Cassius had. You're thinking too much."

"I'm not dangerous, Chief. I'm just trying to remember where I heard of the Mallet Corporation."

"I can't help you. I think they're headquartered down South somewhere. J.W., you did good work finding that car, but now you should go home or go fishing or go to the movies and leave this business to the police."

"I won't get in your way, Chief."

"It's not as though Molly Wood is the only woman who's ever gone missing on the Vineyard. Several have done it in the last five years, but most of them eventually showed up. She probably will, too."

"Not all of them showed up?"

"No."

"I don't want Molly Wood to be an exception."

"You just thought of something," said the Chief, staring up at my face.

I stared back. My mental computer had clicked on. Isle of Dreams was a local consortium, but its mother company was the Mallet Corporation, builder of prestigious golf courses around the country. Luis Martinez and Philip Fredrickson were working with Isle of Dreams, but they were off-islanders, which might just mean that they worked for Mallet. And if they did, they might play on Mallet courses and use Mallet-made gloves.

I ran this by the Chief. When I was through, he tipped his head to one side and raised a brow.

"It's worth a phone call, anyway," I said. "Did your men find anything in Molly's room?"

"You mean like a note saying, 'Help, help, I'm being kidnapped by a golfer'? No, sad to say, they didn't. No address book with a list of suspects, no theater tickets for *La Bohème,* nothing useful. Go home, J.W."

I drove up to Oak Bluffs. First I went to the hospital and found Zee's Jeep. No slashed tires. No suspicious-looking goons hanging around. I was disappointed, and drove back to Circuit Avenue. The Isle of Dreams people had an office over a souvenir shop. A great many second-floor rooms on Circuit Avenue were over souvenir shops, because a great many first-floor rooms on Circuit Avenue are souvenir shops.

I went up the stairs and into the waiting room. A dark-haired man with a black mustache was seated at a desk in front of a computer. He looked up at me and placed a PR smile on his face. "Yes, sir. What may I do for you?" His voice was smooth and his accent was Southern.

"I'm looking for Luis Martinez or Philip Fredrickson."

"I'm Luis Martinez. How can I help you, Mr.—?"

"Jackson. J. W. Jackson. I need to talk with Fredrickson, too. Where can I find him?"

"I'm afraid he's not available right now. He's having a business lunch with colleagues at the Harborview. He should be back by four. Can I help you?"

"Perhaps you can. Do you play golf, Mr. Martinez?"

He chuckled. "Sure I play golf. How about you?"

"No, but I have an interest in Isle of Dreams."

He kept his smile, because even though my clothes might not be what the typical Isle of Dreams customer would wear, nowadays you couldn't be sure that a guy who looked like a tenant farmer wasn't the owner of a computer company. "And what might that interest be, sir?"

"Are you affiliated with the Mallet Corporation?" I said.

He became cautious. "I represent Isle of Dreams."

"All right. I can find out, but I thought I might save a phone call by asking you. Another question, then. Have you lost a golf glove recently?"

"Lost a glove? What do you mean, sir?"

"Did you?"

His smile went away. "Who are you? These are curious questions, and I see no reason to answer them."

"If you don't answer them now, you may have to do it later in a police station. Do you know a woman named Molly Wood?"

He stood up behind the desk. "I don't like your tone, Mr. Jackson. I think you'd better leave."

"Do you know Molly Wood?"

He put his hand on his telephone. His dark eyes were angry. "Get out of here, sir."

He was lifting the phone to his ear when I walked out. I went down to the truck and drove to the Harborview, feeling annoyed. I had let my anger about the slashed tire run over into my interview with Martinez. Not smart.

Chapter Fourteen

Brady

I got back to the Fairchild house after my first-light fishing adventure with J.W. around nine on Wednesday morning and headed straight to bed, and despite all the coffee I'd consumed and the adrenaline that had pumped through my veins and the muscle memory in my shoulders of those tough bluefish pulling on my line and the magic of seeing a new day break over the horizon, I sank instantly into a profound, dreamless sleep.

The next thing I knew, something was prodding and poking at my shoulder. I opened my eyes. It was Eliza.

"Go away," I said. "I just got to sleep."

"There's somebody here to see you," she said.

"Later."

"It's a police officer."

"What time is it?"

"Ten after eleven. I brought you coffee."

"Tell him I'll be down after my coffee," I said. "You entertain him."

"It's a she," she said. "You better get up."

So I got up, got dressed, and took my coffee downstairs.

The officer was sitting on the sofa in the living room. She was wearing her uniform, complete with revolver and radio and nightstick and badge. She had black hair, hot-fudge eyes, olive skin, no makeup. When I entered the room, she stood up and held out her hand. She looked muscular and fit. She couldn't have been more than a couple of inches over five feet tall.

"Sergeant Santonelli," she said. "West Tisbury Police."

I shook her hand. "Brady Coyne. Boston lawyer."

She nodded. "I know. Sorry to get you out of bed at such an uncivilized hour."

I smiled. "I went fishing at three-thirty, got back at nine."

"The Derby?"

I nodded.

"How'd you do?"

"Last I looked, I was at the top of today's board, fly-rod, shore-caught bluefish."

Sergeant Santonelli shrugged, apparently unimpressed with my angling prowess. Probably not an angler herself. She gestured at a chair. "Let's sit."

I sat. I was holding my coffee mug in both hands. I took a sip. "Want some coffee?" I said.

She shook her head and fished a notebook from her hip pocket and a ballpoint pen from her shirt. Then she handed me a photograph. It was a head-and-shoulders shot of Molly Wood. She was wearing a nurse's uniform. The photo appeared to be several years old. Molly's hair was longer.

"Do you recognize this person?" asked Sergeant Santonelli.

"Sure," I said. I gave the photo back to her. "You know I do."

She smiled. "And you know she appears to be missing."

I nodded.

"You had a date with her Monday night and she didn't show up, right?"

"That's right."

"You met her Sunday?"

"I first met her here," I said. "She came in to take care of Mrs. Fairchild. She's a visiting nurse. Then I met her again. Mutual friends, um, fixed us up."

"The Jacksons."

"Yes. Zee. Mrs. Jackson."

"Odd coincidence, isn't it?" she said. "Meeting her here and then having a blind date with her that evening?"

I shrugged. "I guess so."

"And the last time you saw her?"

"Sunday night. Eight o'clock, maybe."

"At the Jacksons."

"Yes."

"And what did you do after that?"

"Me? J.W. and I went fishing."

"Till when?"

I shrugged. "Midnight. A little after that, probably."

"Then what?"

"Then I came home and went to bed."

"Alone?"

I grinned at her. "Unfortunately."

"I mean," she said, "did anybody see you come home and go to bed on Sunday night, or early Monday morning?"

"Not that I know of."

"And when did you arise the next morning?"

"Arise?" I smiled. "I never arise, Sergeant. I stagger and stumble until I've had my coffee. Eliza got me up the next morning. Around eight, as I recall."

"So between the time Mr. Jackson dropped you off here—a little after midnight—and the next morning around eight o'clock, when Elizabeth Fairchild awakened you, you cannot account for your whereabouts. Is that right?"

"I can definitely account for my whereabouts," I said. "I was in bed." I leaned toward Sergeant Santonelli. "Look," I said, "I didn't kill Molly Wood."

"Who said anything about killing her?"

"I did. It's what we're all worried about."

"Who'd want to kill her?"

"Jesus," I muttered. "That's the question, isn't it? If I knew the answer to that question, I'd tell you, believe me. I really don't know much about her beyond the fact that I met her and found her charming and pretty and was looking forward to seeing her again."

"But you didn't."

"See her again?" I shook my head. "No."

"Well, Mr. Coyne," she said, "thank you for your

time, and I'm sorry to interrupt your sleep." She snapped shut the notebook she'd been scribbling in and stood up.

"No problem," I said. I stood up, too. "I'm glad the police are on top of it."

"We're circulating her picture, talking with everybody. All her patients, their families, people at the VNS office. The state police are in charge, but all local police forces on the island are cooperating."

"Any suspects yet?"

Sergeant Santonelli cocked her head at me for an instant before she smiled and shrugged. "I really couldn't tell you."

After Sergeant Santonelli left, I went back to bed. I tossed and turned for a while before I gave up. I figured I'd just have to be tired and grouchy for the rest of the day, and anybody who encountered me would have no choice but to tread softly.

It was sometime in the middle of the afternoon. I'd just finished my late lunch—a bowl of Cheerios with sliced banana, brown sugar, and no milk—and was sipping coffee and smoking a cigarette out on the patio when Eliza came out. She handed me a cordless telephone. "It's J. W. Jackson," she said.

I took the phone. Eliza sat in the chair across from me.

"J.W.?" I said.

"Yeah, it's me," he said.

"Hang on a minute." I put the phone on the table and looked at Eliza. She was wearing sunglasses and a little white tennis outfit. "Do you mind?" I said to her.

"What?" she said. "You're making secret fishing plans, don't want me to hear? Afraid I'll leak your secrets to Nate?"

"Exactly," I said.

She shrugged, stood up, came around the table, and gave my shoulder a squeeze on the way by. "Old poop," she muttered.

I watched until she went into the house. From behind, she could've passed for a teenager in her little short tennis skirt.

I picked up the phone. "Sorry," I said. "What's up?"

"How's Sarah doing?"

"No change."

"If she could talk," he said, "it'd be interesting to know if Molly said anything to her."

"I thought of that."

"Of course you did." He hesitated. "I talked to the cops this morning. It's not encouraging."

"How so?"

"Well, Molly hasn't turned up, either on the island or back home in Scituate. No one at the Vineyard Haven ferry recalls seeing her. Aside from that golf glove, they didn't find a damn thing in her car. They went over to Edna Paul's and didn't come up with anything there, either."

"Like she just walked into the sea," I said.

"Yeah, that happens."

"So now what?"

"You said you'd talk to Edna Paul."

"I didn't say that."

"Sure you did."

"Me and my boyish charm."

"Yes. Your charm plus your power to steer two-hundred prime Vineyard acres to the Marshall Lea Foundation. She'll eat out of your hand, you play it right."

"What about you?" I said.

"Oh, I've got some ideas."

A half hour later I was sitting on a folding chair beside Sarah Fairchild's bed in the Intensive Care Unit at the Martha's Vineyard Hospital. I was holding her hand and telling her how pretty the ocean had looked at first light and how J.W. and I had gotten into a school of blitzing bluefish.

The ICU nurse had told me it would be good to talk to her, but not to say anything upsetting. She wasn't comatose, exactly, the nurse had explained. More like a very deep sleep. They couldn't yet determine what—if anything—Sarah could understand. But she did respond to sounds. She could hear me, and it would probably be comforting for her to hear a familiar voice.

So I told her about how the sky changed color at first light, and how the birds screamed and dived over the school of bluefish, and how J.W. and I had caught a few of them, and how while we were watching, the sun had suddenly cracked the horizon and filled the world with light, and what a pretty early-autumn day we were having here on the Vineyard . . . and it might've been my imagination, but I thought I felt her grip tighten slightly on my hand as I talked to her.

After my allotted five minutes, I told her I had to leave, but I'd be back. I stood up, and as I bent over the railing on her bed to kiss her cheek, I saw her lips move. I put my ear close to her mouth.

"Nathan?" she whispered.

"It's Brady, Sarah."

"Nathan," she repeated.

"Nathan loves you," I said.

I kissed her, gave her hand a final squeeze, turned, and left her cubicle.

Nathan. Her only son. Sarah had always had a prickly relationship with him, and for good reason. He'd given her nothing but trouble throughout his life. He'd been kicked out of several schools. He'd been arrested several times for public drunkenness and disorderly conduct, which the Vineyard newspapers never failed to report with apparent glee. He'd held a few jobs, but had quit or been fired from them all. From what I'd been able to observe, Nathan's only interest in his mother was as a source of handouts to supplement his trust fund.

And there lay Sarah in her ICU bed, asking for her son.

I stopped by the nurses' station. "I was wondering who's visited Mrs. Fairchild since she's been here," I said.

The nurse looked to be in her mid-thirties. She was immensely overweight. Her forearms were thicker than my thighs. "Well, you, of course," she said, "and her daughter, and the other young man."

"Patrick?" I said.

"The grandson, yes. He's been in several times."

"What about her son?"

She shrugged. "No. Just you three."

As I walked out of the hospital into the parking lot, I remembered how J.W. had told Nathan that I was an expert in unarmed combat. I wished it were true. Because right then I wanted to beat the shit out of the ungrateful, inconsiderate, self-centered son of a bitch.

Chapter Fifteen

J.W.

The Harborview Hotel in Edgartown is one of those huge old wooden hotels that a hundred years ago you could find in every resort community on the East Coast. You see photos of them in books about turn-of-the-century spas and vacation spots where the wealthy and the upper middle class fled the heat of the summer or sought the winter warmth of huge fireplaces and hot buttered rum. By the mid-twentieth century, most of them had burned down or fallen down, but a few remain. One is the Harborview. It's been restored and expanded, and it offers the Vineyard's best view of Edgartown's lighthouse and outer harbor. It also offers fine food and drink and many dining areas where groups can meet in private. Phil Fredrickson was in one of those rooms.

"I'm looking for Philip Fredrickson," I said to the woman behind the counter. "He's here at a meeting and I don't want to disturb him, but his colleague, Mr. Martinez, says I can find Mr. Fredrickson here. I must speak with him immediately. Can you have someone slip into Mr. Fredrickson's conference room and give him that message? My name is Jefferson

Jackson. I'll wait for him there." I pointed to a quiet corner of the lobby.

"Yes, sir," said the woman, eyeing my clothing doubtfully, as Luis Martinez had done, but like him, not sure what to make of someone wearing worn shorts, Tevas, and a T-shirt upon which was printed a recipe for piping plover pie. "Could you write that down in a note, sir, so there'll be no confusion?"

"Certainly." She produced a pen and notepaper and I wrote down the message. She took it, waved a young man over to the counter, gave him the note, and sent him on his way.

I sat at a table under a plant that was so realistic that I knew it had to be plastic. In not long at all, a man came down the hall, spoke to the woman at the desk, then followed her pointing finger over to my table.

He was a thirtyish guy with sun-bleached hair and a mouthful of incredibly white teeth. I stood—his handshake was firm and professional—we both sat. "What can I do for you, Mr. Jackson?"

"I hope you'll forgive my appearance," I said, "but I just got a call from Jo-Jo Jones."

He smiled uncertainly. "Jo-Jo?"

"You don't know Jo-Jo? Well, no matter. He's in the Environmental Protection Agency, stationed in Boston. Anyway, I guess it won't hurt to tell you that Jo-Jo is all in favor of the Isle of Dreams proposal to build a first-class golf course here on the island. Jo-Jo's got a place here in Oak Bluffs, and he likes golf."

I paused and looked at him as though he should understand me.

Naturally, he didn't. "I don't follow you, Mr. Jackson."

"Sorry. This is the problem. There are some people in the agency—not Jo-Jo, certainly, and not people like the governor, for instance, either, but other people who have some clout and who don't want this deal to go through. They want to stop further development on Martha's Vineyard and a lot of other places. Well, Jo-Jo wants to head them off at the pass, if you know what I mean, but to do that he's got to know some things, and he's asked me to get the information for him. I'm down here on vacation and I really don't want to be doing this, but I got this call and Jo-Jo says it's important, so I talked with Luis Martinez, and he sent me to you. So here I am."

Fredrickson opened his mouth, but I held up a shushing finger. "Before you say anything, I want you to know that it'll be held in strictest confidence. We don't want certain other people to know what we know or to know that we know what they already know. So here's what I need from you. It doesn't have to be official, you understand, in fact it's better if it isn't. We don't want anything in writing or anything like that. Just some information that will help Jo-Jo and the governor protect the interests of golfers and people trying to do business in Massachusetts."

I showed Fredrickson a toadeater's face. "I should tell you," I added, "that I don't know the significance of the questions Jo-Jo has asked me to ask you, and that, frankly, they make no sense to me, although they may to you. Whatever your answers, however, I will transmit them to Jo-Jo. May I go on?"

"Ask your questions," said Fredrickson cautiously.

"Thank you. The first is: Do you represent the interests of the Mallet Corporation?"

Fredrickson and I both considered his options. If he didn't represent Mallet, there seemed no reason not to say so. If he did, but denied it, there could be complications. Jo-Jo Jones, an apparently powerful supporter of the Isle of Dreams project, might be offended and withdraw his favor. Besides, Jo-Jo probably already had evidence of Mallet's involvement, or he wouldn't be asking for verification.

"Yes," said Fredrickson after a moment. "I work for Mallet, but I'm also a consultant for Isle of Dreams."

"Excellent. Jo-Jo has spoken favorably of the Mallet Corporation and the courses and clubs it has built. I'm sure he'll be pleased when I convey your response to him."

Fredrickson beamed.

I first smiled, then put a slightly confused look on my face. "I really don't understand this one, Mr. Fredrickson, but have you recently lost a golf glove?"

"What? A golf glove?"

I shrugged and shook my head. "Yes, sir. That was Jo-Jo's second question."

Fredrickson's brow wrinkled. "No. As far as I know, I haven't lost a golf glove."

"In that case, Jo-Jo wants to know if you know anyone who has."

"Why would anyone ask a question like that?"

I shrugged. "Perhaps a golf glove has been found in some compromising location such as a married lady's bedroom, and one of those people who oppose your project wants to embarrass Isle of Dreams by some revelation to the press. I'm only guessing, of course, but perhaps Jo-Jo or the governor is trying to preempt that sort of attack on the project."

"Ah, I see. Well, I have all my golf gloves. Tell that to Mr. Jones and anyone else who wants to know." Then he frowned. "At least I had all of them on Saturday. That was the last time I played. I suppose I could have dropped a glove someplace. I could call Farm Neck and see if anyone has found it. Are you saying that someone found one?"

I stayed behind my sycophant face. "I'm sure I don't know, Mr. Fredrickson. I was only told to ask and to report your answer. I have only a few more questions. Again, I don't know their significance. First, do you know a woman named Molly Wood?"

He frowned. "I believe she's a visiting nurse I've seen at the home of Mrs. Sarah Fairchild."

"Fine. Now, pardon me for seeming to intrude upon your private life, but have you ever socialized with her?"

He grew wary. "I don't think that's anyone's business but mine and hers."

"I daresay you're right. I'll convey that answer to Jo-Jo, along with your others. Please forgive me for asking these questions, but I'm only doing it at the governor's—that is, Jo-Jo's—request." I stood. "Thank you for meeting with me, sir. I assure you that it has not been an unimportant conversation."

I put out my hand, but he didn't take it. "Wait. Yes,

I've gone out with Molly Wood. I had supper with her and we went dancing, but that was almost a month ago."

"You only dated her that one time?"

"Yes. Actually, I asked her out again, but she was busy." He looked at his watch. "I really have to get back."

"I assure you, you've been most helpful. Only two things more. Last summer here on the island, or at any other time or place, did you meet a woman named Katherine Bannerman?"

He shook his head. "I wasn't on the Vineyard last summer, and I don't know any woman by that name."

"You've been more than generous with your time, sir," I said. "Here's my final question. Did Luis Martinez date Mrs. Wood?"

Fredrickson seemed relieved to have attention turned to his partner. "Yes, I believe he did. It was just before I went out with her, in fact."

I thanked him profusely. Our hands finally met, squeezed, and parted, and we smiled and went our separate ways. I got into the Land Cruiser and drove home.

The Mallet Corporation had a big interest in the Isle of Dreams proposal. But was it big enough to countenance kidnapping or worse?

Kidnapping or worse. I was no longer thinking there was a simple, nonviolent explanation for the disappearance of Molly Wood, and I didn't like it.

Chapter Sixteen

Brady

From the hospital I headed to Edgartown. I was remembering how Nate had accosted me and my intrepid band of Marshall Lea Foundation members with a shotgun, and how, when I told him I intended to speak to Sarah about the matter of bringing potential buyers onto the property, he'd sneered and said, "I doubt that."

Nathan's response to his mother's stroke was *I doubt that*.

Now she was in the ICU, semicomatose, asking for him.

Bastard.

I still had a couple of hours before cocktails on the Jacksons' balcony, so I followed J.W.'s directions and finally found Summer Street and, near the top of the hill, Edna Paul's house. It was a pretty white clapboard bungalow surrounded by a chest-high stockade fence to separate its yard from its neighbors'. Most of the other dwellings on Summer Street were larger than Edna Paul's, but hers was as trim and tidy as any of them.

I parked on the side of the road in front, got out,

and went through the gate. An oldish Volvo wagon was parked beside the house, and potted geraniums hung on the porch that spanned the front. The geraniums had grown a bit leggy but were still bravely producing some late blooms.

I walked around the side of the house and peeked into the backyard, where a clothesline was stretched between a couple of beech trees. A skimpy two-piece bathing suit hung on it. It was neon pink.

J.W. had told me that Edna Paul was a retired grammar-school teacher. I wondered if she wore pink bikinis.

I returned to the front of the house, climbed the three steps onto the porch, and rang the bell.

A moment later, the inside door opened, and an angular woman with steely hair and rimless glasses peered at me through the screen. Definitely not the bikini type. "What is it?" she said.

"Mrs. Paul?"

"It's Miss Paul, young man."

I smiled. "My name is Brady Coyne. May I talk with you?"

"About what?"

"Your boarder. Molly Wood."

She pursed her lips, then pushed her glasses up on her nose as if to get a better look at me. "What did you say your name was?"

"Coyne. Brady Coyne." I took out my wallet and found one of my business cards. I held it up for her. "I'm a lawyer."

She pushed open the screen door, took the card, and let the door snap shut between us. She squinted at my card, then looked at me. "I know who you are," she said. "My friends Millie and Roberta told me all about you. How you stood up to that awful Nathan Fairchild. You're with the Marshall Lea Foundation." She smiled and pushed open the door. "Please. Come in, come in."

I went in. "I'm not actually with the Marshall Lea Foundation," I said. "I represent Sarah Fairchild."

"Yes," she said, "that's what I meant." She took my arm and steered me into her living room. It smelled vaguely of Lysol. "You're arranging the sale of the Fairchild property to the foundation. How wonderful! That is a beautiful property, and the Marshall Lea Foundation is my favorite cause. I'm delighted to meet you. What about some iced tea?"

"That sounds lovely."

Edna Paul disappeared into the kitchen, leaving me standing in her living room. It was small and cramped with overstuffed furniture. One entire wall was covered with framed black-and-white photographs. They appeared to be class pictures. Each one depicted a couple dozen children lined up in three rows with a woman standing in the middle of the back row, towering over the kids. The woman was Edna Paul. She had been an angular, no-nonsense young woman, and as the photos progressed through the years, she grew into an angular, no-nonsense school marm. She was smiling in none of the pictures.

There were no other photographs—family or otherwise—in the room.

She came back with two tall glasses of iced tea. "My children," she said, jerking her chin at the wall of photos that I was looking at. "Forty-two years' worth of children. Nowadays I walk down the streets of Edgartown and I run into bald men with potbellies and gray-haired women with lined faces. They stop me and say, 'Good morning, Miss Paul.' I'd like to say I recognize all of them, but of course I don't. I say, 'My, how you've grown.' And they always tell me I still look the same. I retired three years ago. I wish I hadn't." She stared at the photographs for a minute, then shrugged and handed me a glass. "Please sit down, Mr. Coyne."

I sat on a pillowy armchair with dark floral upholstery. Edna Paul took a wingback chair beside me.

"Miss Paul—"

"Why don't you call me Edna?"

I smiled. "Fine. Edna. I guess you know that your boarder Molly Wood seems to have disappeared."

"Well, that awful Mr. Jackson tried to ask me about her, and then a policeman came by asking questions. They didn't get anything out of me, I'll tell you. I'm not a gossip."

I smiled and took a sip of iced tea. "Umm, delicious," I said. I put the glass on a cardboard coaster on the table beside me. "Gossip?" I said.

She shook her head. "Oh, I could tell you stories, believe me. But as I always told my children, if you can't say something nice about a person, don't say anything at all."

"Is Mrs. Wood a good tenant?"

Edna tightened her lips. "I would've expected a recent widow to live a quieter life, I don't mind telling you. Oh, she is neat and polite and all, and I suppose she's responsible at her job. She's a visiting nurse, you know."

I nodded.

"I figured, a widow lady, a nurse. Ideal tenant." She shook her head. "I don't brook any hanky-panky, Mr. Coyne. Not in this house."

"Does Mrs. Wood indulge in hanky-panky?"

"Like I said, not in this house. She knows better." Edna leaned toward me. "She attracts men, Mr. Coyne."

"She's an attractive woman," I said.

She frowned.

"Who are these men, do you know?"

"Oh, I try to keep my nose out of where it doesn't belong, don't you know. And they never come into the house. That's against my rules. Don't even come to the door to call on her, the way a proper young man ought to. They pull up in front, toot their horn, and she flounces out of here in her little short skirts, all perfumey and . . . well, you catch my meaning. Sometimes, she goes off to meet them by herself in her own car. Imagine!" She clicked her tongue against her dentures.

"Are they different men?"

"Oh, my, yes. Many different men."

"But you've never met any of them."

She shook her head.

"Could you describe any of them?"

"Lord, no. I never pay any attention."

I wondered how she knew they were different men, then. But I let it pass. "What about their cars?

Those who come to pick her up, have you noticed what kind of cars they drive?"

"No. I wouldn't know one car from another anyway."

"Has Molly ever talked about any of these men?"

"Heavens, no. I've made it perfectly clear that I have no interest whatsoever in her, um, private life."

"Does she ever talk about anything that's bothering her or worrying her? Does she strike you as nervous or fearful?"

Edna removed her glasses, polished them on a handkerchief, then fitted them back on her ears. "We don't have those sorts of conversations, Mr. Coyne. The truth is, we don't have many conversations at all. She works all day and carouses all night, and it seems that she only comes home to change her clothes. She expresses no interest whatsoever in my affairs, and I assure you, I have no interest in hers." She frowned. "Why are you so interested in Mrs. Wood? Are you one of her young men?"

"Me?" I shook my head. "Oh no. Not me. Sarah Fairchild is my client, as you know. Molly Wood is her nurse. Sarah is quite fond of her, and she's very upset that Molly no longer takes care of her. Sarah's concerned about Molly, so . . ."

"So you're playing detective, eh?"

"Detective?" I smiled. "Hardly. I'm just trying to get some answers for Sarah. This business with Molly is distracting her from some important matters she needs to think about. The sooner I can put Sarah's mind to rest about Molly, the sooner we can take care of those other matters." Matters such as the sale of the Fairchild property to the Marshall Lea Foundation, I was hoping to suggest.

Edna Paul seemed to get my suggestion, because she sat back in her chair and nodded. "I do hope you get your answers, then. You don't think something's happened to Mrs. Wood, do you?"

"I don't know. What do you think?"

"I surely don't know, either. But I haven't seen hide or hair of her for three days and three nights now."

"Has she ever done that before?"

"What, not showed up for three days?"

I nodded.

"No. Never before." She shrugged. "But it's her life. I'm not her keeper."

"It's odd," I said slowly, "but I have a rather different impression of Molly. She seems like a very nice person. Not wild at all. Sad, actually. I think she misses her husband."

Edna Paul blinked a couple of times.

"Is she really that wild?" I said.

"I didn't say she was wild."

"I'm sorry," I said. "I guess I misunderstood."

Edna looked past my shoulder to the wall of old photos. "I get lonely sometimes," she said softly. "Sometimes I have unrealistic expectations."

"You hoped Molly would be your friend?"

Her eyes came back to me. "A companion, perhaps. Mrs. Wood—Molly—she's a good tenant and, yes, she is a nice person. I suppose she spends many more nights alone up in her room than she does going out. Sometimes I think I hear her crying up there. And I sit down here wishing she'd come down and talk to me about it. Share with me. And then when she goes out, I feel—I don't know. Betrayed. Angry."

"I understand," I said.

"I do hope she's all right," said Edna. "I truly do."

"Edna," I said. "I wonder if I might take a peek at Molly's room."

She looked at me and frowned. "That Mr. Jackson, he tried to talk me into letting him into her room, and I told him that he had no business in there whatsoever. Then a policeman came around asking a lot of questions. He wanted to look in her room, too. I asked him if he had a search warrant, and he did not but insisted he could get one. I let him go in and look around, but I told him in no uncertain terms that without a warrant he could take nothing away with him. I don't think he liked that very much, but I know the law, Mr. Coyne. So I suppose I could let you in there. But I can't let you take anything, you understand."

"I understand perfectly," I said.

She led me up a narrow flight of stairs. The second floor consisted of two small bedrooms separated by a bathroom. One of the bedrooms, Edna told me, she used for storage. She herself slept in the back bedroom on the first floor. The room that Molly was renting was small, square, and quite pleasant. A large window looked out on to the street where I had parked, giving her a good lookout for young men arriving in automobiles. A twin-sized bed was pushed against one wall, and a chest of drawers stood against the opposite one. There was a closet with a full-length mirror on the door. Another door opened into the adjacent bathroom.

I went into the room. Edna remained in the doorway, vigilant lest I try to steal something.

A bottle of perfume, a comb and brush, a plastic pin-on plaque that read AMELIA WOOD, RN, and a little jewelry box sat on top of the bureau. I resisted the temptation to look inside the jewelry box or to open the drawers and paw through Molly's underwear. I figured Edna would peg me as a pervert.

I did open the closet door. It was a small closet full of cheerfully colored blouses, skirts, jerseys, shorts, sweaters, dresses, and pants, along with a couple of white tennis outfits, all neatly aligned on hangers. A pair of matching suitcases sat on the shelf, and several pairs of shoes and sneakers and sandals, along with two tennis rackets, were on the floor. No golf clubs.

I peeked into the bathroom. A toothbrush and tube of Pepsodent lay on the back of the sink, and a black cosmetics bag sat on the shelf under the mirror.

I saw nothing that hinted at what might've happened to Molly.

I wandered back into the bedroom. A tattered copy of *Sense and Sensibility* sat on the table beside the bed. Jane Austen. Sure. Women love Jane Austen. I guess plenty of men do, too, but I'm not one of them.

I picked up the book and flipped it open. It had been inscribed: "For Molly, who has more sense and sensibility than any woman alive, with love from Ethan." He had dated it "Christmas 1995."

Ethan, I guessed, was her dead husband, and I felt a pang of sadness at the image of Molly lying in this lonely little room on this island at night, separated by ocean and time and life itself from her husband, reading a book given to her by her beloved Ethan, the memories of Christmases past it must have sparked for her, the fact that Ethan had chosen this book for her, that he had known her intimately enough to know she'd cherish it, that he had written in it, and that he had died in a bed beside her.

As I flipped idly through the book, it fell open to a folded piece of notepaper that might have been serving as her bookmark. I turned my back on Edna Paul, who remained in the doorway watching me, and pretended to gaze out the window as I unfolded the note.

It read: "It is not, nor it cannot come to good. But break, my heart, for I must hold my tongue."

The words had been printed in masculine block letters with a black felt-tip pen. The note was undated and unsigned. Not even an initial.

"Break, my heart." A jilted lover?

"I must hold my tongue." A jilted *secret* lover?

"It cannot come to good." A jilted, secret, *unsuitable* lover?

The words seemed vaguely familiar, but I couldn't place them. A quote from somewhere.

I thought of slipping the note into my pocket and turning it over to the Edgartown Police. But it occurred to me that this note could turn out to be evidence, and if it did, my filching it could render it inadmissible in court.

So I memorized the words, slipped it back between the pages of Molly's book, and returned the book to the table.

I turned and smiled at Edna. "It's a nice room."

She nodded. "Thank you."

I spread my hands out. "I didn't take anything."

"I didn't think you would."

I followed her back down the stairs, thanked her for the iced tea, and started for the front door. Then I stopped and said, "Oh, by the way, I noticed a bathing suit on your clothesline. Is that Molly's?"

She pressed her lips together and frowned for an instant. Then, surprisingly, she smiled. "It certainly isn't mine."

I sat in the front seat of Sarah's Range Rover for a few minutes, smoking a cigarette and gazing up at Molly Wood's bedroom window. Aside from the interesting note in her book, I had noticed nothing that might suggest what had happened to her.

I figured one thing that had *not* happened was that she had decided to take an unannounced vacation. There were two suitcases and no empty hangers in the closet. Her treasured copy of *Sense and Sensibility,* her jewelry box, her cosmetics, and her hairbrush had all been left behind. I figured even on the spur of the moment, no woman would go away for three days without bringing at least some of those items along.

Something else was gnawing at me, too, and I'd pulled out of Summer Street and onto Pease's Point Way before I realized what it was. Molly's black nursing bag, the bag I'd seen her carrying the first time I met her at Sarah's, the bag I assumed went everywhere with her, had not been in her room.

Okay, she probably kept it in her car. Or for all I knew, visiting nurses left their bags at the VNS headquarters when they weren't out making house calls.

I glanced at my watch. It was a little before five. I had an hour before cocktails on the Jacksons' balcony.

I found a phone booth beside a gas station, and directory assistance gave me the number for the Visiting Nurse Service. I called it, was told that somebody would be there for another hour, and got directions.

It was in Oak Bluffs right across the street from the high school. It took me fifteen minutes to find the shingled two-story building that housed the Martha's Vineyard Community Services, which included the Visiting Nurse office. Here on the island, I noticed, they called it the Visiting Nurse Service, not Association as they did everywhere else.

When I told the receptionist I was a lawyer representing one of the Visiting Nurse patients, she stared at me for a moment, then buzzed somebody on her intercom.

A moment later, a middle-aged woman wearing a long yellow skirt and a white blouse bustled out from around a corner. She introduced herself as Mrs. Sadler, the intake supervisor.

I told her that I was a lawyer, Sarah Fairchild was my client, and Amelia Wood was Sarah's nurse. Mrs. Sadler nodded. She didn't seem at all worried that I might sue her. She steered me into an empty office, closed the door behind us, and said, "So how can I help you, Mr. Coyne? Does Mrs. Fairchild have a complaint about her care?"

"No. Not at all. She's very fond of Mrs. Wood."

Mrs. Sadler frowned. "You know—"

"Mrs. Wood has gone missing," I said. "I know. I

wondered if you had any thoughts about that."

She smiled quickly. "The police asked the same thing. I told them I had no thoughts about it whatsoever, aside from being very concerned, of course. Molly has been with us for only a few months, but she's always been absolutely reliable. I can't understand it. She's a lovely person. It's very worrisome."

"When did you first realize something might be wrong?"

"Monday morning at eight o'clock," she said. "That's when she was supposed to check in and get her calendar."

"But she didn't check in."

"No. I called her pager at about eight-fifteen, and when another fifteen minutes passed and she didn't call in, I tried her home. There was no answer. I waited awhile, figuring maybe she'd had car trouble or something and had left her beeper somewhere. Finally, I reassigned some nurses to her schedule."

"And you never did hear from her?"

Mrs. Sadler shook her head. "I kept trying her all morning. Home, her beeper. I even called her patients' homes, just to be sure that for some reason she hadn't done her rounds without checking in."

"Did you check with all of them?"

She nodded. "She missed them all. I was reluctant to try her emergency number. I didn't want to upset anybody."

"Did you finally try it?"

She shook her head. "I intended to. But when I looked in her file, I saw that she'd left the space for an emergency contact blank. That slipped by us, I'm afraid. Someone should've noticed that. Look," she said, "is Mrs. Fairchild unhappy with the new nurse we've assigned?"

"Actually," I said, "Mrs. Fairchild is in the ICU at the hospital."

Mrs. Sadler nodded. "That's right. I remember hearing that. How is she?"

"She's unconscious. She had a stroke."

She tsk-tsked and shook her head.

"I'm worried about Molly Wood," I said. "I, um, well, I had a date with her, and she didn't show up."

"She's a very attractive woman."

"Yes, I agree. And it's not that I've never been stood up by an attractive woman, but it does seem that something's happened to Molly."

"How can I help?"

"I don't know." I fished out one of my business cards, scratched the Fairchild phone number on the back of it, and gave it to her. "That's where I'm staying. If you think of something or hear anything, I'd appreciate it if you'd call me."

She took my card, glanced at both sides of it, and tucked it into her skirt pocket. "The police asked me to do the same thing," she said.

"Sure," I said. "They're the important ones." I gave her my best, saddest smile. "Me, I'm just somebody who cares."

Mrs. Sandler reached over, touched my hand, and nodded sympathetically. I'd hit a soft spot. "Anything I hear, I'll call you, I promise," she said.

I thanked her for her time, and she walked me back out into the reception area. When she held out her hand to me, I took it and said, "By the way. Where do your nurses keep their bags?"

"You mean when they're not on duty?"

I nodded.

She shrugged. "At home, or perhaps locked in their vehicles. They're supposed to keep their bags secure. They carry expensive medical equipment in them."

"What about drugs? Do they carry drugs in those bags?"

"No, no meds. Our nurses routinely administer medication, give shots, and so forth. But the patients have their prescriptions with them."

"What about syringes?"

She nodded. "The nurses carry a supply in their bags."

"They don't leave their bags here, then?"

"Here? In the office?" She shook her head. "No. The nurses are responsible for their bags."

It was nearly six o'clock when I climbed into the Range Rover. I pointed it back to Edgartown and decided it was time to start thinking about fishing.

Well, first I'd try to give some thought to putting my feet up on J.W.'s balcony railing and sipping one of his martinis and gazing out over the treetops toward the sea.

But all the way over there Molly Wood's smile kept flashing in my mind, and I could almost hear the tinkle of her laugh in my ear and feel the warmth of her hand and the soft promise of her lips.

Diana and Joshua greeted me in the driveway when I

got to J.W.'s place. They probably figured I'd become a permanent suppertime fixture at their house, and whatever shyness they'd shown me earlier had been replaced with aggressive friendliness. Each of them grabbed one of my hands and dragged me out back to show me all the progress they'd made on their tree house.

I was standing there admiring it when J.W. came around the corner. He held his martini glass aloft. "Started without you."

"Diana and Josh are pretty good carpenters," I said.

"Pa helped a little," said Diana.

"Brady's going to come up to the balcony now," said J.W. "We have adult things to discuss."

I followed J.W. up the stairs to the balcony. Zee was slouched in a chair with her feet up on the railing and a martini glass resting on her belly. Her eyes were closed.

When I took the chair beside her, she looked at me, smiled, and said, "Gonna be some weather tonight."

"Weather," in the parlance of those who live on the edge of the sea, means "bad weather."

"I've always admired you native types," I said. "Living close to the land and sea, intimately attuned to nature and her mysterious ways. I suppose you wet your finger and stick it up in the air, take a deep breath, sniff the air, check out the aches in your joints, and make your predictions."

"No," she said, "I watch the news on television. Hurricane Elinore is heading for the Carolina coast.

South Beach could be hot." She glanced at her watch. "High tide's around ten. I'd like to be there about an hour before that, fish the whole tide."

"Low tide around four," said J.W. "All-nighter, huh?"

"Weather's coming," said Zee.

He shrugged and nodded, as if that explained it all.

Zee pushed herself up and went down to the kitchen. J.W. plopped himself into her chair. "Molly," he said. "Looks grim."

He told me about his conversations with the police and the various other people he'd queried, and I told him about my visit with Edna Paul and the note I'd found in Molly's copy of *Sense and Sensibility*. I shut my eyes for a minute, then quoted it for him: "'It is not, nor it cannot come to good. But break, my heart, for I must hold my tongue.'"

J.W. gazed up at the sky. The stars were beginning to wink on. "I've heard that somewhere."

"I think I have, too," I said. "But damned if I can place it. From a poem? The lyrics to some song? It's got that ba-*bump*-ba-*bump* beat to it. You could dance to it, you know? What the hell is that? Iambic pentameter?"

J.W. lifted both hands and shrugged. "I should've paid better attention in Mrs. Warbuck's English class." He stared off toward the salt pond, where darkness was gathering. "That note was probably written by some admirer, huh?"

"I dunno. Maybe it was from Ethan. Her husband, I'm guessing, who gave her the book."

He shook his head. "'It cannot come to good'? Doesn't sound like something a loving husband would write." He frowned for a minute, then suddenly he slapped the arm of his chair and stood up. "Wait here."

J.W. disappeared down the stairs, and a few minutes later he came back lugging a book about the size of an unabridged dictionary. He sat down and opened it. I craned my neck and read the title. *The Complete Works of Shakespeare.*

"I figured you were more the Captain Marvel type," I said.

"Wile E. Coyote is my favorite," he muttered. "Now shut up."

I lit a cigarette and shut up, and a few minutes later J.W. snapped his fingers. "Got it. 'It is not, nor it cannot come to good. But break, my heart, for I must hold my tongue.'" He poked my arm. "That's what you said, right?"

"Exactly."

"*Hamlet*, act one, scene two," said J.W. "The poor prince is all upset because his father the king just died and his mother the queen is screwing his uncle. He's really pissed at both of them. He thinks it's incestuous, and he thinks his mother is amoral and his uncle is just using her. This quote comes at the end of a soliloquy. Sort of a foreshadowing of all the bad things that will happen in the rest of the play."

"So what do you make of it?" I said.

"We figure out who wrote it, we can ask him." He shut the book and put it on the table. Then he picked up the martini pitcher and topped off both our glasses. "So did you notice anything else?"

"Something I didn't notice," I said. "Molly's bag."

"What bag?"

"Her nurse's bag. She had it the first time I met her at Sarah's. It wasn't anywhere in her room at Edna's, and it wasn't at the VNS headquarters. Was it in her car, did you notice?"

He shrugged. "I didn't see it. The cops didn't mention finding anything but that golf glove. It might've been in the trunk, I guess. Cops can't be counted on to tell you everything."

"Can you check on it?"

"I guess so. You think it's relevant?"

"Could be. The woman at the Visiting Nurse place said they keep syringes in those bags."

"Yeah? What about drugs?"

"No, the patients have their own drugs. But the nurses sometimes do the injections."

"So you're thinking . . . ?"

I shrugged. "I don't know what I'm thinking. Just, if the bag's missing, where the hell is it?"

"A motive to hurt her?" said J.W. "Someone thinks she's got drugs in it, whacks her to steal it?"

"Or maybe just for the syringes," I said.

"Hmm," said J.W. "I can see mugging her, maybe. Giving her a shove, grabbing the bag, running away. But Molly's been missing for three days."

"Guy sees her getting into her car. Or out of it. Sees the bag, tries to snatch it, she resists, he panics, hits her or . . . or stabs her or something . . ."

"Some random guy," said J.W. "Hurts her worse than he meant to."

"Could be, right? You got any cokeheads on the island?"

He laughed. "You kidding?"

"Guys willing to hurt people to get hold of some narcotics?"

"Guys and gals as well," he said.

"Pardon my political incorrectness."

"Most offensive," he said with a grin. "Shocking, in fact."

After dinner, I helped J.W. clean up the kitchen while Zee read stories to the kids. I washed and he dried and put things away, and while we worked he told me about all the people he'd been interviewing. The golf glove they'd found in Molly's car had led him to Eliza Fairchild's two lapdogs, Luis Martinez and Philip Fredrickson, both of whom worked for the company that manufactured the glove, which also happened to be a major backer of the Isle of Dreams Corporation, which wanted to buy Sarah's property.

"So what's the connection?" I said. "I mean, it could be some jealous-lover thing, but Molly didn't even play golf, so I don't see how it could connect to the business end."

J.W. shook his head. "I don't know. Those two were all over Eliza, you said."

I nodded. "You're thinking Martinez and Fredrickson had ulterior motives? You're thinking they were pawing Eliza because they were looking for information?"

"Most likely they were pawing Eliza because Eliza is eminently pawable. Still . . ."

"But it could be all about money," I said, "and they were using Eliza. And you're thinking they could've also been using Molly."

J.W. shrugged. "Suppose Sarah confided something to Molly. You said the two of them were very close."

"Humph," I said. "Sarah didn't confide anything worth killing about to me."

He looked sideways at me. "You sure?"

I shrugged. "Good question, I guess. So you think whatever happened to Molly has something to do with the Fairchild property?"

He shrugged. "All I think is that I don't know what to think, and I'm trying to keep an open and creative mind about it."

"If that is what happened," I said, "then whoever did whatever they did to Molly would most likely also go after somebody else they figured Sarah might confide in, huh?"

He nodded. "If that's what this is all about."

"Someone like Sarah's lawyer."

He shrugged.

"You suggesting that I ought to pretend I know something, set myself up as some kind of decoy, try to smoke out the bad guys?" I said.

"What, and endanger yourself?" J.W. held up both hands. "I am offended. I am your friend. I would never suggest that you endanger yourself."

"You already did," I said.

"No," he said. "I think you did that all by yourself."

"Well," I said, "if I did that and nothing happened, it would probably mean that what happened to Molly was a jealous-lover thing rather than a money thing or a golf thing. That would narrow it down."

"It would indeed," said J.W.

"On the other hand," I said, "if something *did* happen . . ."

"Right," he said. "You gotta think about that."

By the time Zee and I got to South Beach, a cloud bank had blown in. It obscured the stars and the moon, and the night was so black and moist that even a landlubber such as I could smell the storm in the air.

We cast blindly through the thick air into the dark water that I knew was in front of me only by the sound of the surf out there somewhere and the soft lapping of the waves at my feet. Nothing happened for a long time, but Zee and I kept casting. She stood so close beside me that we could talk conversationally, and I could hear the whirr of line spinning off her reel and the little clank when she engaged the bail on her reel. But the darkness was so enveloping that I couldn't see her. She kept reminding me that the ocean is always changing, that wind and tide keep the water in constant motion, and that bluefish and stripers never stop moving in their insatiable quest for food. The next cast could always be the one that intercepted a Derby winner.

Fishing in the ocean at night is an act of blind faith—or blind folly.

Sometime after we'd been there for a few hours, the breeze shifted direction. It felt warmer on my face, and it tasted damper, and it became stronger.

Within minutes after I first noticed the wind shift, I heard Zee grunt.

"Fish?" I said.

"Um. Good one."

I reeled in and fished out my flashlight in time to see Zee backing a very large striped bass up onto the beach.

"Keeper?"

She knelt beside it and measured it against some markings on her rod. "Oh, yeah," she whispered. "Thirty-seven inches. Heigh-ho, heigh-ho. Derby winner, here we go."

She lugged the big fish up to her Jeep, and I returned to my casting with renewed enthusiasm.

A few casts later, I felt a hard pull. But I failed to hook the fish.

Zee returned.

"I had a hit," I said.

"They've arrived," she said. "Time to get serious."

And for the rest of the night—I had no idea how many hours passed—we caught fish. We landed eight or ten nice stripers apiece, though none of them matched Zee's thirty-seven-incher and none of mine was a keeper, and we caught about as many bluefish. I kept a blue that Zee guessed would weigh ten pounds, and she kept all of hers, including one about the same size as mine.

First light came so gradually it was barely noticeable. There was no burst of light on the horizon, because the horizon was packed with heavy clouds. It was, rather, a growing awareness that the sky was a bit less dark than the water, and that I could make out

Zee's silhouette beside me, and that on both sides of us up and down the beach there were other silhouettes casting into the sea.

We quit a little after seven-thirty. My shoulder ached and my poor, sleep-deprived head felt like an overblown balloon, and as we drove to Derby head-quarters to weigh in our fish, I realized that I'd spent the entire night without thinking a single thought of Molly Wood or Sarah Fairchild or my law practice. My mind had registered nothing except the sea and the sky and the air and the rhythms of fishing.

Anyone who doesn't fish could never understand.

Chapter Seventeen

J.W.

Zee and Brady pulled into the yard just before nine-thirty the next morning. In the fish box, awash in the last melting remnants of the ice they'd packed there the night before, were eight or ten nice blues and a keeper bass.

I examined the fish. "Not bad," I said.

"Not bad, but not great, either," said Zee. "The guys right behind us at the weigh-in brought in better ones. You two both got daily thirds yesterday, though, so you outlasted most of the competition and at least made the board. Guess who's leading the overall bass competition."

"Who?"

"Nate Fairchild. Last night he brought in a fifty-six-pounder. From the 'North Shore,' he said, but I think we can be a little more precise than that."

"Fairchild Cove." I looked at Brady. "The tides are getting about right. Let's go up there tonight and give old Nate a run for his money."

"As you may recall, the last time I ran into Nate on the beach, he waved a shotgun in my face." Brady rubbed a red eye and yawned. "He probably thinks that with Sarah in the hospital he can do what he pleases, such as keeping the cove to himself."

"There's a law against waving shotguns at people, isn't there?"

"Maybe catching that bass will soothe his savage breast."

"Maybe it will. We should get there about five. The tide will be rising, and the sun comes up around six. Good time to hunt bass."

"Nate probably thinks the same thing."

"I doubt if Nate will have his shotgun with him that time of day. He probably thinks he's scared you off for good."

"Pretty close to it," said Brady.

But I didn't think he looked very frightened. If anything, he just looked tired, like a lot of other people doing serious Derby fishing. As if he'd read my thought, he looked at his watch. "I'm going to catch a couple hours' sleep, then get back to work. See you at the fork in Sarah's driveway at five?"

"You're on." I thought of meeting Nate on the beach and felt cold and happy.

After Brady drove away, I took the fish out back and filleted them. We were having a good Derby, fish-in-the-freezer-wise, even though we weren't doing too well at getting on the board.

While Zee was sleeping, I loaded the kids in the car and drove down to the Chief's office in Edgartown. He wasn't there. He was downtown, according to Kit Goulart.

"But," she added, "he said if you came by I should give you this." She handed me an envelope. Inside was a photograph of Molly Wood. "I think it came down from Dom Agganis."

Sergeant Dom Agganis was the head of the Massachusetts State Police force on Martha's Vineyard. He and I were not bosom buddies, but I got along with him, which is more than I could say about his underling, Officer Olive Otero, who rubbed me as wrong as I rubbed her.

I found the Chief at the four corners leaning on the side of a bank. He looked as happy as he ever does.

"Thanks for the photo," I said. "I see you're admiring the traffic flow." And indeed, the cars were moving smoothly, in marked contrast to the stops and stalls and creepy-crawling of summertime traffic.

"Agganis got the pictures from somebody on the mainland and sent them to all the departments on the island. The traffic is nice, isn't it? There are even parking places on Main."

"Have you heard anything more about Molly Wood's car?" I said. "Did they find anything else?"

"It's none of your business, but no, they didn't."

"What about Molly Wood's medical bag?"

For the first time, he looked at me seriously. "What bag?"

"Visiting nurses all carry medical bags. According to Brady Coyne, it isn't in her room and it isn't at the offices of the Visiting Nurse Service. If it isn't at either one of those places, it should be in her car."

His eyes roved up and down the street, the way cops' eyes often do. But he wasn't looking for perps. He was thinking. "I'll get in touch with Dom Agganis," he said. He turned and walked up the street.

We went back to the Land Cruiser. It was early, but some people might already be up. I drove to Oak Bluffs and parked on Circuit Avenue, the main drag.

The Atlantic Connection is a favorite Oak Bluffs nightspot, and one of the few places on the Vineyard where you can dance between drinks. It's across the street and a few doors up from the Fireside. It offers a bar and a dance floor and is popular with couples who like to trip the light fantastic.

The Connection wasn't open, but I knew a bartender named Fred who should just about be getting up now, so the kids and I walked up into the campground, between rows of those lovely gingerbread houses, until we came to Fred's tiny, brightly painted place. I banged on his door.

He was, indeed, up, but just barely. He looked at me with red eyes over a cup of coffee. "J.W. *¿Que pasa?* Hi, kids. Come in."

"No thanks. This will only take a minute." I showed him Molly's picture. "Do you remember seeing this woman at the club?"

He peered and nodded. "Yeah. She's been in a few times. Likes to dance."

"She come in alone or with somebody?"

He returned my photo. "With somebody. A couple different somebodies, in fact. Who is she?"

"Her name's Molly Wood. You know any of the men she was with?"

Fred shook his head. "The only one I remember was Shrink Williams. They were in together a time or two."

"I hear that if a woman breaks off from Shrink, he

trails her around. You ever see that happen?"

Bartenders who want to keep their jobs see more than they'll talk about. Diplomatic Fred just shrugged.

I tried another tack. "When were Molly and Shrink together?"

He sipped his coffee and winced. Still pretty hot. "Maybe three weeks back."

"And after that they weren't together? She came into the Connection with somebody else?"

He shrugged again and nodded.

"But not Shrink?"

"No, not Shrink."

"But Shrink did come in."

"Yeah."

"And he'd stay around until she and whoever she was with left and then he'd leave too, right?"

"Maybe. I don't keep track of what everybody does or when they do it."

"Maybe" was all I was going to get from Fred on that subject, so I showed him Kathy Bannerman's photo. "This woman was on the island a year ago. Do you remember seeing her?"

He studied the picture, then cocked his head to one side and studied it some more. "She looks familiar, but last year was a long time ago, and we get a lot of good-looking women coming in during the summers. I'm not sure."

"Maybe she was with the same guy you saw with Molly Wood."

He shook his head. "Could be, could not be." He returned the photo. "Sorry. What's going on, J.W.?"

"We're trying to find these women. We're looking for anybody who knows anything about them."

"Sorry I couldn't help."

He went back to his coffee, and the kids and I walked back to the truck.

"I like these houses," said Diana. "They look like that picture in *Hansel and Gretel*. The witch's house."

"A hundred and fifty years ago, there were tents here," I said. "Then they replaced the tents with these houses and they've been here ever since. They made all those curlicue decorations with special saws."

"Can we have decorations like that on our tree house?"

"Nope. I don't have the right kind of saw or the right kind of skill. The tree house is going to be plain and simple."

They each put a hand into one of mine, and the three of us walked side by side among the pretty gingerbread houses. I was thinking about a woman I knew who worked at the Hot Tin Roof, the island's major nightspot.

I sighted a pay phone on Circuit Avenue, but as I moved toward it a state police cruiser pulled in against the curb. Sergeant Dom Agganis slid his big body out from behind the wheel and said, "Just the man I wanted to see." He produced two lollipops. "Any objection to candy before lunch?"

"No. Do you have one for me?"

"No. Here, kids."

My polite children thanked him nicely.

"You found the car, so that gets you the latest dope on that glove they found in it," said Dom. "It was top of the line. Made by Mallet. It's the kind of glove they make as gifts for special people who they do business with."

"So whose was it?"

"They don't know."

"Well," I said, "a couple guys named Philip Fredrickson and Luis Martinez work for the Mallet Corporation. Mallet is backing the Isle of Dreams outfit, and these guys are trying to help them get their hands on Sarah Fairchild's place up in West Tisbury. Molly Wood is Sarah's visiting nurse."

"Just what we need," said Agganis. "Another golf course. Maybe these guys met the Wood woman up at the Fairchild place. Maybe they played golf together."

"Zee says that Molly doesn't play golf."

He rubbed his chin. "One thing I don't like about this is the Wood woman's description."

"What do you mean?"

He frowned. "She's fortyish, blonde, and attractive. Over the last few years, several people have gone missing from the island. Most of them turned up safe and sound, but some didn't."

"The Chief mentioned that."

He nodded. "A half dozen of our missing people have stayed missing even after people, including us, kept on looking for them. The ones I'm thinking about were good-looking blonde women in their forties. They were all from off-island, and they all dropped out of sight and haven't been seen since. Just like Molly Wood."

"I've been looking for one of them," I said, and told him about the job I'd taken searching for Katherine Bannerman.

He worked his jaw. "Yeah, she's one of them. And now there's Molly Wood. You know anything about her and her friends that I don't know?"

"I don't know what you know," I said, "but I'll tell you what I've heard." And I did.

When I was done, Dom gave me a hard look. "So the Bannerman woman's husband was here last summer, eh?"

"Just about the time she disappeared. He admits it and Bonzo saw him. Bonzo sees a lot. Could be he saw the guy Molly was with."

"I'll talk to Bonzo and I'll talk with Bannerman, too. The Chief called me earlier and told me about that bag Molly Wood carried, so we'll put the squeeze on some of our local druggies, too. And I'll talk with Martinez, Fredrickson, and Shrink Williams. Anybody else on your list of the usual suspects?"

"I'm going to call a woman who works at the Hot Tin Roof and see if she can tell me anything about Molly Wood or Kathy Bannerman, or can corroborate the stories I've been hearing about Shrink. If she tells me anything new, I'll let you know."

"You leave this investigation to the cops. Time for you to go home and be daddy to your kids."

"Pa's helping us build a tree house," said big-eared Joshua.

"Good," said Agganis. "Go build a tree house, J.W."

He opened the door of the cruiser and slid behind the wheel. I pushed the door shut and leaned on the roof.

"I met Molly Wood, and I liked her," I said, "and

225

I've been hired to find Kathy Bannerman. So I'll build the tree house, but I'm also going to nose around and try to get a line on what happened to those women. I'll get in touch with you or the Chief if I find out anything interesting."

"Don't interfere with the investigation, J.W."

"Does that mean that there really is an investigation?"

"As of right now."

I stepped back. "I'm just a citizen asking questions. No law against that."

"A judge might think differently if you get in our way. So long, kids." He eased out of the parking place and drove away.

"Wait here," I said to the children as I dug out money for the phone. They looked into a store window while I made my call.

I didn't hang out in clubs very much, even before I met Zee. But a fisherman I knew had a wife who worked at the Tin Roof. She was home, and I broached my thesis of Shrink Williams as stalker.

"Hell, J.W.," she said with a laugh, "every woman Shrink ever dated knows he does that. He's not dangerous. He just can't imagine that a woman would leave him for somebody else, so he has to check up just to be sure."

"Have you noticed Shrink lately watching a forty-ish blonde woman named Molly Wood?"

"I don't know her name, but it seems to me that he was eyeballing a woman like that recently. She was with a really good-looking guy. Shrink looked green, I thought."

"The man she was with anybody you know?"

"I think I'd remember a guy who looked that good."

"I thought you had eyes only for me."

"Ha!"

"So what'd he look like?"

"Sorry, J.W. I just remember thinking he was good-looking."

"You wouldn't happen to remember seeing the same guy a year ago, with another good-looking fortyish blonde?"

She made a thoughtful, humming sound. "Maybe. I can't really be sure."

"Does this mean that next time you won't remember me, either?"

"Of course not. What was your name again?"

Chapter Eighteen

Brady

I was exhausted after fishing all night with Zee. But I'd caught some fish, and more important, I was winning my bet with Billy. I felt good about that.

As I drove from the Jackson residence to West Tisbury, my thoughts slowly began to turn from fishing to Sarah, in the hospital, and Molly Wood, wherever she was, and my actual job, which was to arrange the sale of the Fairchild property. Given Sarah's condition, I wanted to get that settled quickly. The problem was, I had gone about twenty-four hours without sleep, so the thoughts came at me jumbled and fuzzy. I had strategies to devise and decisions to make, but the last rational corner of my poor old brain told me not to devise a single strategy or make any decisions until I'd gotten a few hours of sleep.

I parked in the turnaround out front and went inside. I heard the whine of a vacuum cleaner and followed the sound to the living room, where I found Patrick pushing the Hoover over the carpet. He was wearing a sleeveless T-shirt and tennis shorts and his feet were bare. No apron.

He hadn't heard me over the noise of the machine, so I went up behind him and yelled, "Hey!"

He whirled around, wide-eyed, stared at me for a moment, then turned off the vacuum cleaner. He fluttered his hand over his heart. "Jeez, Brady," he said. "You scared me."

"Maid's day off?" I said.

"The maid comes in once a week," he said. "The place gets messy after about a day. My darling mother and all her little friends track in sand and leave their empty bottles and dirty glasses and ashtrays all over the house, and Nate splashes fish blood all over the kitchen floor and counters, and . . ." He rolled his eyes. "Somebody's got to take care of the place."

"Well, good for you," I said. "But I have a request."

"Of course," he said.

"Cease with the noisy machine for a few hours. I've been fishing all night, and I've got to sleep."

"Sure," he said. "How'd they bite?"

"We had pretty good fishing," I said. "But your uncle Nate brought in a fifty-six-pounder this morning. So far he's winning the Derby."

"That explains it," said Patrick. "He buzzed through a little while ago, and I thought he must be drunk. He was actually singing. Nate never sings. Mostly, he swears. Especially at me. He didn't even make a nasty comment about my masculinity when he saw me vacuuming. That's totally unlike him."

"Where's Eliza?" I said.

"I don't know and I don't care," he said. "She never came home last night."

"Out on a date?"

"Date?" He laughed sourly. "More like hunting. Or fishing. She sashayed out of here after dinner wearing a little dress that went from here to here." He held one hand at mid-chest and the other at crotch level. "I know what she did. She went to the Fireside or some-place and hiked herself up onto a bar stool. You can figure out the rest."

I shrugged. "I could if I wasn't so tired. What's the news on Sarah?"

Patrick held out his hands, palms up. "No change."

"Still unconscious?"

"She's not technically in a coma, according to the doctors. But mostly she seems to be sleeping. When she opens her eyes, she doesn't recognize you. She whispers nonsense things sometimes. They don't know what's going to happen."

"I'll visit her this afternoon," I said. "After I get some sleep." I patted his shoulder. "You go ahead, fin-ish this room. I've got to make a phone call. Then I'm hitting the hay, and I'd appreciate it if you'd guard my sleep for me."

"No vacuuming," he said.

"And no visitors and no lawn mowers and no slam-ming car doors."

Patrick smiled. "You can count on me."

I turned to leave the room.

"Brady?" said Patrick.

"What?"

"What's happening with your negotiations?"

"The property, you mean?"

He nodded.

"I intend to wind it up in the next few days. Your grandmother's condition is pushing up my timetable."

"You're really going to sell it, huh?"

"It's what she wants."

He nodded.

I went out into the kitchen. I decided not to make myself more coffee. J.W. had given me a mug for the drive home, but I didn't think it would keep me awake much longer. Another mug might.

I found the portable phone, slouched into a wooden chair at the kitchen table, and dialed my office.

Julie answered. "Brady L. Coyne, attorney," she said.

"Hey. It's me."

"Brady," she said. "Do you realize it's Thursday already, and you've been gone almost a week, and you haven't once checked in?"

"Mea culpa, kid," I said. "I figured, anything came up, you'd call me."

"Nothing has come up that I couldn't handle," she said. "That doesn't mean—"

"You're right," I said. "I'm sorry. Has anything come up that, had I been a responsible and mature lawyer, actually present in my office, you would've let me handle?"

She sighed. "No. It's been quiet. It was a good week for you to disappear."

"I didn't disappear. I am highly visible."

"Not to me you're not. You'll be back on Monday, I assume?"

I cleared my throat. "That's why I called."

"I might've known."

"Some things have happened down here," I said. I told her about Sarah Fairchild's stroke and about the disappearance of Molly Wood and about how those two events had conspired to complicate my original mission of arranging for the sale of the Fairchild property.

"Not to mention, the fishing's been good, huh?"

"It's been okay," I said.

"You're supposed to meet with Attorney McPherson Monday afternoon," Julie said.

"What's that? The Reynolds divorce?"

"Right."

"Give Adele a call and reschedule for later in the week. I might be back Monday, but I might not. I think I'm going to need two or three more business days down here. I'll plan to be in the office Wednesday. If anything changes, I'll let you know."

"I've got one new appointment for you," said Julie. "I'm going to write it in for Thursday morning at nine."

"With whom?"

"Me."

"What about?"

"My raise."

"Sweetheart," I said, "give yourself whatever raise you think you deserve. If it's not enough, I'll change it when I get back."

"It couldn't possibly be enough," she said.

"I know. I agree." I yawned. "I've gotta go to bed. I'll catch you later."

"Bed? Brady, it's—"

"The middle of the morning. I know. I was up all night. A lawyer's work is never done."

I think I fell asleep halfway up the stairs. I didn't remember dropping my clothes on the floor, but when I woke up, there they were, in a pile in the middle of the room.

For a minute I had no idea what time it was or what day it was or, for that matter, where I was. I did have a vague recollection of who I was, however, which I took as a positive sign.

Then I realized that somebody was knocking on my door.

"Go away," I grumbled.

"Brady," came Eliza's voice, "I'm sorry, but somebody's here to see you."

"I'm sleeping."

"It's two-thirty in the afternoon. I've got coffee. I think you should wake up."

She pushed the door open and came in before I could either invite her or forbid her. She had a big mug of coffee. She put it on the table beside my bed.

"I told Patrick I did not want to be disturbed," I said. "I thought I was quite emphatic about it."

"So you did," said Eliza. "And he was as emphatic to me about it as he could be, which isn't all that emphatic, poor dear. However, there's a state police officer downstairs, and we have already sent him away once this morning. He left reluctantly then, promising to return, and so he has, and this time he appears to be a man on a mission. I sat him down with

233

some coffee and a newspaper and a promise that I'd fetch you. So why don't you drink your coffee like a good boy and make yourself presentable." She sat on the bed. Her butt pushed against my hip. The warmth of her radiated through the blanket. She bent over me and ran her palm along my cheek. "Presentable might include shaving."

"I should shave for a cop?"

She smiled wickedly and planted a soft kiss on my mouth. "No, silly. For me."

I hitched myself up into a sitting position, plucked the coffee mug from the bedside table, and held it to my lips with both hands. Eliza, apparently, intended to supervise, because she continued sitting there smiling at me.

"I think I can drink my coffee and get dressed on my own," I said.

She patted my knee through the blanket. "Oh, do let me help."

"Patrick said you were out all night."

"Patrick's such a fuddy-duddy."

"So were you?"

She smiled. "You're a fuddy-duddy, too. What if I was?"

I shrugged. "Have fun?"

"I always have fun. It's what I'm good at. It's what I do. I have fun. I can imagine no higher purpose for a person's life than having fun. It will be my epitaph. 'Here lies Eliza. She had fun.'"

"Hit the nightspots?"

"The Vineyard can be quite exciting when the Summer People are around, but I like it even better during Derby time. I rather enjoy fishermen, and they keep such interesting hours." She patted my cheek. "I like the boys who come in after catching a big fish. They tend to be generous and keyed up and smelly and altogether fascinating." She stood up. "But enough about me. Sergeant Agganis is waiting for you. I'm afraid if you don't get yourself downstairs, he'll come barging up here." Eliza blew me a kiss, turned, and walked out of the room, leaving a musky scent in her wake.

I was downstairs ten minutes later. I hadn't bothered to shave, and when I saw the officer sitting at the kitchen table talking with Eliza, I was glad I hadn't. It didn't appear that he'd shaved, either.

I went to the electric coffeepot, refilled my mug, and sat across from him.

He looked at me, nodded once, then turned to Eliza. "Thank you, Ms. Fairchild," he said.

"Am I dismissed?" she said.

"Yes," he said.

He watched her leave the room, then reached his hand across the table. "Dom Agganis," he said. "State cops. We got a mutual friend."

I shook his meaty hand. "Horowitz?"

He nodded. "Roger and I go back a ways. He tells me you and him've been involved in some stuff. He vouches for you."

"Boy," I said, "that's a relief."

"Yeah, it should be." It was hard to tell whether Agganis had any sense of humor whatsoever. "We got a situation going down here, and your name came up, and it rang a bell, so I gave Roger a jingle. He said you were above suspicion, which is a pretty unusual thing for Roger to say about anybody, given the fact that he'd just as soon arrest his own wife. I told him that there were some folks down here who might've said you were under suspicion, and he said that was plain stupid. Jury's out as far as I'm concerned, but still, I figure, give the guy the benefit of the doubt even if he is a lawyer." He patted a manila envelope that I hadn't noticed sitting on the table beside him. "So I understand you had a thing going with Amelia Wood."

"A police officer was around only yesterday, asking me about Molly," I said. "I told her what I knew."

Agganis snorted. "Local cop. Tell me."

So I told him how I'd met Molly, that we'd made a date, and that she'd failed to show up.

"And you been asking questions about her," he said.

I shrugged.

"Her landlady, the place she worked," he continued. "You been snooping. You and your buddy Jackson."

"We haven't noticed that the police are making much progress," I said.

"Yeah, Roger said you could be a smart-ass. So what've you found out? You gonna solve this one for us?"

"Doubt it," I said. "Her black bag is missing. It might've had hypodermic syringes in it. That's about all I know."

Agganis picked up the envelope, reached inside,

and withdrew a sheaf of photographs. He slid one across the table.

I looked at it. "Yes. That's Molly."

He handed me another photo. It was a color eight-by-ten head-and-shoulders shot of a blonde woman, mid- to late thirties. She had blue eyes and a pretty smile. "Who's this?" I said.

He didn't answer. Instead, one by one, he handed me the rest of the photographs. There were five in all, not counting Molly's, and each of them was a head-and-shoulders shot of a pretty blonde woman. Their ages probably ranged from mid-thirties to mid-forties. By no means did they all look alike. But all were pretty and blonde and of an age.

"Who are these people?" I said to Agganis.

"You sure which one is Amelia Wood?"

"Sure." I picked up Molly's photo. "This one."

"You could swear to it?"

"Absolutely."

"Recognize any of the others?"

I shrugged.

"Look at 'em again," he said.

"Come on, Sergeant. What's going on?"

He sighed. "Look on the back of those photos."

One of them did look familiar. I picked it up and turned it over. In felt-tip pen someone had printed: "Katherine Elaine Bannerman, 9/22/97." It was identical to the photo J.W. had shown me.

"J.W.'s looking for this woman," I told Agganis.

He nodded. "What about the others?"

The other photos also had a woman's name and a date printed on the back. The earliest date was 1993.

All were in September or early October. Each was a different year. One woman per year, with a couple of years missing.

I looked up at Agganis. "What is this, a gallery of Miss Martha's Vineyard finalists or something?"

"They're all missing," he said.

I nodded.

"Like Amelia Wood," he said. "Off-islanders who disappeared without a trace. All those others, they've never turned up. They were all here on the island, and then they just . . . disappeared."

"And you followed up to see if—"

"Right. They never showed up at home. They never returned to their jobs. They were all single women. Either divorced or never married, and in one case, a woman who was legally separated from her husband. Ms. Wood is a widow." He arched his eyebrows at me.

I nodded. "You think someone here on the Vineyard is grabbing single women from off-island who are in their thirties or forties. Blonde, attractive women."

"Right."

"Some kind of serial killer with a thing for pretty single blondes in their thirties or forties."

Agganis shrugged.

"And you think Molly Wood . . ."

"It fits," he said. "We could crack this. She's only been missing for a few days. This is the best jump we've gotten on one of these cases, thanks to you and Jackson. Mainly him, rattling all the cages in town, pissing people off, the way he does, me included. These other women, we weren't aware they'd gone missing until weeks had passed." He reached across the table and grabbed my wrist. Intensity burned in his eyes. "Some sick bastard is grabbing women on this island—on *my* island, Mr. Coyne—and he's been doing it for a while, and I want him."

I nodded. "What can I do?"

He let out a big sigh. "Wish I knew," he said. "All I know is, Horowitz said you were pretty good at snooping and you knew how to cooperate with police officers. Jackson's a pretty good snooper, too, and he knows everybody down here, though he's not that good at cooperating. I guess all I wanted to say to you was, go ahead, snoop your asses off, both of you. You come up with any bright ideas—even a dim idea would be okay—you share them with me." He cocked his head. "Got any?"

"Any what?"

"Ideas."

I held up my hands, palms up. "Nothing you don't know. Like I told you, I just met Molly the night before she disappeared."

He fished out a business card and put it on the table. "Just call," he said. "Anytime."

I took the card. It had his home and office and cellular phone numbers on it. "Okay," I said.

He pushed himself away from the table and stood up. He gathered up the photos and slid them back into the envelope, which he then tucked into his armpit.

I started to get up, but he waved me down. "Relax," he said. "I know how to get out of here."

It wasn't until I'd heard his car pull out of the driveway that I remembered the note I'd found in Molly's book. It's what happens after a measly four hours of sleep and only one mug of coffee. So I tried Agganis's cell phone, and when he answered, I told him about the note.

"Shakespeare, huh?" he said. "Whaddya make of it?"

"I don't know," I said, "but if you guys haven't gotten a warrant to search her room, maybe you ought to. If an amateur like me can find something as interesting as that note, who knows what a bunch of experienced law enforcement professionals might turn up."

"Yeah, interesting," he mumbled. "Fact is, we got the warrant this morning, and I'm on my way over there as we speak. Not gonna be fun. That Edna Paul is a pisser and a half."

"Oh," I said. "So I didn't help."

"Good try, though," he said.

Then I called the hospital and asked to be connected to the ICU, where a garrulous nurse—perhaps the large one I'd met there—filled me in on Sarah's condition.

Given the natural tendency for medical people to be upbeat and positive, I hung up gravely worried. Sarah had shown no signs of improvement. The doctors considered her stroke a serious one, and her chances of recovery, given the already ravaged condition of her body and the low level of her resistance after months of chemotherapy, appeared to be slim.

The nurse didn't say it, but it sounded like a death-watch, and there wasn't much anybody could do about it, least of all me.

All I could do was try to carry out her wish, which was to sell her estate to somebody suitable before it fell into the hands of her heirs—who, she believed, were distinctly unsuitable.

So I made two phone calls, one to Lawrence McKenney, the lawyer for the Isle of Dreams Corporation, and the other to Gregory Pinto, the banker who was in charge of the Marshall Lea Foundation. Each had secretaries who were protective of their time. Each connected me instantly when I told them who I was and what I wanted.

I told each of them the same thing: Time was of the essence, negotiations had ended, and I wanted their responses to the conditions I'd specified, their final best offer, plus a good-faith check in my hands by Sunday noon. I would then exercise my power of attorney on Sarah Fairchild's behalf to accept the most attractive offer or to reject them both. If I rejected them, all bets were off. They would have no opportunity to resubmit until or unless Sarah either recovered or died. If she died, they'd have to deal with Eliza, Nate, and Patrick. I didn't need to spell that scenario out to either of them. They'd each done their homework.

Chapter Nineteen

J.W.

On the way home for lunch, I stopped at the state police barracks on Temahigan Avenue. The building had been painted bright blue in days gone by but was now cedar-shingled in the best Vineyard tradition. Dom Agganis wasn't there, but Officer Olive Otero was.

Olive gave me a sour look. "Well?"

I showed her a toothy smile. "A message for Dom. Tell him I talked with a woman who works at the Tin Roof who knows Shrink Williams and says that he has a habit of following his ex-dates around after they stop going out with him. Tell him the woman thinks she saw Molly Wood with a guy while Shrink was snooping around within the past two days. Tell him I said to ask Phil Fredrickson exactly when he dated Molly Wood, and to ask Fredrickson and Luis Martinez if they've seen her with a man in the past week or so. Maybe he can get a description of the man or a name. You get all of that, Olive, or should I say it over again, only slower this time?"

Her lip curled as it usually does when she speaks to me. "I don't think Sergeant Agganis gets paid to do what you think he should be doing, Jackson."

"Just give him the message, Olive. And remember, we civilians pay your salary, and your job is not only to protect and serve us but to be polite while you're at it."

I beat it out the door before she could get her mouth open.

At home, Zee was about to leave for the hospital. "I'll be home for supper. Maybe we can do a little fishing before it gets dark. Any news about Molly?"

I told her about my morning. She frowned. "She never told me much about the men she dated, but maybe she told somebody else. I'll ask around."

She gave me a kiss and drove away.

The children and I ate lunch, and then we spent the afternoon finishing the tree house. When the last nail was in, we admired our work. There was a center room about six by six with windows and a railed porch, and two small attached rooms on adjoining branches, one for each of the house's inhabitants. There was a ladder leading up through a trapdoor in the porch floor, and you could keep out pirates and other villains by shutting the door and securing it with a hasp. There was even a rope tied to a high branch that you could use to swing down to the ground. Tarzan would have been proud.

I said, "Your job whenever you're up here is to be very careful so you don't fall and break your necks."

"We'll be careful, Pa."

"It's like being on the boat. You don't take chances and you don't goof around."

"Okay."

Joshua and Diana climbed in and out and around the house, and up and down the ladder, and swung down on the rope.

"Can we sleep up here, Pa?"

"We'll have to rig up some safety belts so you won't roll out of bed, and it'll be pretty uncomfortable, but I guess you can."

"Good! Can we do it tonight? Can we eat supper up here? Will you sleep up here with us?"

"Not tonight, because I have to get up before sunrise and go fishing with Brady. Maybe tomorrow night, if I can fit into the living room."

"Can we have a dog?"

"No. No dogs."

I watched them climb and play and felt happy and fretful, the way parents do when their children are having fun on the edge of danger. But I could remember when my sister and I were kids, full of confidence and attaching no significance to our father's worries about our welfare, so I kept my mouth shut.

When Zee came home, Joshua and Diana took her out to the tree house and gave her the tour.

"We're gonna have supper and sleep here tomorrow night. Pa's going to sleep with us."

"Is he, now?"

"You come too, Ma!"

"Thanks. I don't know if there'll be room."

"You can sleep with me, Ma."

Zee squinted at Diana's little room. "I don't know if there's space for two in there, sweetheart. We'll see."

"You want to swing down on the rope, Ma?"

"Why not?"

Zee swung down and threw the rope back up. I swung down and put an arm around her waist. "Me Tarzan, you Jane. Them Boy and Girl. How about a martini and then supper and then an hour of fishing?"

"Only an hour?"

"I'm going out with Brady at first light and I need my beauty sleep."

"All you pretty boys think of is your looks."

I slipped a hand down over her hip. "Not quite all."

After supper, while the kids played on the beach behind us, we fished at Metcalf's Hole until it was too dark to see, but we never bent a rod. No matter. Fishing and catching are two different things, and both are fun.

At home in bed, feeling Zee's warm sleeping body against mine and listening to her gentle breath, I thought about Molly Wood and how she played tennis but not golf. Tennis but not golf. I didn't play either game, but maybe the man she dated played both. Maybe it made more sense to think that Molly joined him on a tennis court rather than on a golf course.

Then Frankie Bannerman's voice came floating out from wherever it had been stored in the far corners of my mind, saying that her mother had written that she had been playing tennis with some guy and that there had been a tennis racket in the belongings that Elsie Cohen had shipped back to Connecticut. Her mother must have liked the guy, Frankie said, because before she went away she had never played tennis in her life and always said it was boring.

I was suddenly wide-awake, and I stayed that way for a while, thinking new thoughts.

I didn't know how many tennis courts there were on the island, but there were quite a few. I also didn't know who got to play on them or how many were still open after Labor Day. It was probably un-American to be so ignorant of the sport.

Maybe I'd been asking the wrong people to tell me about Kathy Bannerman and Molly Wood. Tomorrow, after catching the prizewinning bass at Fairchild Cove, I'd do some exploration of the island's tennis courts. I might find somebody who had seen Molly or Kathy whacking the ball around with a man who had a known name.

I sank into uneasy dreams only to be rousted out of them by my alarm clock at 4 A.M. I slapped it silent as Zee stirred.

"Go to sleep," I whispered. "It's just me getting up to go fishing."

"Lucky you," she said in a sleepy voice, and snuggled back down under the covers.

A half hour later, munching on a bagel with a stainless steel thermos of hot coffee on the seat beside me, I drove up our long sandy driveway through a darkness made darker by mist and splats of rain, and headed toward the North Shore. My headlights cut through the night. Behind me, off toward Nantucket, the sky was trying to brighten as the great ball that was Earth rolled eastward. The leading edge of the hurricane was brushing the fringes of our island. It would get worse before it got better. Rotten weather is thought by some to be great for both duck hunting and fishing. I hoped they were right.

Up on Vineyard Sound, just before six, the tides

and the rising sun were going to converge in a perfect harmony at first light and create a rare ideal moment for fishing. Fish, of course, bite when they feel like it, so the ideal moment might end up being as fishless as any other moment. But it offered Brady and me as good a chance for a big fish as we were likely to get. Knowing this, I was filled with anticipation in spite of weariness from a night of restless dreams.

At the Tee in Vineyard Haven, I turned left and drove up-island, feeling—or perhaps imagining—a gradual thinning of the darkness. Above and ahead of me, beyond the slap of my windshield wipers, the fall sky was dark and starless.

I turned into Sarah Fairchild's driveway and then forked off onto the narrow lane that led down to the cove. The gate was closed and locked. I had my key and used it, working in my own headlights. Then I drove through and parked and listened to a country-and-western station from Rhode Island. Garth was singing a sad one about the beaches of Cheyenne. Maybe I should invite him to join Pavarotti, local girl Beverly Sills, Willie Nelson, Emmy Lou, and me in a sextet. Garth was young, but he could probably hold his own.

I decided that when we finished fishing I'd call Dom Agganis and give him my tennis thoughts.

After a while, I poured myself a cup of coffee.

A little later I found my flashlight and used it to look at my watch. Brady was twenty minutes late. Probably overslept. I thought of going up to the house and rousting him, but that would involve waking up everybody else in the house, too. No good. I waited another ten minutes, looking through the mizzle at the slowly brightening sky. Some unformed memory was niggling at the edges of my mind, but I couldn't get hold of it. It was small and it wanted my attention, but I couldn't get my sights on it.

Maybe Brady was already down at the beach. Could be he'd forgotten that we were going to meet and had gone on down alone. I looked at my watch again, wondering whether to be worried about Nate being on the beach, but instead feeling irrationally happy that he might be. There is a beast within us all, and mine had red eyes.

I decided to go on down. If Brady was there, fine. If Nate was there with him, I wanted to be there for Brady, but even more for myself.

If Brady had gotten a late start, he'd probably figure that I had gone on ahead, and he would come down and find me. Besides, if I waited much longer I was going to miss the magic moment, and I couldn't think of a good reason to do that even if Brady stayed in bed all day.

So I put the old Land Cruiser in gear and drove down toward the cove. The empty stone cottage was dimly white against the far trees as I passed it, and from the corner of my eye I saw what I thought was movement in the darkness on its far side. A deer, probably, or perhaps only a product of imagination, for when I turned my head and looked again I saw nothing. In the faint wet light of morning I drove on until I came to the beach.

Nate's pickup was there ahead of me.

I got out and looked around, but saw nobody. I

climbed into my waders, strapped on my utility belt, laden with leaders, lures, a plastic bag of eels, pliers, and fish knife, and got my eleven-foot graphite rod off the roof rack.

No Brady. No Nate.

In the dim predawn light I walked through the drizzle toward Fairchild Point, and as I did I finally saw another figure on the beach. I went toward it, and it came toward me.

"Brady? Is that you?"

"No, it's me, you son of a bitch. Get your ass off of my beach."

Nate Fairchild was full of brimstone and the ethical certainty of all fanatics. He came up to me, tall, wide, and vitriolic. "Get off of my beach, Jackson, or by God I'll feed you to the fish!" He raised an arm and pointed a thick finger back up the road.

I felt a wild joy. "Your mother's not dead yet, Nate," I said, "so this beach isn't yours. Make your casts where you want, but don't tell me where to make mine, and you better not cross my line."

"Bastard!" He stepped closer. In the dim light I could see a devil's smile on his lips, and wondered if I had one on my own. Nate had lost no fights that I knew of and clearly didn't expect to lose this one. He was big and he was strong, but I didn't care.

"I'm looking for Brady Coyne," I said. "Have you seen him?"

"I ain't seen Brady Coyne," said Nate, "but I see you. You been stealing my fish for many a year but you won't do it no more, by God!" And so saying, he threw his rod aside and came at me.

Waders are cumbersome, which probably explains why boxers don't wear them in the ring. I was not the only one wearing them. Nate was also wearing his, which slowed him and allowed me to fade beyond the reach of his first big-fisted swing.

"You've got your reel full of sand, Nate," I said.

"Fuck my reel," he growled, plowing on toward me. His huge hands made huge fists, and those lumpy fists had beaten more than one man into the ground. He swung again, and again I faded beyond his reach. I felt lupine and sure.

He came on, slogging through the sand, fists swinging, strong as an ox. I put a hand to my belt, and when he swung again I tossed my rod away and stepped inside his blow. His arms surrounded me and tried to crush me. I brought the point of my fish knife up to the back of his neck, and his arms hesitated.

"You fight because you love it," I said into his ear, "but I hate it, so if I have to fight, I fight to win any way I can." I pricked his skin with the knife. "Get your hands off me."

"A knife. You cowardly bastard!"

"You slashed the wrong man's tires," I said.

"What the hell are you talking about?"

"Drop your arms, Nate." I cut him deeper and felt something warm flow over my fingers.

He dropped his thick arms to his sides. Our eyes were level. I lifted my free hand and took off my official Derby cap, which was adorned with my official Derby button. "Look at my face, Nate. What do you see?"

"What do you mean?"

"What do you see?" I pricked his neck again.

"Ow! What do you mean, goddammit?"

"Do I look any different to you?"

"No, you look the same. What the hell are you getting at?"

"I'm the same person I've always been," I said, "but you never knew what you were looking at. Now I'm going to take this knife away, and when I do I want you to take three steps back. I don't want any argument." I brought my arm back and stepped away. Nate looked down at the knife. It was pointed at his belly. He took three steps back and put his hand on his own belt knife.

I said, "You've been a lucky man all of your life, Nate. You've beaten the shit out of people who didn't want to fight or know how to do it. I don't ever want to fight, but if somebody like you comes after me or mine, I'll do what I have to do. I'll only say this once, you tire-slashing son of a bitch, so you listen close. If you ever lay a hand on me or threaten my wife or kids, you'd better kill me when you do it, because if you don't, I'll kill you. You understand? No technical knockouts, no saying uncle, none of that. I'll kill you."

He shook his head. "What in hell are you talking about? I ain't slashed no tires, and I don't threaten women and kids. What's got into you?"

He looked so puzzled that for the first time it occurred to me that he might not have done it. But I couldn't bring myself to let the idea go. "You slashed my wife's tire in the hospital parking lot and you left a note threatening to do more. I know it was you, so don't deny it!"

He shook his head again. "I damn well do deny it. I never done any such thing!"

He looked so amazed that I suddenly knew I'd been wrong.

Nate wiped his mouth and put a hand to his neck. It came away red. His eyes were shadowed under the brim of his hat. "Jesus," he said. "You cut me."

"You came at me."

"I came with my fists, not with a knife."

"I don't fight to lose," I said, sheathing my knife. "We're a sorry pair, Nate. We're supposed to be grown men." I picked up my rod. "Have you seen Brady Coyne?" I brushed at the sand on my reel.

Nate seemed to me like some ancient creature from the past, primitive, resentful, fearful, and angry. Not unlike me, I thought.

"No," he said. "I ain't seen anybody. I just got here a minute ago."

"He's supposed to meet me here this morning. If he shows up, I don't want any trouble between you. Tell him I'll be over there, at the foot of Fairchild Point, just this side of the rocks."

"I'm not your slave, Jackson." He picked up his rod and stroked at his reel.

I felt a sudden, unexpected sympathy for him, based, no doubt, on my own sense of guilt. "There's room for the two of us to fish down here," I said. "First

252

light should be perfect. Don't cross my line, I won't cross yours."

"Fuck you."

"Have it your way, but I mean what I say."

He hesitated, then nodded. "All right, but don't crowd me."

"You either." I went down to the water, rinsed my reel, and then walked toward the point. My hands were shaking, and I made myself take deep, even breaths.

The rocks out in the sound at the end of the sandbar were dark against the dark water. Below the rocky point I made my cast. The big swimming lure arced out and splashed in the water. I reeled slowly in, feeling the pull of the swimmer. Off to my right another splash announced Nate's cast.

Come on, bass. Here, fishy, fishy, fishy. Bite my nice lure.

Nothing.

I made six casts.

Nothing.

Beyond the rocks at the far end of the sandbar the sky was reluctantly brightening, and the little memory again came dancing along the margins of my mind. Again I tried and failed to grasp it.

I got an eel out of the plastic bag on my belt, made him fast, and cast him. I felt a nibble, then a little tug, and I lifted the tip of the rod. A vibration came up the line to my fingers. I jerked back to set the hook, but the fish was gone. Damn!

Out at the rocks the light was increasing as the tide

was rising. An odd-looking rock was out there. It looked like a man's head barely poking out of the water.

I squinted.

Christ! It *was* a man's head!

Chapter Twenty

Brady

After my session with Sergeant Agganis, the state policeman, and my phone calls to the prospective buyers of the Fairchild property, I took another mug of coffee and the recent issue of the *Vineyard Gazette* out onto the patio. I slouched in one of the big wooden deck chairs, lit a cigarette, and gazed into the distance, where the ocean looked gray and angry. Fairchild Cove was off to my right a mile or so beyond the rolling meadow and the patches of scrubby pine. That's where J.W. and I would meet in—I looked at my watch and saw that it was nearly five in the afternoon—in twelve hours.

Whitecaps were skidding across the sea, and black clouds were building overhead, and the air tasted of seaweed. A sharp, damp breeze hissed in the pines. It was, I guessed, the leading edge of the hurricane. This "weather," as Zee called it, might rile up the fish, drive them close to the rocks. On the other hand, it could push them out to sea beyond the reach of my fly rod. With fish, you could never be certain, which was one of the reasons I loved fishing. But whatever effect the weather had, I'd be there to find out firsthand.

I scanned the local newspaper. There were some letters to the editor debating presidential vacations, the health of the island water table, and the desirability of building another golf course on Martha's Vineyard. Word had gotten around. Four letters do not constitute a representative survey, but if they did, three quarters of the Vineyard population were all for the Fairchild Country Club. It meant jobs, simple as that.

The odd letter was signed by Edna Paul. It was long and rambling and surprisingly affecting. She wrote about what made Martha's Vineyard charming and special, and she pretty much convinced me that it wasn't golf courses.

I looked for a story about Molly Wood and found none. Either the paper had gone to press before word had gotten out or the police were being uncommunicative. Or maybe the Chamber of Commerce had convinced the editors to keep the lid on bad news.

After an hour or so, I realized I was shivering out there, so I went back inside. Patrick had finished his vacuuming. I found him perched on a kitchen stool sipping a cup of tea and watching a small portable television on the counter.

"Oprah?" I said.

He looked up, grinned, and shook his head. "The news."

"What's the weather report?"

"Stormy. The island's expected to catch the backlash of Hurricane Elinore. Nothing to worry about."

"Not unless you're going fishing," I grumbled. "So what do you folks do about dinner here?"

He shrugged. "When Grandmother was here, we'd take trays out to the sunroom and eat with her."

"We?"

"Me and my mother, anyway. Not Nate."

"What about tonight?"

"I'll cook you something, if you want."

I fished out my wallet and put a couple of twenties on the counter beside Patrick's elbow. "Why don't you go get us all some pizza or something. Let's see if we can get Eliza and Nate to join us. I need to talk with you guys again."

Patrick looked up, arched his eyebrows, then nodded. He picked up the bills and disappeared in the direction of the front of the house.

An hour later, the four of us were sitting around the kitchen table eating pizza. Eliza looked fetching in tight black leggings and a butt-length yellow sweater. Patrick had changed out of his tennis shorts into a pair of pressed chino pants and a cotton polo shirt. He looked rather fetching himself. Nate wore baggy overalls and work boots and a sweat-stained cap bearing the legend COOP'S BAIT AND TACKLE. Decidedly unfetching.

"You're going to win the Derby, huh?" I said to Nate.

"Betcherass," he mumbled around a mouthful of sausage pizza.

"You think that fifty-pounder will hold up?"

"It was fifty-six, actually." He shrugged. "Three weeks to go. I'll get a bigger one."

"Maybe," I said. "Unless I get him first. I'm fishing the cove tonight."

Nate turned and fixed me with a baleful stare. "The hell you are," he said softly.

"The hell I'm not. There's plenty of room for both of us. Your mother would be disappointed if I didn't try it there at least once while I'm here, and I'm going to do it."

He reached for the can of Coors by his elbow and lifted it to his mouth. His throat muscles clenched like a weight lifter's arm as he gulped it. Then he slammed it down and leaned across the table to me. "You got the whole fucking island," he said.

I smiled. "You got a prizewinner from the cove. I want a prizewinner. That's how the Derby's played. I plan to be there at first light, and you better be prepared to share."

"Or what?"

I shrugged with exaggerated nonchalance.

"I hear you were a Marine, huh?" said Nate.

"I don't like to talk about it," I said.

He turned to Eliza. "Mr. Lawyer here was some kind of expert at killing people with his bare hands. You wouldn't know it, lookin' at him, but it's true. Wonder if he's still tough."

"Oh, he's tough," said Eliza. She flashed me a droopy-lidded smile. "Tough and dangerous."

Patrick was watching us with a bemused smile on his face. "Bet he's tougher than you," he said to Nate.

"Lay off," I said to Patrick. "I'm just a mild-mannered city lawyer. I don't like violence." I turned to Nate. "No problems, okay?"

He tugged at the bill of his cap, then glowered at me from under it. "You keep your distance from me.

You cross my line, I don't give a shit what kind of training you got in the Marines."

"Fair enough," I said. I turned to Patrick and Eliza. "I wanted you all to know that I intend to complete negotiations for the sale of the property this weekend. I've told representatives of both the Isle of Dreams golf people and the Marshall Lea Foundation to have their final offers to me on Sunday, and I'll take it from there."

"Meaning what?" said Nate.

"Meaning, whichever offer is most consistent with your mother's wishes and is in her best interest is the one I'll accept."

"Yeah, and what about us?"

I shrugged. "Sarah is my client. I've already explained that to you."

"And you have Mother's power of attorney," said Eliza.

I nodded.

"Meaning, you can do whatever you want," said Patrick.

"You could put it that way," I said. "Though I wouldn't say I'll do what I want. I'll do what I think Sarah wants. As long as she's unable to make her own decisions, I am empowered to make decisions for her. It's my job, whether I like it or not, and I'll do it."

"You don't have to do anything, though, do you?" said Eliza.

"Doing nothing is a decision, too," I said. "It's one I'll have to consider. We'll see what happens on Sunday."

Nate was shaking his head. "It ain't right," he

grumbled. "She's gonna die, and our place is gonna be sold right out from under our feet."

"Oh, cut it out," said Patrick. "You'll inherit the money. It's Grandmother's estate, and it's how she wants it."

"Why don't you shut up, you little pervert." Nate glared at Patrick for a moment, then turned to Eliza. "And you, too, bitch." He looked at me. "You're a smart lawyer. You see it, I bet. These two bloodsuckers. You know what they're doing." Nate stood up and leaned forward with his big hands flat on the table. He looked from Eliza to Patrick. "Both of you," he said, "nosing around my mother, bringing her food, wiping away her spit and drool, pretending to be all worried and lovey-dovey. All the time, all you're really worried about is your money. You don't think she sees through the both of you? You ask her who she loves the most. You know who, don'tcha?" He jammed his thumb against his chest. "Me, that's who. I'm her son, and by Jesus, I'm the one who . . . who loves her the most." He ran his hand over his sun-bleached beard and blinked a couple of times. "She's gonna die. Nothin' we can do about it. She doesn't recognize anybody, huh? Guess what? I was at the hospital today, and guess whose name she said? Yours?" He pointed a finger at Eliza. "Not hardly. Or you?" He jutted his chin at Patrick. "No fuckin' way." He nodded. "Me, that's who. She's asking for me. Nathan, she says. That you, Nathan? So fuck you, all of you."

Nate straightened up so suddenly that his chair toppled over backward and crashed to the floor. He stood there rolling his big shoulders and clenching his fists, glowering at Eliza and Patrick. After a minute, he shook his head and sighed. "Mr. Lawyer," he said to me, "I know you got a job to do. Just keep in mind that I'm the last Fairchild son, and that property's been in my family for more than two hundred years, and by Jesus, after my mother, I'm the only goddam Fairchild left who cares about it. I love this place. It's rightfully mine. I don't want some goddam bird lovers from New Jersey or something prowling around acting like it's theirs, and I sure as hell don't want bull-dozers coming along, cutting the tops off these pretty hills and filling in the gullies and uprooting the trees that've been here longer than my mother."

"Nate, listen," I said. "I—"

"No, goddammit, you listen. My mother hasn't been right since she got the cancer, and whatever she's been tellin' you, it's not her. You understand?"

I looked up at him and nodded. "I'll keep it in mind."

He continued to glare down at me for a minute. Then the air seemed to go out of him. He sighed heavily, looked at all three of us, one after the other, then shook his head, turned, and left the room.

I helped Patrick and Eliza clean up the kitchen. None of us spoke. Nate's outburst still hung in the air.

When we finished, each of us wandered off in a different direction. I assembled my fishing gear on the porch outside the front door, fixed the electric cof-feepot to start brewing at four-fifteen in the morning, and went up to my room.

It was not quite nine in the evening. Normally I turn out my light at midnight, but I figured after all the sleep I'd been missing this week I'd be able to conk off in time to give me some rest before my alarm went off.

I read for half an hour, and then, despite the fact that I didn't really feel sleepy, I turned off the light.

I lay there in the dark with my eyes squeezed shut, listening to the wind wheeze through the trees outside my open window, willing myself to relax. Easier said than done. Nate's tirade kept replaying itself in my head. What if he was right? What if Sarah's urgent desire to sell her property did not represent her true feelings? What if I sold her property, and then she recovered and told me I'd made a terrible mistake?

Nate was a gruff, grouchy, hostile son of a bitch. But it was hard to ignore the emotion he'd revealed in the kitchen. It occurred to me that of the three of them, he was the one who loved Sarah without reservation or expectation.

I remembered when I'd visited Sarah she had seemed to be asking for Nate. Did she really want to take from him the only thing he cared about?

Well, she'd repeatedly told me exactly what she wanted, and she'd given me her durable power of attorney. I couldn't second-guess Sarah Fairchild, and I couldn't second-guess myself.

I had a job to do.

I'd nearly drifted off to sleep when there came a soft rapping on my door. I tried to ignore it, but it continued. Finally, I said, "Eliza, goddammit, I'm trying to sleep. Go away."

"How'd you know it was me?"

"Not even Nate has the bad manners to wake up a man who's getting up at four-thirty in the morning."

"I need to talk to you."

"Try the door. You'll notice that for once I had the foresight to lock it. I mean it. Go away. Whatever it is can wait."

I heard her chuckle through the door. "It's been waiting too long already," she said.

"Eliza, dammit . . ."

"Okay, okay," she said. "Your loss."

By now I was wide-awake. I listened for a few minutes and concluded that Eliza had left my door. I got a cigarette lit and lay there on my back, smoking in the dark and fuming at Eliza.

At the same time, I remembered how her rump felt warm and soft against my leg when she sat on my bed, and how her lips moved on mine and her breasts pressed against my chest when she bent to me and brushed me with a kiss, and I was briefly tempted to get up and track her down and take her hand and bring her back to my room.

I was positive I'd be able to sleep peacefully after making love with Eliza.

But I stayed right where I was. I finished my cigarette, stubbed it out in the ashtray beside my bed, rechecked the alarm clock, then rolled over.

After a while, I fell asleep.

When I was a kid, the fishing season opened on the third Saturday in April, and on Opening Day morning I always woke up before the alarm. But as the years passed, I pretty much outgrew that restless anticipation of a day of fishing. Too many disappointments, maybe.

I don't know what woke me up this time. Maybe it was nerves. Maybe it was the thought that I was going to fish the same water where Nate had landed a fifty-six-pound striper. Maybe it was fear of over-sleeping and losing my bet with Billy. In any case, the glow-in-the-dark clock beside my bed read three-thirty and, for better or for worse, I was wide-awake.

So I got dressed, went down to the kitchen, turned on the coffeepot, and waited for it to do its job. Then I filled a thermos, went out the front door, gathered up my fishing gear, got my flashlight turned on, and headed to the beach.

A sandy path ran from the back of the Fairchild house through a patch of woods and across the meadow to the dirt road that led down to the water. It was a dark night, no moon or stars, and my flash-light beam cut a narrow tunnel in the blackness. The wind was up, and the air was saturated with mois-ture that wasn't quite yet rain but felt like it soon would be.

I'd promised J.W. I'd wait for him at the fork in the road. He was worried about encountering Nate. But Nate didn't scare me. I figured that all his bluster and hostility were his macho way of covering his actual feelings. The man just loved his mother and loved his land and loved his solitude. Nothing wrong with any of that.

Besides, he thought I was a tough Marine.

J.W. wouldn't be here for a while. So I headed to the water. About halfway down the long slope I passed the old tumbledown stone hut. I stopped and shone my flashlight over it. Empty windows, caved-in roof, vines, and scrubby bushes growing over it. It looked deserted and lifeless and spooky.

I continued down to the beach. The wind was sharper down there. Fly casting would be difficult, as the wind would be blowing against my right shoulder. Out in the darkness, I could hear the surf crashing over a sandbar and against some rocks. The tide, I recalled, had turned barely an hour earlier. It would be coming in, filling the cove, crawling up over the sand, rising over the rocks, and, I hoped, drawing in schools of bait with hordes of marauding predatory fish right behind them. The wind was right, the tide was right, the time was right.

And here I was, in the right place.

I rigged up by flashlight. I tested my knots and honed the points of my hooks. If I encountered a fish to rival Nate's, I might not land it. But I didn't want to lose it because I'd failed to take sensible precautions.

By the time I'd pulled my waders on, the moisture in the air had, indeed, turned into a steady, misty, cold rain. First light on this morning would not come in a great burst of brilliance. It would be a slow, almost imperceptible evaporation of the darkness.

I waded out to my hips and began casting. Fly casting in the dark is never easy. I like to see the water, see where my fly hits, see the line as I throw it back over my shoulder and then as it unfurls on my forward cast. Casting in the dark—even without wind—makes me feel awkward and amateurish.

Tonight, with the wind quartering in against the front of my casting shoulder, it was doubly difficult.

Short casts, I kept telling myself. Keep your rhythm. Don't force it.

Easy to say.

Easy to forget.

There was, I remembered, a drop-off out there in front of me. Just where the bass would be lurking at this tide. So I lengthened my line to try to reach it.

But I was fighting the wind, and when I tried to give my forward cast an extra oomph, I did what I've done a hundred times. I lost control of my line, which wrapped itself around my neck and snagged my fly on my waders.

Blame the wind. Blame the darkness. Blame my sloppy casting. It didn't matter. I'd made a mess.

I was glad J.W. hadn't yet arrived to witness it. As it was, he already gave me too much shit about the ineffectual and effete art of fly casting.

I backed out of the water and turned on my flashlight to assess the damages. My fly had embedded itself up to the bend in my neoprene waders just below my left buttock, and my line was tangled around my shoulders and torso and both my legs, and rainwater was seeping down the back of my neck.

This was my punishment for trying to get the jump on J.W. I should've waited for him.

I found my thermos where I'd left it on the sand and shuffled up to the stone hut, carrying my rod and thermos and dragging my fly line behind me. I could escape the rain inside the hut, wiggle out of my waders, get myself untangled, and sip some coffee while I waited for J.W. I'd pretend I had just arrived. What he didn't know he couldn't tease me about.

Two wooden steps led up to a rickety porch that spanned the front of the hut. I could imagine the time half a century ago when gentlemanly surf casters and duck hunters sat in rocking chairs here, their feet up on the railing, a glass of single malt in their hands, gazing out over the ocean and telling each other stories about the good old days.

Now a thick oak door hung half off its hinges, and there was rotting wood planking on the porch floor. I shone the light inside. I wondered what kinds of critters had taken up residence in there. Swallows and owls probably built nests up in the eaves, and skunks and mice and lizards and snakes. . . .

Once upon a time there had been a solid wood floor inside, but now some of the floorboards had grown soft with rot. There was a big wooden table, several wooden chairs, a soot-blackened old wood-stove, and a big soapstone sink hanging off one wall.

I stepped inside. Despite a few holes in the roof, it was comparatively dry in there. I shone my flashlight around the inside. No glittery eyes stared back at me. There was some junk scattered around, evidence that trespassers had used the place. Beer cans, old newspapers, odd items of old clothing, rusty hunks of iron, and the sour smell of some animal that had crawled inside to die. About what one would expect.

I laid my flashlight on the seat of one of the chairs and adjusted it so I could see what I was doing. Then I leaned my rod against the table and started to slither out of my waders.

I had them down around my hips when something hard and heavy crashed against the back of my neck.

What the hell?

My first thought was that a beam had fallen from the roof. The force of the blow slammed me face-down on the floor. Pain zipped into my eyes and explosions ricocheted around inside my skull.

I tried to push myself up. I couldn't. I had no strength. My arms wouldn't cooperate. They felt numb.

The rational part of my brain whispered the word "paralyzed."

A blow to the back of the neck, right where those exposed and vulnerable little knuckles of vertebrae pushed against the skin—one good whack in just the right place, and it's Hello, wheelchair.

Before I could further analyze my prognosis or survey the condition of my extremities, something heavy rammed into the small of my back and stayed there, pinning me to the floor. It took me a moment to realize it was a man—or a woman, for all I knew—kneeling on me. I heard him breathing through his mouth, a little breathlessly, and I felt his hand, rough on the back of my head, pushing my face onto the floor.

"Hey," I tried to yell.

It came out as a muffled grunt.

He didn't say a word. He was kneeling on me, gripping my right shoulder, and then I felt a sudden sharp pain high on the back of my arm, and then a kind of thickening feeling in the muscle.

A needle! The bastard had stuck a needle in me, and he was pumping something into me.

I could almost follow the course of the drug as it entered my bloodstream and seeped into my brain. I waited, but nothing was happening. He kept his weight on my back, and I couldn't move. And gradually I realized I didn't have the will to move. I was quite happy lying there with that weight on me. It wasn't an unpleasant weight, in fact. It didn't hurt. Nothing hurt, and I didn't care if I moved or not, didn't care about anything, oh no, everything was just fine, wonderful, actually, and then I was spinning, down, down, down a long, spiraling tunnel, black and bottomless and peaceful and utterly silent.

Chapter Twenty-one

J.W.

The wind was blowing the rain into my eyes, but there was no doubt about it. There was a human head out there, with the wind-driven waves of the rising tide slapping at its face.

"Nate!" I yelled. "Somebody's out there on the rocks!"

I put my rod on the beach and stripped off my utility belt and waders.

"That's crazy," said Nate's voice.

I threw a look at him. He was keeping his eyes on his line as he reeled in. "I mean it, Nate," I said. "Somebody's out there and he's in trouble if he's still alive. I'm going out there."

The wind and rain were cold as I waded out along the sandbar. I felt the pressure of the east-flowing tide. It was as though it possessed a malignant will to push me into deeper water and wash me away toward Woods Hole. By the time I was halfway to the rocks, the water was deep enough to have filled my waders had I still been wearing them. To keep myself from being carried off the sandbar, I stroked with both hands like a swimmer.

I was on my tiptoes, and was sure I was losing my battle against the tide, when suddenly the sandbar was higher and firmer beneath my feet, and I was able to reach the rocks.

I was frightened and irked at the idiot who had gotten himself out here alone in the middle of the night, and now had gotten me in trouble, too. He was on the far side of a large boulder, and I worked my way around it, pushing against the waves and tide.

Jesus! It was Brady.

His eyes were shut and his face was white. I couldn't tell if he was dead or alive. I got an arm under him but couldn't lift him above the slapping waves. Somehow he'd managed to get himself tangled against the rocks with his own line. My fish knife was on the belt I'd left on the beach, but I had my pocketknife. I dug it out, opened it, reached down into the water, found the line, and blindly began cutting it. There were more loops than should have been possible, but I kept at it, and the moment came when Brady's body was suddenly loose.

I grabbed at him and lifted him higher. He weighed a ton.

I put a finger to his neck and felt a pulse. I got an arm around him and felt the push of the tide against the two of us. I'd never be able to get him back to shore.

"Nate!" I yelled. "It's Brady Coyne. He's hurt, and I can't get us back. Help us."

In the rising light I could see Nate stare out at us, then suddenly lope nearer. He wiped rain from his face and looked again, then shouted, "I see you. Can you hold on for a minute?"

I held Brady with one arm, got the other around a rock, and shouted, "Yeah, but I don't know how long."

"Hang on." He turned and ran down the beach toward our trucks.

I looked at Brady's face. His eyes were open. They were blank and unfocused, but they were open. I felt a rush of hope, and forced the fatigue from my arms.

Nate came lumbering back, carrying a coil of rope. He put the rope on the sand, cut the lure from his fishing line, and attached something in its place. "Catch this," he shouted and made his cast.

The line came over my head, and I let go of the rock and grabbed it. He'd made a perfect cast with a three-ounce sinker. The tide shoved against us, nearly carrying me off my feet, and I grabbed again at the rock.

On shore, Nate cut his line and tied his end of it to the rope. "Haul out, Jackson, and I'll pull you in."

I badly needed another two hands. Lacking them, I took a deep breath, then quickly let go of the rock, put the sinker in my mouth, ducked down, got both arms around Brady's body, and hoisted him as high as I could.

The tide washed hard against us, but as Brady's body rose in the water, his weight gave me the traction I needed to lift him partially atop the rock. I climbed up there with him and pulled the rope across as Nate fed it to us from the beach.

"Make it fast around both of you," yelled Nate.

"You sure you can pull us both in?"

"Hell, I've caught bass bigger than the two of you combined. Now tie that rope around you, and let me get you in here."

I tied the rope, then slid the two of us back into the water. The tide immediately swept us east. I was too cold and tired to be afraid. I hung on to Brady with one arm and swam with the other, and we arced toward the shore as Nate pulled us steadily toward safety.

Then there was sand beneath my feet, and Nate was there in the water, dragging us both ashore. I was so tired I could barely move.

"You two are a sorry-looking pair," said Nate, untying the rope. "You okay?"

"I'm okay."

Nate got on his knees beside Brady. "Well, well. Looks like your lawyer friend must have slipped out there and banged his head." He brought a bloody hand from the back of Brady's neck. "Damned fool should never have gone out to those rocks. Not with the tide coming in." He glanced inland. "He's probably suffering from hypothermia. We better get him up to the cottage out of the wind and rain. Then we should get a doctor to look at him. He may have a concussion."

I climbed to my feet, and the two of us half-carried, half-dragged Brady up to the cottage. Inside, we found rotted floorboards supporting a battered table, a couple of chairs, empty beer cans, a pile of what had once been clothing, and other clutter.

"Let's get him onto the table," said Nate. "We can use those rags to rub him dry after we get him out of these waders."

Brady's close-fitting neoprene waders had, in fact, kept him fairly dry below the waist. We stripped them off and then got rid of his wet shirt and rubbed him dry. By the time we had gotten a ragged, smelly, moth-eaten shirt on him, his eyes were again open, this time with more life in them.

We transferred him to a chair.

"Look at this. Just what we need." Nate had found a thermos. "Coffee's still hot."

I recognized the container. "That's Brady's. He must have been up here before he went out to the rocks."

"Let's get some of it inside him. That ought to perk him up."

We got him to swallow some coffee, and a bit of color came back to his face.

"Brady?" I put my face close to his. "Brady, can you hear me?"

He seemed to think that over, then, in a faraway voice, he said, "Needle."

I felt happy. Brady might not be coherent, but apparently he could hear. "You're going to be okay."

"Can't cast worth a damn," said Brady.

"Sure you can," I said. "You'll be back on your feet in no time."

"Hooked in the ass," said Brady. "Too much wind."

"He's out of his head," said Nate. "We'd better get him up to the house and call a doc."

"Needle," said Brady. He sounded irritated.

"Don't worry about the needle," I said. "There's no needle here."

"Haystack," said Brady. "Hooked in the haystack."

"He's got his needles and his hooks mixed up," said

Nate. "Come on, let's get him up to the house."

"Give him a couple more minutes." I looked at Nate. "You know what you've done, don't you? You saved both our lives."

He tried to put fierceness in his face. "It don't mean nothing. I'd have done the same for a dog."

"There's an old Chinese saying that if you save someone's life, you have to take care of him forever. I'm afraid you're stuck with that job."

"Damned if I am."

I put out my hand. "Thanks, Nate. I owe you my life."

"You don't owe me nothing."

I left my hand out. He glared at it, then gave it a quick, rough shake. "Damn it all to hell," he said. "This don't mean we're pals, you know."

"You may not be my pal," I said, "but you can count on me to be yours when you need one. And Brady will tell you the same."

"I don't need no goddamned Boston lawyer for a pal. Nor you either, J. W. Jackson."

"Well, you've got us whether you want us or not, Nate. How are you feeling, Brady?"

"Needle," mumbled Brady.

Nate looked around the room. "That's the third time he's said that. What in hell's he raving about? We supposed to look for some needle?"

I put a hand on Brady's forehead. He seemed warmer than he had been when we'd first gotten to the cottage. "He's about ready for the trip up to the house," I said to Nate.

"Finding a needle in this mess would be like finding it in a damned haystack," growled Nate.

"There's no needle," I said. "Brady's not really conscious. He doesn't know what he's saying."

"I ain't been in here for a while," said Nate as if he hadn't heard me. "Place is gone to hell." He went through a door into an adjoining room.

Brady seemed comfortable enough where he was, and I was curious about the cottage, so I followed. The next room was even messier than the first, although the floor was in better shape. There were old bunk beds against the far wall. Their rotting mattresses were black with mouse dung and covered with litter.

"There's a cellar back this way," said Nate, going through another doorway.

I kicked aside an empty whiskey bottle.

A moment later Nate was back. "Damnedest thing," he said. "There's a padlock on the cellar door. Now, who the hell would put a lock back there?"

"Somebody who doesn't want other people in the cellar, I guess."

"Yeah. But why? No matter. I got a sledgehammer that'll solve that little mystery." Nate glared back toward the offending cellar, then irritably opened the sagging door of a closet and peered inside.

"Any needles in there?" I asked.

"Coyne's out of his head," said Nate sourly. "There ain't no needles here or anyplace else. He banged his head on the rocks and now he's dreaming his own private dreams." He pushed the door shut. "Let's get him up to the house. This place stinks."

He was right about the smell. Dirt, rot, mouse

droppings, and other foul odors permeated the whole cottage. I remembered reading somewhere that after Edward II was taken prisoner, his captors in Berkeley Castle tried to kill him with poisonous fumes from a pit where they threw dead animals. Edward didn't die, so they resorted to even less pleasant means to get the job done. I didn't think the smells in the cottage would kill Brady, either, but they weren't making our stay pleasant.

"I'll get the Land Cruiser," I said. "We can take him up in that."

Nate nodded, although he looked big enough to carry both Brady and me to the top of Everest if he wanted to.

Chapter Twenty-two

Brady

I don't think I ever entirely lost consciousness after that needle rammed into my arm. The drug seeped into my brain and then gradually spread its pleasant numbness through my limbs, and I felt as if I were resting on a warm, feathery bed, or perhaps a bed of clouds, surrounded by a liquid, incredibly soothing darkness.

I thought, Isn't this nice!

I didn't have a care in the world. Whatever happened would be just peachy with me.

Jumbled thoughts, fragmented memories . . .

Arms under mine, helping me to my feet. Nice man. Helping me up. Whispering to me. "Brady." He calls me Brady.

What's your name? I like you.

I want to cooperate. My feet. They are down there somewhere. Miles away. They're not mine. Pretty funny. I laugh, I think. Somebody else's feet way out there on the end of my legs? That's funny.

My legs don't work. I talk to them. Come on, legs. But they don't listen to me. That's how it is with legs.

They never listen to you. They just do their own silly thing. Funny old legs.

We're outside. Wet. Dark. I can see that. I can see the black. Can you see black? I can. It's a color all its own, full of texture.

He's got his arm around my back, holding me up, helping me down to the beach. I can hear the ocean. It's crashing, crashing. A beautiful, wet sound. A million drops of water bumping into each other. I can hear each individual drop as it collides with all the others.

Time? I don't know. Hours? Minutes? Maybe a week. We're in the water. No. I'm in the water. Very comfortable indeed. Yes, indeed. Sitting, now, leaning back. Very comfortable. Beautiful.

Bright light in my eyes. "Relax," says the nice man. "Take it easy, Brady. Everything's going to be wonderful."

Brady. That's me. Who are you? Who is this nice man? I can't see his face. Maybe he's a girl. But he's nice.

I'm relaxed. Just as relaxed as I can be. Nobody could be more relaxed. I'm the most relaxed person in the universe.

I want to tell this nice man how great everything is, but I don't think the words actually come out of my mouth. But so what? It doesn't matter. Nothing matters.

He's gone and I'm alone and it's peaceful and dark and liquid again, and I'm surrounded by crashing and sloshing and water. Water all around. Water drops bumping into each other. A symphony.

I miss my friend. Where is he? That nice man.
Very comfortable, thank you.
What a beautiful world. Couldn't be better.

J.W. helped me sit up. He was holding a cup to my lips, urging me to drink. Images were whirling around in my brain, scattered and disconnected and elusive. I tried to slow them down and get a fix on them one at a time, but I didn't seem to have the energy for it.

I was very cold. Mostly, I just wanted to sleep.

But J.W. wouldn't let me sleep. He kept talking to me and making me sip the coffee. I remembered getting hit on the back of the neck, something suddenly pricking my arm.

A needle. That's what it was.

And J.W. was telling me how he saw me out there in the water, only my head sticking up. He thought I was dead.

So did I. But I didn't care.

Nate was there. Scowling Nate. Good old Nate.

They saved my life. Okay. Thanks, I guess. It didn't much matter.

The coffee was hot. It scalded its way down to my stomach. It made a fiery spot in my stomach, like a hot marble.

The rest of me was cold.

My brain was numb.

I just wanted to go back to sleep.

When I opened my eyes, the colors were so vivid and

the light was so bright that I closed them again. I tried to shift my position, and pain zipped down my left arm. I groaned.

I felt something warm and soft on my face. I opened my eyes again. Eliza. She was bending close to me. Her hand was touching my cheek.

"Are you awake?" she said.

I narrowed my eyes, and the light didn't hurt so much. "I guess so," I said.

"How do you feel?"

"I don't know. My arm hurts. So's my head. What happened?"

"Nate and J.W. saved your life. You were wading out among the rocks in the dark. It was windy and the surf was high and the tide was coming in, and you got tangled in your line and fell and hit your head, and those guys came along just in the nick of time. Another fifteen minutes and the tide would've covered you over."

I tried to shake my head, and an arrow of pain jabbed into my neck. "That's not what happened," I said.

"Nate said you had some weird story about somebody hitting you and sticking a needle into you and then dragging you out into the water and leaving you to drown."

"That's what happened, I think," I said. "I sorta remember something like that. It's very fuzzy." I realized I was in bed, covered by blankets. "Did they bring me home?"

She smiled. "Yes, they did. I've called a doctor. He

should be here pretty soon." She laid the back of her hand against my forehead. "Can I get you something?"

"Sleepy," I said.

Her face came close to mine. I closed my eyes, and I felt her lips brush my eyelids. "It's okay," she whispered. "Sleep. Eliza is here."

I guess I slept some more.

Then somebody was prying my eyelids open and shining a light into them. A deep man's voice was saying, ". . . morphine would be my guess."

The light went away, and I blinked. He had sparse white hair and round, rosy cheeks. Santa Claus without his beard.

"How're you feeling?" he said.

"Sleepy, mainly."

"What about pain?"

I shifted my shoulders. "In my neck and arm, a little. Darts of pain. Sort of numb in my fingers."

He nodded. "Ever have a cervical injury? Whiplash?"

I thought for a minute. "Yeah. Several years ago."

He nodded. "Can you tell me what happened this morning?"

"Somebody hit me on the back of the neck and stuck a needle into me." I tried to rotate my head. It hurt, and I groaned.

"It's that old injury flaring up. You'll be fine." He cleared his throat. "That needle. You were drugged. Did you know that?"

"Vaguely."

"It's about worn off. We figure it happened eight or ten hours ago."

"What time is it?"

He glanced at his wristwatch. "A little after three in the afternoon."

"What day?"

He smiled. "Friday."

"I've been asleep all this time?"

"Drugged, Mr. Coyne. You had a close call. You nearly drowned, and you were hypothermic. Eliza, here, has been taking good care of you."

"I'm okay, though?"

"Yep. You'll probably be sleepy and a bit disoriented for another day or so, and you may never remember what happened very clearly. But otherwise, you're going to be fine." He turned to Eliza, who was standing beside the bed smiling down at me. "Hot liquids for a while. He might have trouble keeping down his food, so nothing spicy. Chicken noodle soup, tea, like that. You know how to reach me if you need to. But I don't think there'll be any complications."

She nodded.

He turned to me. "I'll notify the police."

I shrugged and closed my eyes.

The next time I woke up, I felt stiff and achy and a bit more clearheaded. I lay there in the darkness thinking about what had happened, and for the first time, I realized that someone had tried to kill me.

I pondered the two most obvious questions— who? and why?—without much luck.

After a while, my door creaked open, and Eliza was standing there in the doorway, silhouetted against the light in the hallway. She was wearing something transparent. Backlit as she was, it revealed the womanly shape of her body.

"Are you awake?" she whispered.

"Come on in."

The silk of her gown hissed in the darkness. She left the door open a crack. The light from the hallway lit up the wall beside me, leaving the rest of the room dim.

Eliza sat on the edge of the bed. "The police were here," she said. "I sent them away. They'll be back tomorrow." She smelled clean. I reached up and felt her hair. It was damp.

She touched my face. "How are you feeling now?"

"Worse," I said. "Which means I'm better, I guess. Less fuzzy. More achy. It feels as if I'm battered and bruised all over."

"The drug's worn off," she said. "Can I get you something? Soup? Hot tea?"

"I don't know. I'm not sure I could stomach anything just now." I tried to hitch myself into a sitting position. It hurt all over to move, and I grunted with the effort.

"I've got an idea," said Eliza. "How about a nice back rub?"

"A nice back rub sounds . . . nice."

She got off the bed. "You've got to roll over," she said.

I did. It hurt.

I bunched a pillow under my face, and I felt Eliza strip the sheet and blankets off me.

I was wearing a pair of boxer shorts and a T-shirt.

She tugged at the shirt and helped me get it off. Then she slid my shorts off.

I felt her hands on me. She'd squeezed some kind of warm lotion on to them, and they moved over my shoulders and neck, softly at first, then more firmly. Her fingers poked and massaged the knots of muscle, and I groaned.

"Am I hurting you?" she said softly.

"It feels great."

After a minute, she said, "This is awkward for me." I felt her weight on the bed, and then she was straddling me, sitting lightly on the backs of my thighs, and I know I wasn't mistaken—she was wearing nothing under that gown, and she'd hitched it up around her hips.

Her warm, slippery hands were moving in circles over my shoulders, tracing my spine, pushing back up along my sides. She was bending over me, her bare thighs clamped against mine, and I could feel her hair brushing my back as she reached up to massage the muscles in my neck.

I realized I was responding to her.

"Jesus, Eliza," I whispered. "You're—"

At that moment, the room was suddenly filled with light. I opened my eyes, turned my head, and looked at the doorway. A man's shape was silhouetted there.

"What the hell do you think you're doing?" It was Patrick.

"I'm just giving poor Brady a back rub," said Eliza.

"Like hell you are," he said. "You're fucking him."

"No, I'm not, honey," she said.

Patrick came into the room, grabbed Eliza's arm, and yanked her off me.

She tumbled off the bed and onto the floor.

Patrick loomed over her. "You're a whore," he growled. "You've always been a whore."

Eliza pushed herself to her feet. She stood there for a moment, facing him. Then she reached out a hand to him.

He slapped it away. "Don't try that," he said.

"Oh, baby," murmured Eliza. "Be nice to Mommy." She stepped closer to him and reached out her hand again. "Come on, baby boy. Mommy loves you best."

This time, Patrick did not slap her hand away. Eliza took his hand, and Patrick just stood there. She lifted his hand to her mouth, kissed his palm, and then slowly lowered it to her breast.

Patrick stood there motionless. Eliza was pressing his hand against her breast, smiling up at him, and Patrick's eyes were closed. She slid closer to him. He didn't move. She leaned her body against his, and I could see her hips moving rhythmically against him.

Patrick moaned softly.

Eliza lifted her hand to the back of her son's neck and guided his mouth down to hers, and it was a long, deep, openmouthed kiss.

I was transfixed.

I was horrified.

Suddenly, Patrick shoved her away from him. She fell against the bed and crumpled onto the floor.

He stood over her. His face was twisted, and his

fists were clenching and unclenching. "Whore," he whispered.

Then he reached down, grabbed her arm, hauled her to her feet, and backhanded her on the side of her head, sending her toppling backward.

"Hey!" I said.

Patrick ignored me. He went after Eliza, grabbed her hair, and yanked her onto her feet again. She fell against him and tried to hug him. She was moaning and crying. "Baby boy . . . Mommy loves you . . . be nice to Mommy . . . Mommy will keep you safe . . ."

Patrick swatted her away, and again she toppled down. Then he bent down and grabbed her throat in both hands and began throttling her. Eliza's eyes bulged and her face was turning red and she was making gurgling noises in her throat.

"Patrick," I said. "Jesus! Cut it out."

He ignored me.

I scrambled out of the bed. A shaft of pain zinged up into the center of my brain, and I staggered, momentarily dizzy. Then I righted myself and went after Patrick. I grabbed his shoulder. He shoved Eliza away, turned, and punched me on the point of my chin.

Lights exploded in my head, and I stumbled backward, crashed against the wall, and slumped down.

I blinked. The room was spinning. Vaguely, I saw Patrick go back after Eliza. He knelt down, grabbed her throat, and started banging her head against the floor. It seemed to be happening in slow motion, and I couldn't move, could only watch Patrick Fairchild kill his mother. . . .

And then I heard a growl, saw a fast shadowy movement in the doorway, and in an instant Nate had his forearm around Patrick's throat. He hauled him off Eliza and clubbed him on the side of the head. Patrick crashed against the wall, and Nate went after him, picked him up by the front of his shirt, and clubbed him again, and Eliza was screaming and Patrick was slumped on the floor, moaning, and Nate was cursing, going after him again, and then Eliza threw herself onto Nate's back and wrapped her arms around his throat. She was crying. Tears were streaming down her cheeks. "Leave my baby alone," she kept saying. "Don't hurt him. Don't hurt my little boy."

And then, abruptly, it was over. Nate shrugged his sister off his back, nodded a couple of times, sighed, and sat down on the edge of my bed. Eliza knelt beside Patrick. She bent close to him, stroked his face, kissed his eyelids, whispered to him.

Nate's big chest was heaving, and his face was wet with sweat. He looked at me, shook his head, and muttered, "Jesus Christ." Then he narrowed his eyes. "You okay?"

I nodded. "You better call the police."

"Police?" Nate shook his head. "This is family business, Mr. Lawyer."

"He was trying to kill her," I said.

Nate laughed quickly. "Not hardly."

I looked over to where Eliza was tending to Patrick. She was helping him to his feet. He staggered for a moment and put his arm on Eliza's shoulder for support. He looked at me and Nate, nodded to each of us as if he were seeing us for the first time, and gave us a quick, apologetic smile.

Then he looked at Eliza and shook his head sadly. "'Frailty,'" he said, "'thy name is woman.'" Then he walked out of the room.

Chapter Twenty-three

J.W.

I got the old Land Cruiser into four-wheel drive and slithered through the rain up the slope to the cottage. There, Nate and I loaded Brady aboard and took him up to the big house. Brady was semiconscious, articulating an occasional clear word, but mostly mumbling about things I couldn't understand. I was worried about concussion and hypothermia.

Eliza met us as we carried Brady inside. Her hand flew to her mouth and she gave a cry, but then, almost instantly, she turned cool and efficient, the way many women behave when there's no time for faint nerves. "This way. We'll get him into his bed and call the doctor. What happened?"

We got Brady to his room and told Eliza what we knew and what Brady had been saying.

"He's got needles on his brain," said Nate. "A hit on the head can make you pretty wacky."

His sister gave him an angry look. "You're an angel of sympathy, as usual. The poor man's hurt."

"I saved his ass, sister dear, which is more than you could have managed. Do something useful for a change, and call a doctor while J.W. and I get

Brady into bed. Or would you rather undress him yourself?"

"You're hateful!" Eliza stomped out of the room, and Nate and I got Brady out of his clothes and into dry briefs and a T-shirt we found in his bureau drawer. We had him tucked under the covers when Eliza came back into the room.

"The doctor is on his way." She went straight to the bed and looked down at Brady.

"Good," I said. "When he gets here, tell him everything—where we found him, how he's been mumbling, everything."

"Where you gonna be?" asked Nate.

"I'm going home to change my clothes, then I have to visit some tennis courts."

Eliza took her eyes off Brady long enough to look at me. "Tennis courts?"

"Molly Wood and another woman I've been looking for are both tennis players, and I want to find out if anybody remembers seeing them play or remembers their partners. If they do, I want to talk with the partners." I had a thought. "You play, don't you? Did you ever see Molly playing with anyone?"

Eliza lifted her chin just a bit. "I only play at the Chappaquonsett Club. I don't think Molly Wood is a member."

"No, probably not." According to the local papers, the Chappaquonsett Club had once allowed the vacationing family of the President of the United States to play there, even though they weren't members, but I doubted that they'd extend a similar invitation to a widowed visiting nurse from Scituate.

"I'll be back later," I said. "Call me if Brady takes a bad turn."

Eliza nodded, but she was already back to eyeing Brady. As I went out, I thought she had a slightly predatory look on her face.

The heater of the Land Cruiser didn't work too well, and I was wet and cold, but before going home I drove down to the beach and collected my rod and waders. I stood there in the wind and rain and looked out at the rocks. The waves now slapped above the spot where Brady's head had been not long ago. He had come within a whisker of drowning.

That thought gave me another kind of shiver as I drove home.

Zee took one look at me as I came into the house and said, "What happened?"

I told her while I stripped, and then I climbed into the shower and let the warm water wash the chill from my bones. When I came out, Zee had clean clothes laid out on the bed. I got into them.

"Maybe I should go up to the Fairchild place," said Zee, handing me a cup of coffee. "I have the day off, and Brady could probably use a nurse."

"The doctor should be there soon, and Eliza acted like she was never going to leave Brady's side again, so he should be in good hands. But I'll take the kids with me if you want to go. I'm going out again as soon as I give Dom Agganis a call." I told her about my recollection of Frankie Bannerman's remarks about Kathy playing tennis.

"It's another link between her and Molly, isn't it?" She made up her mind. "You're probably right about

292

Brady having all the help he needs, so I'll go with you. I played a little tennis when I first came down here. Maybe I can show you some courts you don't know about. You make your call, then let's take my car. It's got a heater that works."

"I don't have high hopes that we'll learn much."

"A long shot is better than no shot at all," said Zee.

So I made my telephone call, then we loaded Joshua and Diana into the backseat and, with Zee driving and me riding shotgun, we started the hunt.

There are a lot of tennis courts on Martha's Vineyard, some open to the public, some belonging to clubs, and some belonging to individual families. I couldn't guess where Kathy Bannerman had played—somewhere up-island, maybe, since that was where she'd lived—but it seemed most likely to me that both she and Molly had played on public courts and least likely that they'd played on family-owned ones, although that was always possible. At the club courts, members could bring guests. Molly and Kathy could very well have met somebody who belonged to a club and been invited to play there.

Since Molly lived in Edgartown, we started at Katama, and, with Zee as guide to the island's tennis domains, we worked our way through Edgartown.

Our big problem was quickly established. The courts were generally empty of players that rainy day, and most of the pros who had given lessons all summer were, after Labor Day, now plying their trade in warmer climes.

Still, we visited every court we knew of, on the off chance that someone useful would be there.

The Katama courts were empty. There were two rainproof women playing between the puddles at the Edgartown public courts out by the Boys' and Girls' Club, but neither of them recognized Molly Wood or Kathy Bannerman when I showed them their pictures. Neither did the groundskeepers at the Edgartown Yacht Club courts. There were some family-owned courts in town, but not one of them was being used as we drove by.

Next we headed for Oak Bluffs. "Your forehead is wrinkled," Zee said. "What are you thinking about?"

I unwrinkled. "I'm trying to remember something, and can't. And when I'm not doing that, I'm thinking about everything else. Molly going missing, the tennis link, if there really is one, Brady almost drowning, Myrtle Eldridge's drug-using friends, your slashed tire, the note. Everything. The problem is, all my thinking is doing no good for me or anybody else."

"I've been thinking about Molly's black bag," said Zee.

"It could be anywhere," I said. "In fact, it's not a bad bet that one of the local druggies is involved with Molly's disappearance. That black bag would have looked like a gift from the gods to him. Did Molly ever talk to you about any addicts she may have met while she's been down here?"

"No, but I see a lot of the local users when I'm working in the ER. They're a pretty forlorn bunch. I don't think any of them would kill someone."

"Anybody will kill under the right circumstances."

"I don't believe that. What about Gandhi? What about Jesus?"

Jesus had been pretty rough on those moneylenders, I thought. "Neither of them was a drug addict, as far as I know," I said. "Anyway, the cops can investigate the drug users and pushers. They already know who they are and where they live."

We drove along the road with Sengekontacket on our left and Nantucket Sound on our right. The rain was beginning to let up, and there was brighter sky over above Cape Cod. The morning was reaching toward noon.

The Oak Bluffs public courts were empty, and Molly Wood and Kathy Bannerman were unknown to anyone at Farm Neck or at the other private courts where we found players. My voyage of discovery was a trip to nowhere.

"Pa."

"I know. You're hungry. Okay, we'll stop and have lunch."

"Oh, good! Can we have ice cream afterward?"

"Sure."

Small arms circled my neck from behind. "Thanks, Pa."

"Hey," said Zee. "Don't I get any hugs?"

She got two.

We ate beside Oak Bluffs Harbor and looked at the boats. The lovely little Folk Boat that I always admired was out there on her mooring. Several Folk Boats have circumnavigated the world, usually piloted by single-handers. Once I'd given thought to making such a trip, but I'd never gotten around to it. Now my mind was on other things.

We got ice cream, then climbed back into the Jeep.

It was after one in the afternoon.

"You three don't have to keep this up," I said. "We can go home and I'll keep going alone, if you'd rather."

"We wouldn't rather," said Zee. "We still have four towns to go, and we have nothing better to do. Besides, we can go by the Fairchild place and see Brady when we start looking around up-island."

In Vineyard Haven, we visited several courts in vain. Eventually we came to the Chappaquonsett Club courts, out toward the entrance to Lake Tashmoo, where some people were working in the office and on the grounds. One of the people in the office was an athletic man in whites who identified himself as the club pro.

"You're just the guy we're looking for," I said, digging my photos out of my pocket.

"Your timing is right." He grinned. "This is my last day here. Tomorrow I'll be in Atlantic City for the fall season."

I handed him the photos. "You ever see these women playing here?"

He looked first at Molly's picture, but Eliza had been right about Molly not being a member of the Chappaquonsett Club. And she'd apparently not been a guest either, because the pro never hesitated. "Nope. Never saw her in my life."

He looked at Kathy's photo and shook his head again. "A year ago, you say? Well, maybe she was here a year ago, but if she was, I don't remember her. Sorry."

We thanked him and drove away.

"I don't know about this plan," I said. The afternoon was wearing on, and we were no wiser than we'd been when we'd left the house that morning.

"There's a place out near Mink Meadows," said Zee. "I played out there a couple of times. It's a private club, but nonmembers can play for a price." She found Franklin Street and headed north.

There were a lot of places on Martha's Vineyard where I'd never been, and this tennis club was one of them. It was tucked back in the trees at the end of a narrow, sandy road. You'd never have known it was there unless you knew it was there.

There was a handsome young man alone in the clubhouse. He gave me a very friendly smile. "Hi," he said.

"Maybe you can help me," I said.

"I certainly hope so. My name's Larry. I'm the club pro."

"I'm J. W. Jackson." I glanced at Zee. She was standing off to one side smiling a wide, amused smile. I showed Larry Molly's photograph. "Have you seen this woman? She plays tennis."

His hand touched mine as he took the photo. "Why, yes," he said. "I certainly have."

"Was she here with a partner?"

"Yes, indeed."

"When did you last see her?"

"I don't know. Five or six days ago, maybe. She was here more than once."

"Was she with a man?"

He smiled a perfect white-toothed smile. "She certainly was. She has hair like the sun. Looked natural, too. They came together. He's the reason I remember

297

her, in fact. He's a handsome fellow. On the other hand, he apparently prefers good-looking, fortyish blonde ladies. Worse luck, darn it." He returned my photo.

"Do you know the man's name?" I asked, tucking the photo back in my pocket.

"No, but I wish I did. He's in his late twenties, early thirties, I'd say, and he has a sort of semi-Southern accent. You know, one of those accents a Northerner gets when he moves South and then comes back North again. I've heard him talking about golf and his beach and about Hilton Head. I was inspired to think I might go down there this winter and see if I can find some work." He tilted his head to one side and smiled. "What would you advise?"

"I've never been to Hilton Head," I said, "but if you decide to go down there, I'll bet things will work out for you. You said the man apparently likes forty-ish blonde women. What do you mean?"

"I've seen him before. He plays here every year."

I felt a little rush of excitement and handed him the photo of Kathy Bannerman. "This woman was on the island last year. Do you remember her?"

"Sure," said Larry. "He brought her here several times. How could I forget?"

I was suddenly aware of the clean smell of him. "Is that Enchanté that you're wearing?"

He smiled. "Yes, it is. Do you like it?" He leaned forward so I could sniff.

"It's very nice, but not my style, I'm afraid."

"Too bad. Say, I'll be back up here again next summer. Do you play?"

"No, I don't." I nodded toward Zee. "But my wife does. Maybe you can give her lessons."

"I'd love to." He smiled at Zee almost as broadly as she was smiling at me.

"Is this man still around?" I asked.

"He was around a few days ago."

"If he shows up again, try to get his name. If you can't manage that, get the license-plate number of his car, and then give me a call." I scribbled my name and number on a piece of paper and gave it to him.

"What's he done, Mr. Jackson?"

"Maybe nothing. It's the women I'm interested in."

Larry sighed. "I should have known. All right, I'll give you a buzz if I see him."

The Jacksons got into the Jeep, and Zee drove west toward the Fairchild house.

"I think you're Larry's type," she said. "Maybe you should take up tennis. You need a safe sport."

"You're my type, and I believe I'll stick to fishing."

I sat back, thinking about what Larry had told me and feeling excited by the first solid link between the missing women. Both had played tennis with the same man. Dom Agganis was going to want to talk with Larry, that was for sure.

I felt good. Answers seemed not far in the future.

Zee drove fast and well over the still-damp asphalt as the setting sun broke through the clouds and painted the island with the lovely slanting light of late afternoon.

And as the light danced on the hood of the Jeep, a little memory also danced into view. When Frankie Bannerman had mentioned the man her mother was dating, she didn't remember much, but she did remember that they'd gone to his beach and played tennis.

His beach, she'd said.

And Larry had just put the same words into the blond man's mouth.

Chapter Twenty-four

Brady

Eliza combed her fingers through her hair, smoothed her gown over her hips, gave Nate and me a quick smile, and followed Patrick out of my bedroom.

Nate was standing there, his thick arms folded across his chest, staring at the doorway. He sighed, then turned to me, and a smile spread across his face. "Maybe you oughta get dressed," he said.

Eliza had undressed me for my back rub. I was sitting there on the edge of my bed, stark naked.

"Good idea," I said.

"I gotta get the hell outta here," mumbled Nate, and he turned and left.

I picked up my underwear, which Eliza had tossed onto the floor, found a clean pair of jeans and a flannel shirt, and took them across the hall to the bathroom. I still felt a bit light-headed, but aside from general stiffness in my joints and an assortment of aches and pains, I decided I was pretty much back to what passed as normal for me.

I stood under the steamy shower for a long time, letting the wet heat seep into my pores, and I thought about what I had witnessed. "Family business," Nate had called it, without a hint of irony.

I gathered from Nate's reaction that Patrick's attack on Eliza wasn't all that unusual. I remembered a few days earlier when she'd worn sunglasses to hide the discoloration around her eye.

It had looked to me as if Patrick was trying to kill her.

I decided to talk with Eliza, explain her options, offer to help her.

She'd say it was none of my business, of course. Abuse victims generally did. They blamed themselves, defended their abusers, and believed that they deserved it.

You could separate a woman from her husband or boyfriend. Dealing with a mother and her adult son would be trickier. But something should be done.

I felt less achy after my shower. I toweled myself dry, wiped the steam off the mirror, dragged a razor across my face, got dressed, and went downstairs.

I heard voices coming from the kitchen and followed them. J.W. and Zee and Diana and Joshua were all sitting around the table sipping hot chocolate. Eliza was leaning back against the counter talking with them. She had changed into a pair of blue jeans and a pink sweatshirt. She'd scrubbed her face and brushed her hair and redone her makeup, and now she was smiling and chatting as if nothing had happened.

Hell, had I imagined it? Was all that another one of those weird morphine dreams?

Then Eliza glanced over and saw me standing in the doorway, and the quick frown that passed across her face told me that what I'd seen had been real.

She arched her eyebrows and held my eyes for a moment, and I knew she was begging me not to say anything.

I nodded at her, then turned to the Jackson family. "Hi, gang," I said. "What brings you around?"

"We wanted to see how you were doing," said Zee.

"I'm okay," I said. I turned to Eliza. "That hot chocolate smells good."

"Coming right up," she said.

I sat at the table.

J.W. said, "We gotta talk."

I nodded.

"Think you could drive me home a little later?"

"Sure," I said. "I'm fine."

He glanced at his watch, then turned to Zee. "Why don't you take the kids back, honey? It's getting on to their bedtime, and Brady and I have got some business to do."

"But, Pa," said Diana.

Zee stood up. "Come on, gang. You father will be right along."

"You said you'd sleep in our tree house with us," said Joshua.

"I don't know about that," said J.W. "It might rain some more."

"But you promised . . ."

J.W. tucked his chin against his chest and gave his two kids a look that clearly said: "That's enough."

Zee kissed my cheek, then herded the kids toward the front door. J.W. said, "Be right back," and followed them.

Then I was alone in the kitchen with Eliza.

She put a mug of hot chocolate in front of me and sat down across the table. "Please don't say anything," she said.

"We need to talk."

"No," she said, "what I mean is, don't say anything to me. Just forget it, okay?"

"Eliza—"

She reached across the table and put her hand on top of mine. "Please."

I shrugged. "Where's Patrick?"

"I don't know. He went out. He's upset."

"How about you?" I said. "Are you upset?"

"I told you I didn't want to talk about it."

"Right," I said. "Sorry. Where's Nate?"

"Probably went fishing. What else does he do?"

"He saves your ass."

"Brady," said Eliza, "I mean it. Change the damn subject."

I shrugged. "Tell me how your mother's doing."

Eliza looked down at the table. "Worse. They don't know what's going to happen. I—"

At that moment, J.W. came back. He stood in the doorway. "Am I interrupting?"

Eliza stood up. "No. You two guys go ahead, talk your manly talk. The water's hot if you want some more cocoa or something. There's leftover pizza in the fridge. Help yourselves."

"Thanks," said J.W.

Eliza ran her fingers across my cheek as she walked past me. "Umm," she said. "You shaved."

When she was gone, I looked at J.W. He was grinning.

"It's not what you think," I said.

"I don't care what it is," he said. "So how are you really feeling?"

"Not that bad. Like somebody stuffed me into a giant bowling ball and rolled a few games. I was drugged, you know."

"Yeah? You really were? You were mumbling something about needles, but I figured you'd banged your head. You weren't making much sense."

"You saved my life," I said.

"Nate, actually. He saved both of us. So what happened down there?"

I told him, as best as I could recall, how I'd been hit from behind and zapped with a needle and dragged out into the water and left to drown.

"You sure you're not making that up?" he said. "Looked to us like you waded out too far, got your line tangled around your legs, fell and hit your head."

I smiled. "I admit it all feels pretty hallucinatory. But the doctor said it was morphine, so I guess it happened."

"Don't suppose you got a look at your assailant?"

I shook my head. "He surprised me, got me from behind. It was dark."

"Did he say anything?"

"Yeah, seems to me he did. But not until after he hit me with the drug. All I remember is whispering. I'd never recognize his voice."

"You sure it was a guy?"

"No, I'm not. But he—or she—dragged me out into the water. If it was a woman, she was a strong one."

"So who'd do something like that?" said J.W.

"That's the question, all right. My first thought would be Nate. He's pretty jealous of his beach."

"Then he'd turn around and save your life?"

I shrugged. "Maybe he would."

"Could've been anybody, when you think about it," said J.W. "Somebody's been hanging around that cottage. You might've surprised them."

I nodded. "Fishermen poaching on Nate's beach, or maybe teenagers, drinking beer, getting laid."

"Doubt if teenagers or stray fishermen would bother padlocking the cellar door." J.W. scratched his chin. "I want to take a look down there. But the reason I came over was I wanted to talk to you about Molly Wood."

"I thought you wanted to see how I was feeling."

"Right," he said. "That, too. But Molly's missing and you're not, so now that I see you're okay, I'm more concerned about her than you."

"So am I," I said. "What can you tell me?"

"I found out today that she's been playing tennis with a good-looking blond-haired guy. Kathy Bannerman played tennis with the same guy."

I laughed sourly. "That narrows it down to what, about five thousand men on the island?" I said. "That's good work."

He gave me a sarcastic smile. "Thanks. This might not be the bad guy. But if he dated these two women, he probably can tell us something. The fellow who saw them together thought he might've heard some mention of Hilton Head."

"That's where the Isle of Dreams Development Corporation, the people who want to buy this land, are located," I said. "Philip Fredrickson is one of their representatives. He's blond."

J.W. nodded. "There was a golf glove in Molly's car. It was made by the Mallet Company. The Isle of Dreams is a subsidiary of Mallet."

"Five thousand blond guys, five million golf gloves," I said.

J.W. nodded. "This Larry fellow I talked to said he thought he heard the blond guy mention a private beach to Molly. It sounded like they were setting up a rendezvous. Midnight swim or something."

I stared at J.W. for a minute. "Private beach," I repeated. "And you're thinking . . ."

"We were on a private beach last night," he said.

"How many private beaches are there on the island?"

"Dozens," he said. "But there's only one where you got drugged and dragged into the water and left to die." He looked around. "Where's Nate?"

I shrugged. "Eliza thought he went fishing."

"Probably right back on his beach. You and I cost him a prime tide of fishing this morning. Whatever I might've thought of Nate Fairchild, he was pretty damned heroic. I think I'll mosey along down there, talk to Nate, now that we're on speaking terms. He spends a lot of time on that beach. Maybe he's seen something."

"I'll come with you," I said.

J.W. waved his hand. "You sit tight. I don't want to be slowed down by some invalid just out of a sickbed. I can take care of this myself."

"Christ," I said. "I'm fine. Let's go." I shoved myself back from the table and stood up . . . and a sudden wave of dizziness and nausea forced me to grab the back of the chair for balance. I sat back down.

"Yep," said J.W. "You're fine, all right." He stood up. "You take it easy. I won't be long. You can drive me home when I get back, if you're up to it."

"Give me a few minutes," I said. "I just need to get something in my stomach."

"I want to get home in time to read to the kids before bed," he said. "You just relax. You're looking a little green around the gills."

The truth was, I felt a little green around the gills. I nodded. "Okay. You go ahead. I should be okay to drive you home. If I'm not, I'm sure Eliza would be happy to."

He grinned. "You better not leave me alone with that woman."

I flashed on the scene in my bedroom. "I'd never do that," I said.

I followed J.W. to the door, and as he was leaving, I said, "Look around the cottage for a hypodermic needle, while you're there."

He nodded. "You're thinking of Molly's medical bag?"

"Yes. Visiting nurses keep needles in them."

"Well," said J.W., "that's the connection, isn't

it? Between what happened to you and Molly's disappearance?"

"Could be," I said.

After he left, I went back to the kitchen. I looked into the refrigerator, but the thought of warmed-up pizza gave my stomach a jolt, so I settled for the can of Progresso chicken soup that I found in a cabinet.

I heated it in the microwave, and while I sat at the table slurping it off my spoon, I tried to figure out why Molly Wood's abductor—or, for all we knew, her killer—would be hanging around the tumbledown stone cottage on the Fairchilds' beach at five o'clock on a rainy morning, waiting to whack me across the back of my neck and zap me in the shoulder with a syringe full of morphine and drag me into the stormy sea and leave me to drown under the rising tide.

The soup went down easily and seemed to settle comfortably in my stomach. When I finished it, I stood up from the table warily. I was pleased to observe that I felt steady and sturdy and clearheaded.

I didn't come up with any answers about Molly and needles and people who wanted to kill me, though.

I glanced at my watch. J.W. had been gone about half an hour. I decided to walk down to the beach, see what he was doing. I agreed with him. That cottage might hold some answers. Anyway, a stroll in the salty evening air would feel good.

I went upstairs, got a pack of cigarettes and a flashlight, fetched my jacket, and looked around for Eliza. She wasn't up there. When I got back downstairs, I called for her. She didn't answer, so I scribbled a note and left it on the kitchen table. "Went down to the beach," it said. "Back soon."

Then I went outside.

All the family cars were lined up in the turnaround in front—Sarah's Range Rover, which I'd been using, Nate's battered old pickup, Eliza's Saab convertible, Patrick's BMW. Warm orange lights glowed from the windows of the Fairchild family homestead.

It looked homey as hell.

Some home.

A sharp, damp breeze was blowing in off the water, but the rain had stopped and wispy clouds were skidding across the new moon. I paused on the back lawn to light a cigarette, then drew the smoke experimentally into my lungs. Ah, nicotine! I'd been a long time without a hit, and I was delighted to observe that it didn't make me feel dizzy or nauseated.

I smoked half of it, then ground it out under my heel. I didn't need the damn cigarette. I could quit any time.

Ha!

I blinked a few times until my eyes adjusted to the darkness. The sky was bright enough to illuminate the sandy pathway that wandered away from the house to the beach, so I left the flashlight in my pocket.

It was about a fifteen-minute walk to the cottage from the house, mostly downhill, but by the time I had topped the last rise and saw the cottage and the beach below me, I was a little winded.

It was the morphine, of course. Totally unrelated to cigarettes or middle age.

It was about then that I latched on to the fragment of thought that had been niggling at me.

Patrick's car was parked out front. But he wasn't in the house.

So where the hell was he?

And just about the time I asked myself that question, another pellet of insight that had been ricocheting around in my head slowed down enough for me to catch up with it.

What had he said? "'Frailty, thy name is woman.'" *Hamlet.*

The note I'd found in Molly Wood's book. That had been a quote from *Hamlet,* too.

Hamlet thought his mother was amoral.

So did Patrick.

Jesus.

I stood there, catching my breath, and as I did, mingled with the muffled crashing of the waves on the beach and the hiss of the breeze in the scrubby pines, I thought I heard voices. They seemed to be coming from the direction of the cottage, and although I didn't recognize them, I could tell they were men's voices, and they sounded angry.

I hurried down the slope and around to the front of the cottage where it faced the ocean. The voices had been coming from inside. I climbed the steps onto the rickety old porch and pulled out my flashlight. Just as I was about to flick it on, I heard a voice. The tone was calm, the way a parent might try to soothe a child who'd scraped her knee, and it echoed from somewhere deep inside the cottage.

The voice was muffled, but I could make out the words. "It's all over," he was saying. "Time to give it up."

It was J.W.

I flicked on the flashlight, and as I stepped inside, I heard a loud clanging noise, as if somebody had smashed a steel pipe against the hood of a car. Then there was a grunt and a thump and a curse and another clang.

I hurried inside, following the sounds through the front room into a center room, and from there I saw a door hanging ajar in the room beyond. It was lit a dim orange color, as if a fire was burning inside.

I went over to the doorway. It opened onto a set of crude wooden steps leading down into a cellar. The sounds of scuffling feet, grunts, and muttered curses came from down there.

I hesitated at the top of those steps, suddenly aware of a foul, putrid odor wafting up to me. My stomach lurched, and for an instant I thought I was going to puke.

I turned my head, took a deep breath through my mouth, then started down the steps.

The first thing I noticed were two men. One of them had his back to me. He held a long-handled spade-shaped shovel in both hands, and he had it cocked back like a baseball bat. The other man was J.W. He'd fallen backward and was lying on the dirt floor with his arms crossed defensively over his face.

The second thing I noticed was that awful odor. It was more foul than an open septic tank, more acrid than rotten garbage, and it made me gag.

The third thing I noticed was that some of the dirt

floor had been recently dug. There were mounds of loose dirt, several digging implements lying around, and on one of the mounds of dirt sat a kerosene lantern, casting its flickering orange light around the old cellar.

Both J.W. and the man with the shovel were caked with mud as if they'd been rolling around on the dirt floor, and as I watched, the man stepped forward, raised the shovel high over his head, and smashed it down. J.W. tried to roll away from it, but its flat side grazed off the back of his head, and J.W. groaned and pulled himself into a fetal position.

I jumped off the bottom step and grabbed the first thing my hand found. It was a pickax, the kind with one pointed end and one end shaped like a hoe. It was heavier than I expected, but then a jolt of adrenaline hit me, and I hefted it as if it were weightless and went after the guy.

He was standing over J.W., raising the shovel over his head again. J.W. was staring up at him. His eyes were glazed over and unfocused, and his breath was coming in quick, strained spurts, and his scalp was bloody.

"No!" I yelled.

The guy with the shovel whirled around and in the same motion swung that sharp-bladed shovel at my head. I managed to duck away from it. The momentum of his swing momentarily threw the guy off balance, and that's when I hit him with the pickax. I swung it up at him like a golf club, as hard as I could. He lurched right into it, and the hoe-bladed end crashed against the left side of his rib cage.

He uttered a little wet gasp, took two steps, then fell facedown on the dirt. I went over to him and lifted the pickax. I was ready to hit him again, to hit him as many times as it took, to smash in the back of his skull, to destroy him, to—

"Brady, don't!"

It was J.W. His voice was small and strangled with pain.

I hesitated, let out a long breath, and dropped the pickax. I looked at J.W. He didn't look good. I went over and knelt beside him. "You okay, man?" I said.

He blinked up at me. "Did you kill him?" he whispered.

"I don't know and I don't care. He was trying to kill you."

"Came damn close to it," he said. "But I'm okay. See if he's alive."

I went back to the guy. He was sprawled spread-eagled with his face in the dirt.

I grabbed his shoulder. He was heavy, like dead-weight, but I managed to roll him onto his back. His chest was rising and falling rapidly. The entire left side, where I'd caught him with the pickax, was wet and black with mingled blood and dirt, and his face and hair were coated with mud.

At first I didn't recognize him. A mud-stained pale green surgical mask covered his mouth and nose. But I could see that his hair was blond.

I pulled down the surgical mask, turned, and eased J.W. up to his feet. "It's Patrick Fairchild," I said, "and he's still alive. You wanna tell me what the hell happened?"

Chapter Twenty-five

J.W.

I carried a flashlight with me as I left the house and headed down toward the beach to find Nate. I didn't feel so smart about other things, particularly the blond man. At the far edges of my mind some semiformed idea about him frustrated me by refusing to take real shape. I'd had the same experience with logic problems, when I had all of the information that I needed to solve them, but was just too dense to put it together. It wasn't quite maddening, but it was irritating.

In the fading light I walked fast in the darkness along the driveway, then took the fork and headed toward the beach. I figured there might be a shorter route leading from the house down past the cottage, but I didn't know where it was and didn't want to waste any time finding it. I wanted to locate Nate and have him and his sledgehammer go with me to the cottage so I could find out what was behind that padlocked cellar door.

By the time I reached the beach, the stars were beginning to come out, and there was a moon in the eastern sky. They cast only the faintest shimmer on the dark waters of Vineyard Sound that lapped against the sands of Fairchild Cove and against the now invisible rocks where Brady had been left to drown.

Nate wasn't on the beach.

I turned and looked up toward the cottage. I could barely see it in the darkening night. I started up the hill.

The sagging porch facing the sea opened into the room where Nate and I had carried Brady. I ignored that door and walked around the building. Then I heard something and stopped, feeling that little shiver that runs through you when you're in a strange place and don't quite know what's going on. The sound seemed to be coming from inside the cottage. I flicked off my flashlight, eased around the far corner, and looked in the window. There was a sliver of orange light coming through the cellar door.

I crept around to the front of the cottage and slipped inside.

Maybe Nate and his lock-breaking sledgehammer were ahead of me.

Maybe not.

I floated to the cellar door and saw that the new padlock was unlocked. I took a breath of sickeningly foul air, pulled the door open, and started down the stairs.

Light from a kerosene lantern flooded up through the dusty air. With it came a terrible stench. The lantern sat on a mound of dirt, and then I saw a man working with a shovel. His back was to me. The sounds I'd heard were those of dirt being dug and tossed aside.

I almost gagged, and I dug my handkerchief out of a pocket. I recognized the stench. It was the smell of death. Long ago, when I'd been on the Boston PD, I'd smelled that smell when I'd been on a team that had entered an apartment where an old woman had died alone many days before.

Holding my handkerchief over my nose and mouth, I looked around for other people, but the man was alone. I went down the remaining steps to the reeking cellar floor.

I could see blond hair between the man's cap and his collar.

"Hello," I said, and he spun around. He was wearing a surgical mask over his face, but I recognized him instantly. "Patrick. What in blazes is going on?"

His eyes were bright in the lantern light.

"J.W.!" His voice was sharp. He grasped the shovel like a battle-ax.

I looked around. Almost at my feet, half covered with dirt, was a black medical bag. I knew instantly that he was digging a hole to bury it.

"Christ," I said, filled with bitter certainty. "It's you. You're the one. You killed Molly, and you tried to kill Brady. And you killed Kathy Bannerman and those other women, too." I gestured toward the awful floor. "You buried them all here."

He shook his head. "No! No, it wasn't me. It was . . . it was Nate. I used to see him come down here. I never trusted him. I tried to get in here before, but he'd locked the door. Tonight I got in and . . . and I found this. It's terrible. Terrible!" His voice was a wail.

"No," I said. "It wasn't Nate. It was you. You play

317

golf and tennis. Nate doesn't. And you use that Enchanté cologne. Nate doesn't. I remember smelling it on you. You smelled like you'd just come out of the shower. And you have that hint of the South in your voice. Nate doesn't. You're blond. You're the one. It's time to give it up. It's all over."

He crouched, wide-eyed. "Who's that with you? There, right behind you?"

It was a sucker's trick, but if there really was somebody there, I needed to know who it was. I wasn't about to turn my back on Patrick and his shovel, though, so I took a quick step to the side and gave a fast glance behind me. The quick step was a mistake. I had just enough time to see there was no one in back of me and to whip my eyes toward Patrick again, when my foot landed on Molly's medical bag. It turned beneath my weight, and I was instantly off balance.

At that moment Patrick leaped forward and swung the shovel. He didn't kill me with that first blow because the shovel hit a beam as he swung it, and the beam slowed it and turned it so the flat side, not the sharp side, hit me. I went down like the '29 stock market.

My head was ringing. The shovel went up and came down again as I rolled. But Patrick had hurried this blow, and the shovel glanced off the back of my skull. He swung again and hit me as I rolled into a depression in the floor. Trapped there, dizzy and almost blind, I tried to get my arms and legs up between me and that deadly shovel. This time Patrick was patient. He lifted the shovel. I felt fatalistic but also incredibly stupid and irritated. It seemed like a particularly dumb way to die.

Then suddenly Brady Coyne was there behind Patrick, a pickax in his hands. He shouted, "No!" and Patrick spun and swung the shovel at his head instead of mine. Brady ducked and swung the pickax and Patrick staggered and fell.

Brady's face had the look of death. He stepped toward Patrick and lifted the pickax again.

"Brady," I gasped. "Don't!"

Somehow he stopped his blow. He looked toward me and the madness went out of his eyes. He tossed the pickax aside and came to me. "You okay, man?"

I didn't have much of a voice. "Did you kill him?"

"I don't know and I don't care. He was trying to kill you."

"Came damn close to it. But I'm okay. See if he's alive."

Brady eased me up to my feet and then took a look at Patrick. "It's Patrick Fairchild, and he's still alive," he said. "You wanna tell me what the hell happened?"

I touched my head and looked at the blood on my hand. "Well, the most important thing from my point of view is that you just saved my bacon. First Nate, and now you. Zee said maybe I should take up safer sports than fishing, and maybe I should." Then I told him what had happened and what I thought, and why. I pointed to the floor. "That smell tells you something's buried down here, and he was about to add the black bag. I think he killed several women and buried them here, although I'm no shrink, so I can't explain why. All I know is that they all looked something like Molly Wood. They were all fortyish and blonde and pretty."

Brady listened as he looked at the hole Patrick had been digging and the medical bag, and then nodded. "I may have an insight about that." He described what he'd seen happen between Patrick and Eliza in his bedroom, then wrinkled his nose and said, "Let's get out of here before we die from this air."

We weren't as gentle with Patrick as we might have been, but we got him up the stairs and out onto the grass. I waited with him under the stars and moon while Brady went to the house and called the police. I wanted no more part in discovering what the cellar might reveal.

After they'd cleaned me up at the hospital, I called Zee from the state police barracks and told her I'd be late getting home. And I was, because Dom Agganis was at the crime scene and Officer Olive Otero was asking me the questions, and Olive did not go out of her way to be kind and gentle with me. Finally, however, she let me go, but only after warning me not to leave the island.

"Warning me not to leave is like warning the tide to keep rising and falling. While you're at it, maybe you should do that," I said grumpily as I went out.

At home, Zee was awake and anxious. She looked at the bandages on my head and held my face in front of hers. "Are you really all right? Don't lie."

"I am, really."

"Then let's get into bed and you can tell me everything that happened."

In bed, she wrapped her arms around me as if she thought I might slip away and do something else that was stupid and dangerous. "Talk," she said.

I did, telling her everything she didn't already know, including Brady's incest theory. "It's up to the cops and the DA from here on out," I said, "but if I'm right, they'll nail Patrick. They'll find bodies in the cellar, including Molly Wood's and Kathy Bannerman's. They'll track down people who saw Patrick with Molly, and Patrick with Kathy, and maybe Patrick with some of those other missing women just before the women disappeared. They'll have the cologne and the note Brady found at Edna Paul's place and the one you found under your windshield wiper, and they'll be in touch with the detectives down on Hilton Head about women there who may have dated Patrick and then disappeared. They'll know about Eliza chasing after every man she meets, and Patrick being crazy with jealousy. Then they'll have their shrinks dueling with his shrinks about the psychological implications of the relationship. I'd guess they'll argue that Patrick killed women like Molly, who looked like his mother, because he couldn't bring himself to kill her, which is what he really wanted to do. You can get a shrink to say anything in court."

"Spooky." She shivered.

We lay together in silence, our arms around the grief of the ages. Then Zee said, "I'm glad you're home safe." She gave me a sharp squeeze. "Don't you ever do anything dangerous again."

"I promise," I said. "Never again."

The next day, at noon, I waded out to the rocks in Fairchild Cove. It was low tide and I had my quahog rake and Buck Rogers with me. Normally I only used the peep sight during scallop season when I was dip netting, but now I used it to scan the bottom of the cove in search of other treasures. And I found them. There, not far from the rocks, lay Brady's fancy fly rod and reel. As I'd guessed, murderous but smart Patrick, when preparing Brady for his "accidental" drowning, had made sure that the fly rod would be near the body.

I raked up the rod and waded back to shore.

"Well," said Brady, when I met him at the house, "I was sure I'd never see this again."

"It's an effete, East Coast, pointy-headed little toy," I said, "but I figured that since you saved my life, the least I could do was save your fishing pole."

"You're a crude fellow, like all surf casters," said Brady. "Maybe when you finally realize that truly manly men use fly rods, I'll show you the proper way to catch fish. It may surprise you to learn that you don't have to use an eleven-foot club to do it."

"Just because you've caught more fish than I have during this Derby," I said, "you don't have to rub it in. How about supper tonight? Zee thinks she owes you a meal for coldcocking Patrick in the nick of time. Afterward, if you have more energy than I have, you can go fishing with her while I stay home with the kids."

"You're on," he said.

I drove home, thinking about the contradictions inherent in life—how brutal Nate Fairchild saved Brady and me in spite of his hatred of us; how handsome, personable Patrick, who seemingly had many blessings many people might dream of, was a mass murderer; how Brady and I, who saw ourselves as peaceful and gentle people, nevertheless had the capacity for murderous rage.

And I thought of little Diana's insistence, when she first saw it, that the stone cottage was haunted by ghosts.

Such complexities were, for some, evidence that there is no God. For others, they were the best evidence that there is.

I parked in front of our little house.

The kids came running out. "Can we sleep in the tree house tonight? It's not raining."

The sun was low in the west, but the sky was clear.

"Your mother's going fishing with Brady."

"Just you and us, then, Pa. Can we?"

Their small faces looked up into mine, bright with innocence and eagerness, green and golden in the heyday of Time's eyes.

"Sure," I said.

And that night, under the simple stars, we three slept until the sun grew round again and the world was born anew.

Chapter Twenty-six

Brady

I didn't wake up until close to noon the next day. When I staggered downstairs, I found Nate sitting at the kitchen table cradling a mug of coffee in his big hands.

He looked up at me with his eyebrows arched.

I nodded, went to the coffeepot, poured myself a mugful, and sat across from him. "You heard, huh?" I said.

"Always thought that boy was wound pretty tight," he said. "They've been digging corpses out of my cottage all morning. Place is swarming with cops. Wouldn't let me near my own beach."

"Where's Eliza?"

"Scrounging around for a lawyer for her son." Nate cocked his head at me and grinned. "Guess she doesn't trust you."

I lit a cigarette. "Tell me about Eliza and Patrick," I said.

He flapped his hands. "What's to tell? It's been her and him since his father killed himself back when he was a toddler. She dragged the boy around with her, moving here and there, resorts, fancy places, chasing one guy after another, marrying and divorcing and never settling down, always trying to live the good life. Who knows what he saw growing up? She always treated him like a baby. Hell, I'm no shrink, but I can tell you this. It's no wonder he got messed up."

"They figure he killed Molly Wood, huh?"

"Her and half a dozen others, sounds like."

"And buried them in the cellar."

Nate nodded. "He's been jumpy ever since my mother started talking about selling this place. Guess he figured whoever bought it would bulldoze the cottage and find all those bodies."

"That's why he wanted to kill me," I said. "With Sarah in the hospital, incompetent to agree to a deal herself, and me with her power of attorney, if I was out of commission, no deal would be done."

Nate shrugged. "Don't ask me. All I know is, the hospital called this morning. My mother's in a coma. She's getting worse, not better."

"I'm sorry, Nate."

"Yeah, well, she's a tough old bird, but she's had a lot of pain from the cancer, and maybe this is better." He smiled quickly. "I'm gonna miss her, I'll tell you that."

I nodded. "Me, too."

"You still planning on selling the place?"

"It's what Sarah wants," I said. "The Isle of Dreams and the Marshall Lea folks are supposed to submit their final offers tomorrow. I'll look them over and try to make a decision."

He shook his head. "Any way you can write in a little clause giving me access to my beach, at least?"

"Believe it or not," I said, "I already thought of that.

325

Of course, I'd expect you to share access with a certain visiting Boston lawyer from time to time, and also with the Jackson family."

"You're a mean son of a bitch," grumbled Nate. "Never should've hauled you out of the water. Should've let you and Jackson drift away on that tide. All my problems would've been over."

"Well," I said, "you showed your true colors yesterday morning. Far as I'm concerned, you're a hero."

He smiled. "You better not tell anybody," he said. "I got a reputation to protect."

I was refilling my mug when the doorbell rang. Nate went to answer it, and a minute later he came back. J.W. was with him, and he had my fly rod.

"Zee thinks we still owe you. She wants to take you fishing tonight, if you're up to it."

And that's when I remembered. I'd lost my bet with Billy. So what if I'd had a morphine hangover after nearly dying and then squandered an entire night saving J.W.'s life when I could have been fishing? Billy would accept no weak excuses. A bet was a bet.

"Sure," I told J.W. "I'm always up for fishing."

"Come for dinner. Supposed to be a nice night. Zee wants to try Wasque again. Tide and wind should both be right."

"Just stay the hell off my beach," said Nate.

A school of bluefish came blitzing through the rip at Wasque right at sunset, and for about an hour Zee and I and a dozen other Derby competitors caught fish as fast as we could cast into the water and haul them out.

They all ran to a size—five or six pounds—not worth entering into the competition, but as Zee pointed out, they were perfect eating size, and soon there were bluefish flopping in the sand all up and down the beach.

It ended as abruptly as it had begun, and one by one we all stopped casting.

Zee and I sat on the sand watching the water as the darkness gathered over the sea. The sky was clear and infinite, and a million stars filled it with light. They were huge balls of fire, but so distant that to us on our little, faraway planet they were mere yellow specks. Some of them had burned out eons ago, but their light was still traveling through space and time.

We talked about Molly Wood and the other blonde, middle-aged women whom Patrick had seduced, strangled, and buried in the cellar.

Zee was an emergency room nurse. She'd seen a lot of death and tragedy and craziness. But she had no philosophy for what Patrick Fairchild had done, and neither did I. She kept talking about her kids, the world she'd brought them into and her responsibility for them, and it took me a while to realize that she was really thinking of Eliza, and what she'd done to Patrick, and how so many other lives had been affected, and how Eliza had been shaped by Sarah, her own mother, and how parents and children were connected back through the generations.

And as I sat there on the Martha's Vineyard sand, I thought of my own boys, Billy out in Idaho rowing rich fly-fishing clients downriver in the summer and teaching rich people how to ski in the winter, and Joey studying law at Stanford, and I hoped I'd done okay by them.

I thought I had. But you never knew for sure.

Sarah Fairchild died that night sometime while I was sitting on the beach with Zee gazing at the stars and sharing infinite thoughts.

I spent Sunday morning with Eliza and Nate, helping them agree on arrangements for their mother's memorial service and burial. The two of them were solemn, and at one point when tears began dribbling down Eliza's cheeks, Nate put his arm around her and cried, too.

I called the representatives of both the Marshall Lea Foundation and the Isle of Dreams Development Corporation and told them that the Fairchild property was off the market, at least for the foreseeable future. When Sarah died, so did my power of attorney. Now my job was to execute her will. Once that was done, the only people authorized to sell the property would be Sarah's rightful heirs, Eliza and Nate and, depending on what happened to him, Patrick.

J.W. drove me to the ferry on Monday morning. Joshua and Diana came with us. They were bubbling about their tree house. Diana told me that she was trying to persuade her father to install a woodstove so they could live in it all winter. She invited me to be her guest next summer when I visited.

J.W. allowed as how it was pretty comfy, though they hadn't quite worked out the plumbing yet.

An hour later I was sneaking a cigarette at the stern

on the top deck of the ferry. We had chugged halfway across the sound to Woods Hole, and the island of Martha's Vineyard was a blurry green mound rising out of the sea on the horizon. It looked bountiful and peaceful, the way it must have looked to its early settlers when they first sighted it from their wooden sailing vessels. A refuge. A good place to live and raise children and grow old surrounded by people you loved.

I flipped my cigarette into the wake of the ferry, gave the Vineyard a final glance, then walked up to the front. From there I watched the mainland of America grow larger, and I turned my thoughts to my law practice, to Boston, to home.

RECIPES

Seafood St. Jacques à la J. W. Jackson

(Serves eight)

Note: This dish is most commonly cooked as Coquilles St. Jacques, which is made with scallops. Here it's made with a combination of fish or shellfish. Scallops are the classic element, of course.

1. Bring to boil: ½ pound sliced mushrooms, 4 tablespoons butter, 1 cup dry white wine, 1 minced onion, 1 bay leaf, 1 teaspoon thyme, juice of 1 lemon.
2. Simmer 3 minutes, then add 2 pounds of any combination of fish or shellfish and simmer 2 minutes more. Drain, reserving liquid.
3. Make white roux: melt 4 tablespoons butter, stir in 4 tablespoons flour, stir in 1 cup milk, then continue to stir until thickened slightly.
4. Add roux to reserved liquid and whisk until thickened. Add 1 teaspoon salt and 1 teaspoon pepper.
5. Beat 4 egg yolks and 1 cup cream or milk, then

slowly whisk egg mixture into roux. Bring up to a boil but do not boil. Sauce should coat spoon.

6. Put fish mixture in ovenproof pan, remove bay leaf, and spoon on sauce. Cover with mixture of 1 cup Parmesan cheese and 1 cup bread crumbs, and dribble with 2 tablespoons melted butter. (Note: At this point the dish may be refrigerated or frozen.)

7. Bring to room temperature if prepared in advance, bake uncovered in 350° oven until hot (20 minutes, more or less).

8. Glaze under broiler and serve with rice or potatoes.

NANA'S STEAMED PUDDING FROM J.W.

1. Sift together: 2 cups flour, 1 teaspoon cinnamon, 1 teaspoon baking powder, 1 teaspoon powdered cloves, 1 teaspoon salt.

2. Mix: 1 cup New Orleans molasses (light), 1 cup melted butter or margarine, 1 cup warm milk, 2 beaten eggs.

3. Add dry ingredients to wet in stages.

4. Add to batter: 1 cup seedless raisins (plumped in hot water, dried, and floured), 1 pint jar candied mixed fruit (floured).

5. Add 1 jigger good brandy.

6. Put in a well-greased and -floured steamer mold. Tie on lid. Place steamer mold in boiling water in a pan and cover. Water should be ⅔ of the way up the side of the mold. Steam, boiling continuously, for 2 hours. Serve with hard sauce or other sauce.

Brady's Thanksgiving Sea Duck

Sea ducks such as eiders, scoters, and old squaw (not to be confused with puddle ducks such as mallards, and nothing at all like the bland, fatty domestic duck served in restaurants) abound at the Vineyard. Sea ducks have an undeservedly bad reputation as table fare. As a result, J.W.'s duck-hunting friends like to give away what they manage to shoot. I happen to think sea ducks are delish, and J.W. and Zee agree with me. They are strong-flavored, dark-meated, and decidedly gamy, but prepared properly they're a feast. We believe a dinner of sea ducks with all the trimmings is a suitable way to remember our first settlers, who lived off the land and probably considered sea ducks delish, too.

Sea ducks should be prepared the day before you intend to serve them, as you need to marinate the meat for about 36 hours.

1. Remove the breasts including the skin and discard the rest of the ducks. One eider breast feeds two. With smaller ducks such as old squaw, figure one breast per person.
2. Slice the meat off the breasts. The slices should be about ½ inch thick.
3. Spread the breast slices in a high-sided platter and cover with milk. Cover the platter with aluminum foil and marinate in the refrigerator all day, for about 12 hours. The evening before your feast, drain off the milk, rinse the meat, pat it dry on paper towels, then cover again in fresh milk and marinate overnight, 8 to 12 hours. The two

rounds of milk marinade will neutralize the gaminess and bring out the distinctive flavor of sea ducks.

4. The morning before you plan to serve it, drain off the milk, rinse and pat dry again, and cover the meat with a robust red wine. Let it marinate in the refrigerator for about 6 hours.

5. Drain the meat and pat it dry with paper towels. Do not rinse it this time.

6. Rub both sides of the meat with salt, fresh-ground black pepper, ground red pepper, and dried sage and rosemary.

7. In a very hot skillet coated with olive oil sear the meat on both sides. Do not overcook. It should be rare on the inside.

8. Serve with cranberry sauce or chutney, wild rice, fresh green vegetables (steamed asparagus would be my choice, but it's not in season in New England in November), a green salad, and an excellent red wine.

ABOUT THE AUTHORS

William G. Tapply is a retired high school history teacher who now teaches writing at Emerson College, Clark University, and for The Writers Digest School. The author of eighteen Brady Coyne novels as well as five volumes on outdoor living and fishing, he is a contributing editor to *Field and Stream* magazine. He lives in Pepperell, Massachusetts.

Philip R. Craig grew up on a small cattle ranch southeast of Durango, Colorado. He earned his M.F.A. at the University of Iowa Writers' Workshop and is a professor emeritus of literature at Wheelock College in Boston. He is the author of thirteen J. W. Jackson/Martha's Vineyard mysteries. He and his wife live on Martha's Vineyard.